Also by Johanna Lindsey

THE HEIR

Johanna Lindsey

The Heir

BOOKSPAN LARGE PRINT EDITION

HarperLargePrint

An Imprint of HarperCollins*Publishers*

A hardcover edition of this book was published in 2000 by WILLIAM MORROW AND COMPANY, *An Imprint of* HarperCollins *Publishers*.

Cover design by Patricia Barrow
Cover illustration by Fredericka Ribes
Cover logotype by Dave Gatti

© BOOKSPAN

ISBN 0-7394-0991-3
Printed in the U.S.A.

**This Large Print Book carries the
Seal of Approval of N.A.V.H.**

For Alex
and smiles that melt the heart

THE HEIR

1

They stared out the window at the bleak, winter-touched garden where the girl walked. It was small, though the town house was large and in a fashionable area of London—there simply wasn't much land available to any of the houses along the block, to devote to a "country look."

Lady Mary Reid, their hostess, had done well with her small section of garden, when most of her neighbors didn't bother with other than grass. And trust their niece, Sabrina, who loved the outdoors no matter the time of year, to be found out in that little piece of earth.

The two women continued to watch Sabrina, silently, pensively. Alice Lambert wore a frown. Her sister Hilary, the elder by one year, looked rather despondent.

"I don't think I've ever been this nervous, Hilary," Alice whispered to her sister.

"Me either, if you must know," Hilary answered with a drawn-out sigh.

It was hard to tell they were sisters by looking at them. Hilary took after their father, tall, narrow of frame to the point of extreme thinness, with dull brown hair and light blue eyes. Alice was nearly an exact copy of their mother, on the short side and rather plump, but with dark hair of a lustrous brown and dark blue eyes tinged occasionally with a violet hue.

They were sisters who didn't get along too well. Bickering was common. Yet for once they were in agreement. The niece they had pretty much raised was having her come-out in London society tonight, and they were both worried. Unfortunately, they had good reason to be worried.

It wasn't that Sabrina might not stand out or make a good showing. Though she wasn't a great beauty like Mary's daughter Ophelia, who was also having her come-out this Season, Sabrina did have her good points. It wasn't their lack of consequence, either. Sabrina's grandfather had been an earl, her great-grandfather had been a duke. Her own title was merely Honorable, but then they weren't hoping to catch a lofty title for her, nor even great wealth. Any husband of good standing would do as far as the Lambert sisters were concerned.

No, it wasn't any of the normal worries that one might expect when dealing with a country girl being put on the marriage block in high society. It was much, much more personal and had to do with why the two sisters had never married themselves. They each feared that the old scandal that had haunted their family for three generations might surface again after all these years.

But neither of the two women would mention what was at the heart of their nervousness. By mutual accord, the long-ago tragedies were never spoken of.

"D'you think she's warm enough in that woolen coat?" Alice asked, still frowning.

"D'you think she cares?"

"But her cheeks are going to get wind-chapped, and how will that look at her first ball?"

As they continued to watch their niece, a dead leaf, overlooked by Lady Mary's gardener, drifted toward Sabrina and stopped at her feet. The girl, having noticed it, assumed the pose of a fencer and, as if she had a real rapier in hand rather than an imaginary one, made a stab for the leaf. She then laughed at herself and scooped the leaf up, tossing it into the air where the brisk winter wind caught it and carried it away.

"She doesn't take this marriage thing seriously," Hilary said now.

Sabrina *should* have been just as nervous as her aunts were, if for different reasons, but instead, she appeared not to have a care in the world.

"How can she take it seriously when she knows we didn't marry and it didn't hurt either of us?"

"I'm afraid we've given her the wrong impression. It's not as if we didn't want or hope to marry when we were her age, just that now we're rather glad we didn't."

Which wasn't putting a good face on it. Neither woman truly regretted not having a spouse. What they might have regretted was not bearing any children themselves, but Sabrina, having come to them to raise when she was barely three, had thoroughly satisfied their maternal instincts. Many might call them old maids and claim their sour-grapes bickering stemmed from that, but that was hardly the case. The two sisters had been bickering since they were children. It was rather ingrained.

As if Hilary suddenly realized she had been participating in an unspoken truce, she said abruptly, "Call her in. It's time to prepare her."

"This soon?" Alice protested. "We've still hours yet before—"

"It will take hours to do her up properly," Hilary cut in.

"Oh, posh, it might take *you* hours, but—"

"And what d'you know about it, when you didn't even have a come-out yourself?" Hilary interrupted yet again.

"And you did?" Alice shot back.

"Doesn't signify. Mary has mentioned many times in her letters that she starts preparing herself as soon as she gets out of bed in the morning."

"It would take her all day just to stuff herself into her corset."

Hilary flushed with color, unable to deny that charge about her childhood friend who had been kind enough to offer them her residence for the Season, since they didn't own property in London themselves. Mary *had* grown exceedingly plump over the years, so much so that Hilary had barely recognized her old friend when they arrived in London yesterday.

She countered instead, "Even her daughter begins readying herself at noon."

"Ophelia just likes staring at herself in her mirror, no doubt," Alice snorted.

"I'll have you know . . ."

The words trailed off as the sisters left the room, this squabbling a much more normal state of affairs for these two. No one who had heard them talking in whispers and in such agreement for those few moments would have believed it, certainly not the niece they had been discussing.

2

Sabrina Lambert *was* nervous, but for her aunts' sake, she tried her best not to show it. Her come-out had been a year in the planning, which included several trips to Manchester for fittings for her new wardrobe. And she knew her aunts had such high hopes for her. That was why she was nervous. She really didn't want them to be disappointed, when they'd put so much effort into this launch.

But she was realistic even if they weren't. She didn't expect to find a husband here in London. The people here were much too sophisticated, while she was just a simple country girl. She was used to conversations about crops and tenants and the weather, while the London *ton* thrived on gossip, salacious gossip—about each other. And there would be dozens of other hopeful young misses all descending on London for the same purpose. It was considered *the* place to find a husband.

But Sabrina began to relax as the evening progressed. It helped that she had a friend in Ophelia, who was so very popular. But then Ophelia had been born and raised in London. She already knew everyone, was already aware of all the current *on-dits,* and even helped to spread the latest gossip—even if it was about herself. The London girl was in her element. And she'd also had her launch at the very start of the Season three weeks prior.

Not that arriving in time for the first ball of the Season would have made much of a difference, when Ophelia was destined to be *the* success of the Season, as beautiful as she was. And ironically, she wasn't even shopping for a husband, already had a fiancé, although she'd never met him. Her own launch was merely a matter of course—at least Sabrina had thought so until she found out that Ophelia wasn't exactly happy with the husband her parents had arranged for her, and had every intention of finding a better match.

How she was setting about accomplishing that, which was to slander and ridicule
her fiancé every chance she got and to
anyone who would listen, Sabrina found
highly distasteful. But for all she knew, that
was how it was done in London, the getting rid of one's unwanted fiancé, that is.

And she might have personally felt sorry
for the man in question, who apparently
wasn't even in England and so couldn't put
a stop to the rumors that Ophelia was
spreading about him, but it wasn't her
place to defend him. It could all be true,
after all. How was she to know?

Besides, Ophelia's mother was their
hostess and Aunt Hilary's good friend.
While Lady Mary might want to know what
her daughter was up to so she could put
a stop to it, Sabrina wouldn't feel right being the one to tell her. Ophelia had befriended her, was introducing her to all her
friends. It would be like betraying her. And
furthermore, her own aunts didn't like the
man's grandfather . . .

That was the strange part, and probably
why Sabrina felt sorry for Ophelia's fiancé.
He was actually her neighbor, or rather, his
grandfather was. The "old coot," her aunts

called him, "the recluse," and when they thought she wasn't listening, "the old bastard." Sabrina had never met him herself. He really was a recluse who rarely left his estate. And it had certainly been news to them that he had a grandson. Her aunts had actually scoffed when they learned that Ophelia had been affianced to this heretofore unknown heir. What grandson? They'd never met or even heard of him.

According to Lady Mary, however, it was the marquis himself who had contacted her husband and made the arrangements for the marriage on his grandson's behalf. And of course, the Reids had jumped at the chance for their daughter to be married to such a lofty title, which the grandson was going to inherit. It didn't hurt, either, that the marquis was quite rich and all that wealth would be coming to the grandson as well. It was only Ophelia who was unhappy with the match, well, Ophelia and her many ardent admirers.

She had those in abundance. The young men flocked about her, utterly entranced by her beauty, and apparently that had been the case at each affair she had thus far attended. But how could they not be?

She was blond and blue eyed. You couldn't be much more fashionable than that. But she also had the most exquisitely lovely features, and a figure that, unlike her mother's, was willowy thin.

Sabrina, now, could claim none of those appealing attributes. She was on the short side at only a couple inches above five feet, which wouldn't be so bad if she didn't have such plump breasts or such wide hips, which made her altogether too curvaceous with her narrow waist.

But even that wouldn't have been so bad if her coloring were at least fashionable, but it was just the opposite. Her hair was a dull brown, not even a lustrous brown or a rich brown, but utterly dull, and her eyes, which really were her best feature, or so she used to think, were the color of spring lilacs, yet ringed with a darker violet, so they were actually quite startling when first noticed.

She found out just how startling when everyone she met, men and women alike, stared at her eyes an embarrassingly long time, as if they couldn't quite believe they were the color they were. And to top all that off, her features were rather plain, not ugly by any means, but not what one would call pretty either. *Plain* did describe them very well.

Actually, Sabrina had never been quite so unhappy with her own looks—until she met Ophelia and saw what a real beauty looked like. Like night and day, there was no comparison between the two of them. Which was quite possibly why Sabrina began to relax soon after they arrived at her first ball that night, and completely forget her previous nervousness. She was realistic enough to know that she couldn't possibly compete for the young gentlemen's attention with Ophelia there, and so she gave up any hope of even trying. And once she did relax, she was able to be herself rather than the stiff, timid little mouse she had been feeling like.

Sabrina enjoyed a good laugh as much as anyone, and made an effort to bring laughter to others. She could be outspoken, but she also had a teasing nature. She had a gift for lightening someone's mood when it was most sour. With two grumbling, always bickering aunts, she'd had many years to perfect that gift, and had little trouble ending their little fights when she chose to intervene.

The gentlemen who asked her to dance that night might have done so only so they could question her about Ophelia and her fiancé. But since she didn't know Ophelia very well yet, and her fiancé not at all, she could hardly answer their questions. She made them laugh, though. A few of them even asked her to dance again for that very reason—she was amusing. And at one point in the evening she actually had three young men wanting to dance with her at the same time.

Unfortunately, Ophelia happened to notice that . . .

3

Ophelia was standing across the ballroom with three of her closest friends, well, two friends and one girl who secretly despised her, but was loath to leave the circle of her popularity. Each of the three was pretty in her own way, though not nearly as beautiful as Ophelia. Nor did any of the three outrank Ophelia in title. She was the only lady among them, her father being an earl, their fathers having less prestigious titles. But then Ophelia couldn't stand for any female in her circle to outrank or outshine her.

Ophelia was unaware of Mavis Newbolt's dislike. She might not care for some of Mavis's snide or catty remarks, but she would never attribute them to dislike. How could anyone dislike her, after all, as eminently popular as she was?

And she had known she would be. There had never been any doubt that she would reign supreme this Season and have her pick of every single eligible bachelor in town. She did have that pick. They all adored her. But to what purpose, when her parents had let the Marquis of Birmingdale woo them with his blasted title?

She hated old Neville Thackeray for thinking of her. Why did he have to pick her for his grandson, just because her mother had once lived near him and thus he felt he knew her personally? Why couldn't he have picked the dowdy Sabrina instead, who still lived near him? Of course, she knew why Sabrina hadn't been considered for the Birmingdale heir.

She knew the Lamberts' family history from her mother's account of it. Everyone from Yorkshire had likely heard the story at one time or another, though it was an old scandal and probably forgotten by most.

They were fools, her parents. Ophelia could have landed a dukedom. Beauty like hers didn't come along often. But they had settled for a mere marquis. She wouldn't, though. She *was* going to get out of marrying the Birmingdale heir. Good God, he wasn't even an Englishman—well, not a pure one anyway. But it was no wonder the marquis felt he had to do the bride-picking himself, in an age when arranged marriages were nearly unheard-of. The grandson had been raised by barbarians!

She shuddered at the thought. And if shaming him didn't work, and showing him that he'd never have anything from her except her utter contempt, then she would just have to think of some other way to be rid of him. But she'd have a new fiancé by the end of the Season, and one of *her* choosing. She didn't doubt that for a moment.

However, at that particular moment Ophelia was staring at her mother's young houseguest, and was briefly disconcerted seeing the gentlemen hovering near Sabrina, who *should* have been dancing attendance on her instead. But because there weren't any men within hearing distance just then, she was able to speak her mind without worrying about how it would reflect on her, and she was surprised enough by what she was seeing across the room to do so.

"Would you look at that," Ophelia said,

directing the other girls' attention to Sabrina and the three men speaking with her. "What can she possibly be saying to them, to keep them so enthralled?"

"She's your houseguest, Ophelia," Edith Ward offered soothingly, recognizing the signs of jealousy in her friend, and adept at defusing it. All three girls, at one time or another, had been burned by Ophelia's unwarranted jealousy. "They no doubt just want to talk to her about you."

Ophelia began to look appeased until Mavis said in supposed innocence, "It looks to me like she's garnered a few admirers, but then I'm not surprised. She does have remarkably beautiful eyes."

"Those peculiar eyes of hers are hardly a saving grace, Mavis, when she's utterly drab otherwise," Ophelia replied tersely. But she immediately regretted her harsh tone, which might make her sound jealous, which she wasn't, of course.

So she added, with what she thought was a sincere sigh but came out sounding more like a huff, "I do pity her, though, poor girl."

"Why? Because she isn't pretty?"

"Not just that, but she comes from bad

blood, you know. Oh, dear, I shouldn't have mentioned that. You are *not* to let that go any further. My mother would have a fit. Lady Hilary Lambert is her dear friend, after all."

Since they all knew that Ophelia was quite displeased with her mother at the moment, that last bit was redundant. Ophelia wouldn't mind at all if her mother had a fit. But then the admonishment not to repeat what they were hearing was just as redundant, since both the other two girls thrived on gossip, just as their mothers did, and they were sure to tell their mothers every single word they'd heard. Mavis deplored gossip herself, but in the *ton* you really did have to keep up with it.

"Bad?" Jane Sanderson asked avidly. "You don't mean the wrong side of the blanket?"

Ophelia appeared to give that some thought, but must have decided against that particular scandal because she said, "No, worse than that, actually."

"What can be worse—?"

"No, really, I've said too much already," Ophelia protested lightly.

"Ophelia!" Edith, the oldest of the four

girls, exclaimed. "You can't leave us in suspense like that."

"Oh, all right," Ophelia complained, as if they were dragging the information out of her, when nothing would have stopped her at that point from telling all. "But this is *only* between us, and *only* because you are my best friends and I trust you not to repeat it."

She continued in a whisper. The two friends who were actually her friends had wide eyes by the time she finished the tale. Mavis, knowing Ophelia as she did, didn't know whether to believe her. But then she knew that Ophelia felt no qualms at all about lying, if she thought it might get her what she wanted. And apparently what she wanted at the moment was to completely ruin Sabrina Lambert's chance of finding a husband in London.

Two reputations blackened this evening, and both by the same woman. Mavis felt truly sorry for both people, their only fault that Ophelia didn't like them. The Birmingdale heir would undoubtedly weather the storm. He was merely being made a laughingstock by Ophelia's ridicule of him, so that her parents would be mortified enough to break off the engagement they had arranged. But with a title like his and the huge estate that came with it, he'd still easily find another bride.

Not so the Lambert girl. Bad blood was bad blood that might be passed along to heirs, and what gentleman would want to take that chance by marrying her? Which was really too bad. Mavis had genuinely liked the girl. She was nice, a simple, innocent quality hard to encounter in London, and amusing besides, once she'd opened up. And Mavis felt partly responsible for turning Ophelia against her, by mentioning her remarkably pretty eyes.

Mavis shook her head mentally in disgust. She really was going to have to find a new group of companions. Being friends with Ophelia Reid was simply too detrimental to one's well-being. Spiteful, vain bitch. Mavis hoped, she really did, that Ophelia would have to marry the Birmingdale heir after all. Serve her right to have a husband whom she'd managed to get all of London to scorn.

4

It was not a night to be traveling abroad, was possibly the worst night of the year, with snow swirling in ever-thickening gusts, preventing visibility even with a lantern held aloft. And cold. Sir Henry Myron had never in his life experienced such bone-chilling cold.

The weather wouldn't have been so extreme in England. He would probably have thought nothing of a little snow. But so far north in the Scottish Highlands, he would have been hard-pressed not to freeze even without the snow trying to help him toward that end. How anyone could live in such a harsh climate and *like* it was a wonder to Sir Henry, who had been tasked with coming here.

The worst part of the trail had been

passed, a narrow path across a low mountain. Henry wouldn't have called it a mountain. It seemed more like a gigantic rock jutting out of the ground, bare of trees, grass, even dirt, just a big granite thing blocking the way that needed to be passed, and the only way to do so was to climb over it by foot or on horse.

He'd had to leave his carriage behind at a nearby kirk. But then he'd been warned by his guide that he would have to, and so had rented a mount for the last leg of the journey along its narrow trails.

They should have stayed the night at that kirk. The churchman there had offered them beds for the night. But they were so close to the end of the journey, just an hour away, that Henry had insisted on going on. Of course, it hadn't been snowing then. The snow had come from the other side of that huge rock, or rather, low mountain, blasting them with stinging flakes as soon as they topped the rise.

Henry was beginning to worry that they would both be lost and freeze to death, their bodies not found until the spring thaw. It was impossible to see even two feet in front of them, yet the guide continued on, as if he could still see the path, now covered in snow, as if he knew exactly where he was going. And so he did . . .

The large stone manor house loomed out of the white-speckled darkness so suddenly, they were at the door before Sir Henry had even noticed they had reached their destination. The guide was pounding on that door. Henry barely heard it, the wind was shrieking so loudly. But the door opened and warmth gushed out, and they were both ushered straightaway to a large crackling fire.

Henry was numbed. After a short while, though, he began to thaw, and the shivering began just after that. A woman was fussing over them and tsking about the foolishness of being out in such a storm— at least he thought that was what she was saying. He wasn't quite sure, though, her Scots brogue was so thick. But she piled heavy woolen blankets over his shoulders, and wrapped his stiff fingers around a cup of hot whisky, staying to make sure he drank every drop of it, which he was glad to do.

A short while later, he began to think that he and his frozen toes might survive after all, a painful discovery as feeling began to return to those extremities, but welcome nonetheless. And he finally began to take closer note of his surroundings.

He was surprised. Henry wasn't sure what he had expected to find at the home of a rich Highland lord, and one so isolated as this one was—well, to be truthful, he had expected something medieval, an old, crumbling fortress perhaps, or merely a big farm. The MacTavishes were sheep farmers, after all, or so he'd been told.

But what he was seeing was something altogether different, not quite a manor house that he might have passed in the shires of England, yet surely in that design. Built all of stone—Scotland wasn't known for its abundance of lumber—it could have been furnished in the style and comfort of a manor house, yet what should have been a large drawing room looked like an old medieval hall instead.

The house was modern in design. The occupants weren't, apparently. It was as if whoever had built it had done so in protest, that he had been raised in one of the older-style castles and that was the feel he was most comfortable with and was going to adhere to.

Trestle tables, of all things, and wooden benches lined the floral-papered walls. He didn't doubt that they were pulled out for dinner to accommodate the household all sitting down at once to eat, just as in days of old. The windows weren't covered with drapery, but with sheepskins still thick with fleece. He might allow the skins would keep out the cold better than any drapery could, but *sheepskins?* There wasn't a sofa or comfortable chair to be seen, just a few more unpadded benches near the fire. And hay on the floor.

When he noticed it he simply stared, then finally shook his head. He'd been right, after all. The MacTavish Highlanders did live medievally.

But there were no MacTavishes about, nor anyone else for that matter, though the hour was still early in the evening. The large *Great Hall* was empty, except for the woman who was returning now with two more cups of hot whisky. But she wasn't alone, not this time. On her heels came a tall young man who stopped in the door-way to give Henry's guide a nod—they were apparently acquainted, but then the guide had said he'd been here before. The man then stared at Henry.

After having a good look at what should have been a modern drawing room but wasn't, Henry might have expected at that point to see people wearing bearskins, or rather, *sheep*skins, but no, the Scotsman was dressed in trousers and frock coat. He could have walked down a fashionable London street without gaining undue notice—except for his height perhaps, and the large body that went with a six-foot frame.

He said nothing, though, and he didn't look too pleased that an unknown guest had arrived. Or perhaps the unfriendly look he wore was normal for him.

It was quite disconcerting for Henry, though. Nearly twice the boy's age, yet he was briefly intimidated . . . Well, no wonder. Highland Scots were nothing like the agreeable Lowlanders in the South who had been dealing with the English for centuries. Social progress was stagnant in these far reaches of the realm, so isolated due to the rugged land itself, and the weather besides. Many of the northern clans lived just as they had in days of old, in hardship but in strict obedience to their clan chief.

Lord Archibald MacTavish wasn't a clan chief, but he was head of his small branch of the clan, and certainly head of his family, which was extensive in distant cousins, but unfortunately, very lacking in an immediate heir, since he had outlived all four of his sons. And this was the reason Henry's visit was not going to be received very well. He would be lucky if he wasn't kicked back out into the storm, once he made it clear why he was there.

But the young man in the doorway couldn't know why he was there, thus his unwelcoming demeanor was unrelated, was perhaps natural, or perhaps only reserved for Englishmen. And he'd know Henry was English, since he had spoken to the woman who had aided him, and she'd obviously gone to fetch the boy.

And then he came forward, abruptly. And as he neared the light from the fire and the two torches burning on either side of the mantel—the only light in the entire room—Henry was able to see that he wasn't as young as he'd first thought. In his mid-twenties was more likely. At least there was a maturity in his look that spoke of an older age, even if from a distance he looked much younger.

"If the laddie here wasna wi' you, mon"—the young man nodded toward Henry's guide—"I'd be thinking you're lost. So what's a Sassenach wanting wi' Archie MacTavish?"

Henry was quick to introduce himself, but his answer was suitably grave. "I'm here on a matter of urgency and no small importance. I am employed by Lord Neville Thackeray as his solicitor, who is the—"

"I ken who Thackeray is," the young man cut in impatiently. "He's still living then?"

"Well, yes, at least he was when I left England, but it's uncertain how much longer that will be true. He hasn't been well, you see, and at his advanced age, there is no telling when he will take a turn for the worst."

The young Scot nodded curtly, then said in his light brogue, "Come tae my office where 'tis warmer. Damned drafty in here."

"*Your* office?"

Henry sounded so surprised that it was

no wonder the man raised a questioning brow at him, but then unexpectedly, he burst out laughing. "Dinna tell me you've been caught by auld Archie's prank."

Stiffly, because he wasn't used to being the butt of any jokes, Henry replied, "And what prank would that be?"

"This room, o' course," the man replied, still grinning. "He insists that any strangers be shown here, rather than tae the normal part o' the house. Thinks it's funny, he does, what they end up thinking aboot him."

Henry blushed profusely, having apparently been caught by the prank. "I take it this room isn't used much then—except for visitors?"

"Och, nay, it gets its use, when the sheep o'erbreed and there's no' enough room for them all in the barns when the snows come. And o' course, during shearing season, when MacTavishes come from afar, we're needing a big room tae feed them all in, and this one does well enough."

Henry couldn't tell if what had just been said was part of the prank or not. Frankly, he'd rather not find out, and the mention of that warm office did sound inviting, so he readily followed the young man, who led the way to it.

The rest of the house was indeed comfortably furnished and what one would expect of its grand style. If Henry hadn't been in such a hurry to get to a fire, and the entryway not so dark that time of night, he might have noticed that before he'd been whisked into that strange drawing room›turned›stable. But it was easy to see, now that a lamp had been left on a table in the hall, the other rooms leading off of it and glimpses of the fine furnishings within.

The office he was directed to was small but neat—and warmed by a large brazier in the corner, indicating it had been in use by the young man when he had arrived. Henry was beginning to think it was Archibald's factor or estate manager who had come to meet him, but he'd made enough assumptions, wrong ones at that, so he asked pointedly who the man was just as soon as he settled into the thickly stuffed leather chair across from his desk.

The answer, "I'm a MacTavish, o' course," wasn't all that enlightening, particularly when everyone on the property likely bore that name, but Henry was too tired by then from the journey and the battering the weather had added to it to press for further explanation.

"Has Lord Archibald been informed of my arrival?" he asked instead.

"The auld mon is abed by now, early riser that he is," was the reply. "But you can be telling me what it is you're wanting wi' him."

Whether factor or secretary, the man did indeed appear to handle Archibald's affairs for him, even had an office in his house, so Henry could find no reason not to answer him. "I'm here to collect Lord Neville's grandson."

Oddly, that seemed to amuse this Mac-Tavish. There was a slight curling of the lips, barely noticeable, but there nonetheless. His tone, however, was more obvious. Definite humor there.

"Are you indeed?" he replied slowly. "And what if his grandson doesna want tae be collected?"

Henry sighed mentally. He should have known better than to try to deal with employees.

"I really should be discussing this with Lord Archibald," he said.

"D'you think so? When the grandson is of an age tae be deciding things for hisself?"

Henry was just tired enough to get annoyed. "There is nothing to decide here, young man," he said crisply. "A promise was made and Lord Neville demands it be fulfilled."

At that, the young man sat forward. And the frown he wore now was quite disconcerting. "What promise?"

"Lord Archibald is aware of it, and aware that the time has come—"

"What . . . blasted . . . promise? I'm the grandson o' them both, and I'll be deciding if there was a promise that needs fulfilling if it concerns me."

"*You're* Duncan MacTavish?"

"Aye, and you'll be telling me what the hell this is all aboot."

5

"Good God, you were never told?"

Duncan MacTavish was standing behind his desk now, leaning partially across it, and nearly shouting, "Does it sound like I ken what you're talking aboot?"

Henry was incredulous. Duncan was twenty-one years of age. He knew that for a fact. And in all his years no one had told him, not even his parents? Nor had Lord Neville warned him that his grandson didn't know. He had to wonder now if Neville was even aware of that himself.

Henry also admonished himself for not realizing sooner who Duncan was. His eyes, after all, were exact copies of Neville's, a dark midnight blue. The nose, also, had that patrician slant that the Thackerays were known for; at least, each ancestor portrayed in the gallery at Summers Glade sported that exact same nose. Nothing else about the young Duncan, though, resembled the marquis. Although Henry hadn't known Neville when he was a young man, he'd seen the portrait of him done when he was this same age.

There was nothing remarkable about Neville Thackeray, fourth Marquis of Birmingdale, to stand out and draw particular notice to him. He'd been a plain-looking aristocrat in his youth, and had not improved much with age, now that he was in his late seventies. His young grandson, however, was quite the opposite.

Duncan's brawny size and height must come from the MacTavishes. His dark red hair certainly did. And he was handsome, very much so, in a rugged sort of way. It was that very ruggedness, a harsh masculinity, coupled with his size, that belied his youthful age.

Henry *knew* how old the lad was, yet if he didn't, he'd swear he was much older. Perhaps the Highlands aged one prematurely, the harsh clime, the hardships entailed with living in such an isolated place.

As for the question that had been directed at him, Henry really wished that Archibald MacTavish were present at the moment. *He* knew of the promise, and the others added to it, that the two old men had finally, after many heated letters sent between them, agreed upon. He should have explained the situation to young Duncan before now.

"It was a promise made by your mother before you were born," Henry said at last. "Without making it, she wouldn't have been allowed to marry your father. She made it gladly, though. She loved your father. And no one objected at the time, not your father, who wanted her any way he could have her—he loved her too—nor his father, Archibald."

"Sir Henry, if you dinna spit it oout, what that promise was, I'm liable tae toss you back intae that storm this verra second."

It was said calmly. Even Duncan's expression had turned inscrutable. Yet Henry didn't doubt that the lad meant every word. And he could hardly blame him for his upset. *Why* hadn't anyone told him before now?

"You, or rather, your mother's firstborn son, which turned out to be you, were promised to Lord Neville for his heir, if he sired no other heirs, which he never did."

Duncan sat back down. "Is that all?"

Henry wasn't sure now how to proceed with the lad. Any other young man would undoubtedly feel that this was the luckiest day of his life, to be a great lord's heir when he hadn't known he would be. But he also knew how Highlanders felt about the English, and Duncan MacTavish had been raised a Highlander. He had also never met his English grandfather, nor ever stepped foot in England.

"Do you realize what a great honor this is, Lord Duncan?" Henry tried to point out.

"I'm no' a laird, so dinna be calling me—"

"Actually, you are," Henry was quick to interrupt. "One of Lord Neville's lesser titles has already been bestowed on you, as well as the estate—"

"Be damned if it has!" Duncan was on his feet again. "You willna be turning me into an Englishmon just because that auld mon wants it so."

"You *are* half English."

That gained Henry a seriously disgusted look that had him flinching, but Duncan's reply was again a quiet one. It was amazing how easily he could switch from fury to calm and back again.

"You ken that I dinna have tae accept that English title?" Duncan said.

"Do *you* understand that you will become the Marquis of Birmingdale whether you want to be or not?"

There was a long, uncomfortable—at least for Henry—moment of silence, which included a bit of teeth grinding on Duncan's part before he said, "So why are you here tae tell o' this now, when, as you said, the marquis isna dead yet?"

"You have come of age. Part of your mother's promise was that you would be sent to Lord Neville at this time, if he was still living, which he is, so that he could himself instruct you on your responsibilities, and also so that he can see you settled properly before he dies."

"Settled?"

"Married."

"I suppose, then, he'd even be picking me a bride?" Duncan said sarcastically.

"Well, yes, actually, he has," Henry replied with the utmost reluctance.

But it was at that point that Duncan MacTavish burst out laughing.

6

Duncan had been amused because he hadn't believed that his English grandfather's gall could actually affect him. Neville Thackeray could pick for him a dozen brides. Who was to force him to marry any of them? He was his own man. If Neville had wanted to direct and control him as his solicitor was claiming, he should have sent for him sooner, before any and all decisions were his own to make.

The entire situation was incredible. Archibald had turned over to Duncan the running of the farms, the mines, and the other MacTavish enterprises when he'd turned eighteen. Why would he have done that if he'd known all along that Duncan wouldn't be there to carry on? A promise made before he was born, that everyone knew of—except him. Utterly incredible.

He had nothing against the English personally. His own mother had been English, after all, though after she became a Mac-Tavish, that was pretty much overlooked. It was an ingrained animosity for him, the result of the distrust and dislike he'd witnessed all his life. Yet he was expected to go to England, to live among the English? Even to marry one? Be damned if he would.

His amusement didn't last long after he turned the little Englishman over to Archibald's housekeeper to put to bed. And he spent a restless night himself, by turns amazed and infuriated over the magnitude of what had been kept secret from him. In the end, though, he decided that Archibald must have a plan to get him out of fulfilling that long-ago promise. Nothing else made sense to him. And he'd find out what it was first thing in the morning.

As expected, Archibald was already in the kitchen while dawn was still making its first appearance. Duncan joined him there as he did each morning. They were both early risers. And the kitchen, the warmest room in the house at that hour, was where they took their meals, the formal dining room too big and drafty for just the two of them.

Such had been the case ever since the last of Archibald's four sons had died fourteen years ago. The last had been Duncan's father. Two of the sons had died due to pure carelessness, two due to nature's fury. Duncan's parents died together. They had been sailing to France to sign contracts for a new market for MacTavish wool. Such a short trip, yet the storm had been so sudden and so violent, the ship never made it to its French port.

Duncan would have been on that ship as well if he hadn't experienced such a horrid bout of seasickness before it even set sail. Archie, there that day to see his kin on their way, had insisted he stay behind. Duncan had been disappointed. He had wanted to travel. At seven years of age, it would have been his first trip so far from home—and his last.

Being the last of Archibald's direct line, Duncan had been coddled thereafter, and so overprotected, he often felt stifled by Archie's concern. He couldn't blame the

old man, though. It couldn't be easy, outliving all your children. And Duncan was
his only grandchild.

Two of Archibald's other sons had been
married before they died, but three preg-
nancies between them had gone bad, so
the two wives, both being childless, had
returned to their parents when their hus-
bands died. The last son had become a
priest. It was falling off the roof of his kirk
when he'd been repairing it that had taken
his life.

Archie had experienced much tragedy in
his life. Duncan had as well, having known
all but one of his uncles. It was amazing,
though, that Archibald wasn't a bitter old
man. He wasn't even that old, though he
was certainly referred to as the "auld" man
by one and all. But he'd married young
himself, and his four sons had each been
born on the heels of the other, in the four
years following his marriage. His wife likely
would have given him many more children
if she hadn't herself died giving birth to the
last.

He'd never remarried, though he certainly could have, and still could. He was
only sixty-two this year. Most of his red hair

was still red, if somewhat faded, the gray at his temples and in his beard giving him a distinguished look, or it did when he took the time to fancy himself up. Having retired, though, when he turned over his many concerns to Duncan, he rarely left home these days, and at home he was usually a bit on the unkempt side.

Having no one to impress other than the cook, whom he'd kept up a long-standing flirtation with, and who, unfortunately, never took him seriously, Archie could often still be found in his bedclothes in the middle of the day.

Today he was fully dressed, combed, and scrubbed, and he wasn't looking too pleased when Duncan joined him in the kitchen. So he'd been told of the solicitor's arrival. Good. It allowed Duncan to get right to the point of his own concern the moment he sat down.

"Why did you no' tell me, Archie?"

Archibald grimaced, and not because Duncan used his first name. That wasn't a matter of disrespect, but as he would have it. And he didn't try to evade the question by pretending he didn't know what Duncan was talking about.

"Because I didna want ye dividing yer loyalties afore ye needed tae."

"What dividing? My loyalty is here and will always be here."

Archie smiled at that, looking rather smug for a moment. But then he sighed.

"Ye hae tae ken how it was, laddie. My Donald was fair smitten by yer muther. There was nothing for it but that he hae her, despite her being English. But she was a young lassie, no' even eighteen yet. And her da was no' happy that she had her heart set on Donald as well. Nor did he want her living sae far from home. He refused tae let them marry. For nigh a year he refused. But he loved his daughter, and couldna help but see she was dying o' heartbreak. Sae he compromised. He demanded Donald's heir, *my* heir, be sent tae him at his—yer—majority. If she'd promise that, then she could marry Donald."

"I ken why the promise was made, I dinna ken why I'm the last tae know aboot it."

"Tae be honest, lad, I'd been hoping that auld bastard would die long afore now, and his solicitors wouldna know aboot ye. Surely he mun have some other kin *some-*

where, that they could've been finding tae give his damn title tae. But nay, he's going tae bluidy well outlive us all."

The last was said in such disgust, Duncan might have laughed if he weren't at the center of this dilemma. And he hadn't heard yet what Archie's plan was, to get him out of it. But neither had Archie finished answering his question.

He reminded him, "And my mother? Why did she keep it a secret from me?"

" 'Twas ne'er a secret. Ye were just tae young afore she died, lad. She would hae told ye when ye were a bit aulder. She was no' unhappy wi' her promise. She was English, after all, and pleased that ye would be the next Marquis o' Birmingdale following her da. She held much stock in titles, ye ken. Most o' the English do."

"*You* should have told me, Archie. You shouldna have let it come tae the day o' collecting, wi' me no' knowing. And what am I tae do wi' that wee Englishmon upstairs who thinks I'll be going wi' him?"

"But ye will be going wi' him."

"The devil I will!"

Duncan shot out of his chair so quickly, it toppled over to the floor, startling the cook across the room into dropping a knife, which caused her to shriek when it almost stabbed her toes. She cast Duncan a glare. He didn't notice, glaring himself at his grandfather. Archibald, wisely, kept his eyes on the table.

"You canna sit there and tell me you've no' figured a way oout o' this," Duncan continued hotly. "I willna believe it! Who's tae manage here, then, if I go?"

"I managed well enough afore ye took o'er. I'm no' sae auld—"

"You'll drive yourself intae an early grave—"

It was Archie's chuckle, this time, that cut Duncan off. "Dinna think tha' my giving ye the reins meant I was ready tae retire. Nay, ye just needed the learning, laddie, and hands on was the best way tae get it."

"For what purpose then? So I could go off and be a blasted marquis instead?"

"Nay, sae ye'd hae firsthand knowledge tha' ye could teach tae yer son."

"What son?"

7

There had been many letters between the two old men—and much arguing. This was explained to Duncan that morning as he ignored the breakfast Cook set before him, and asked for a dram of whisky instead, ignoring, too, the stern look the old girl gave him for imbibing so early of a morn. The arguing had not been over whether Duncan would go to England, but over who would lay claim to his firstborn son.

"The one that'll be taking o'er here," Archie explained. "Nae one expects ye tae divide yerself, Duncan lad. We've tae many businesses here, and there'll be tae many duties there in England for ye tae assume. That'd be tae much for any mon, and tae long a journey for ye tae be making constantly back and forth."

They both wanted him wed posthaste so that he'd have a bairn by next year that would be farmed out—just as he was being. They didn't care what he thought of their arranging his life for him. They'd already agreed between the two of them that with Neville getting him, it was only fair that Archie get his firstborn.

He had a good mind to board a ship to some far-off place and to hell with both of them. But he loved Archie. He was furious with him at the moment, but he still loved him and could never break his heart that way.

Yet he felt like his life had never been his to live. They'd decided long ago that he would do as he was told to do, and that was that. Perhaps if he'd been raised differently, it might not have bothered him at all, to be so controlled. But Scotsmen were a fiercely independent lot, and Highlanders even more so. Which was why he *still* couldn't believe that Archie had ever had any intention of honoring that damned promise. Agree to it, aye, to keep the peace and get Donald his bride, but in the end, he should have ignored it.

Yet he found out why Archie was resigned to honor the promise when he'd asked him directly, "And what if I refuse tae go?"

Archie sighed and said forlornly, "I loved yer muther like a daughter. I didna think I would, her being English, but she was the sweetest lass, and she grew on me verra quickly. I realized long ago, afore she died, that I couldna dishonor her by breaking her promise. Even after she died, and the choice was truly mine, I still couldna dishonor her memory."

"The choice is *mine,* Archie, no' yours tae be making for me."

"Nae, ye dinna hae any more choice than I did, because ye loved yer muther, tae, and wouldna put such a stain on her memory, would ye now?"

Duncan didn't answer that. What he wanted to say stuck in his craw. Of course he couldn't dishonor his mother. But he was hating her at the moment, for putting him in this despicable position, and that put another knot in his throat that was nigh choking him.

His silence, however, prompted Archie to add, "Yer no' seeing the benefits yet, that I gained for ye by delaying yer going. Had auld Neville got ye when he wanted ye, three years ago, ye'd hae been at his complete mercy. Now he'll find that he mun be careful in what he asks o' ye, tha' he could as easily get a nay from ye as a yea. For yer muther's sake, ye'll be taking over the duties she was sae happy tae dump on ye, but ye can accomplish wha' needs doing in yer own way, no' as Neville would hae it."

As appeasements went, that one didn't hit the mark for Duncan, when what he wanted was to kick Henry Myron on his way back to England—without him. That thought was so appealing, he almost left the kitchen to do just that. None of them, not his mother nor either grandfather, had taken his own preferences into account. He'd lived all his life in the Highlands. How could any of them think he could possibly want to live anywhere else? Title or not, great wealth or not, he did *not* want to live in England.

But if there was an easy way to manipulate Neville Thackeray as Archie had apparently done, he wanted to know it. So he picked up his chair and sat again, asking Archie, "And just how did you manage putting this off?"

Archie smiled then, proud of his accomplishment and how he'd gone about it. "First I pointed oout tha' yer my heir as well, and since I already had ye, he'd hae a bluidy hard time getting ye away from me."

"When you already planned tae sacrifice me?" Duncan said bitterly.

"Och, laddie, I wish ye werena sae upset by this. 'Twas a bluff, aye, wha' I told him, but he didna know tha'. Nigh six months o' some serious threats passed atween us, then anither nine months o' arguing when I told him I'd settle for yer firstborn, that he didna want tae relinquish. I ken he was thinking tha' if ye didna settle in proper like, he'd hae yer bairn tae mold tae take yer place. The mon wasna thinking clearly, though, if he thought he'd live long enough tae do any molding."

"And you will?"

Archie chuckled. "Yer no' thinking clearly yerself, Duncan lad. As my heir, as well as his, ye'll be glad o' a son or tae or three, tae pass on all we're leaving ye. Tae send yer firstborn here early will only be tae his benefit. But aye, I'll be outliving that auld bastard by many a year, and he knows it."

"You mentioned only fifteen months," Duncan mumbled. "What put him off till now?"

"Well now, the talk o' bairns naturally led tae talk o' brides. He was insisting ye marry an English lass. He wouldna budge on that, though anither five months passed while we . . . er, 'discussed' it. Then I insisted the lassie be the most bonny tae be found, and it took him a good long while tae find her."

"An English lady, I suppose?"

Archie chuckled. "Aye, tha's wha' took sae long. Titled and the most bonny was no' easy tae come by."

"Yet a pure waste o' time," Duncan replied, adding, "I may go tae England, but I'll no' be marrying some handpicked lass that I've ne'er set eyes on."

"Dinna fash yerself on tha' account, laddie. 'Twas only anither delay on my part, insisting he find ye a bride. If ye dinna want tae marry the prettiest lass in all o' England oout o' stubbornness, nae one is going tae insist on it—well, Neville might, but as I said, yer auld enough tae be telling him nay and meaning it."

" 'Tis nothing tae do wi' stubbornness," Duncan said, his tone rising in annoyance.

"O' course it isna."

That condescending tone got Archie a glare. "I'll be picking my own bride, is all, nae more'n any mon expects tae do, yourself included."

"And glad I am tae hear it. But why burn the bridge afore ye cross it? Hae a look at the wench Neville found for ye first afore ye decline her. Ye may like her well enough. But if ye dinna, at least make an effort tae find anither."

Duncan snorted. "I've nothing again' marriage, Archie, but I'm a bit young tae be thinking o' it yet."

"And I'm a bit tae auld for ye no' tae be. I may outlive Neville, and I'll find someone tae help me here in the meantime, but I willna feel comfortable retiring completely again till yer son is auld enough tae take o'er."

Which meant that Archie was in complete agreement with Neville, that Duncan marry immediately. One of the major undertakings of his life, and they both wanted him to rush into it.

Duncan left the kitchen in disgust. He'd go to England. But he wondered if his grandfather Neville would be glad of his coming.

8

It was quite possibly the most gloomy, forlorn-looking place Duncan had ever seen. He supposed the thick carpet of fog that rose several feet above the ground might be responsible, as well as the leafless trees that could be dead as not, for all he knew. Or perhaps the early hour of the morning was why it looked so deserted.

On the other hand, Duncan truly doubted that any small bit of sunshine would impress him much in his current mood, nor any bright fauna if there was any to be found this time of the year. He was in a state of mind to hate Summers Glade, and hate it, he would.

Sir Henry had wanted to arrive last night, which would have been easily done since the inn they had stayed at had been less than twenty minutes away at a steady clip. But Duncan wasn't about to meet this English grandfather of his for the first time after a full day of traveling. He wanted to be at his most alert, not tired and thinking only of a hot bath and bed.

He hadn't planned to arrive before Neville Thackeray was even out of bed, though, which turned out to be the case, and was a letdown, since he was primed for a confrontation with his grandfather. And the place wasn't deserted, as he'd almost been hoping by the look of it. Inside it was teeming with servants, more than ten large families could possibly make use of, all there to wait on one old man.

To be fair, though, Duncan allowed it was a very large house the marquis lived in, which might be needing a few extra servants to see to the care of it. He also allowed the English might be a wee bit pampered, great lords like his grandfather in particular, and so they might think they needed huge staffs when they really didn't.

But for all the bleakness on the outside of the old estate, there was much bright grandeur to be found on the inside. The furniture in most of the rooms that Duncan had a glance of in passing was old-style French, the delicate, overly carved kind. It was well preserved for its age, but so ornamented as to give the place a gay, if gaudy, feel.

Mirrors and pictures were in gold-leafed frames that were nearly as wide as what they framed. Chandeliers were so large and with so much dangling crystal, they were likely to blind anyone unfortunate enough to look up at them when fully lit. And there were flowers in each room, suggesting that there was a hothouse on the estate somewhere.

All in all, Summers Glade, at least on the inside of it, certainly wasn't what Duncan had been expecting from an old English marquis, and certainly not after the dour look of the outside. Staid, unpretentious, heavy pieces had been his guess for what Neville would surround himself with, not the frivolous decor of the previous century.

But since Neville *had* lived in the last century, it wasn't all that surprising, after a bit of thought, that he might prefer the gaily carved and painted look of it that he had no doubt been raised with. Duncan would not be a bit surprised now if his grandfather showed up in one of those silly, puffy old white wigs, which had been the rage of the day when such furnishings had been in high style.

It took four servants—the haughty butler, who turned him over to a downstairs maid, who then turned him over to an upstairs maid, and finally the no-nonsense housekeeper—to show Duncan to his room in the upper regions. He'd almost been laughing by the time the housekeeper arrived to welcome him, that it had taken so many people to get him upstairs, when any one of them could have just pointed the way. But that was by no means the end of the procession.

A new maid showed up to light the fire in his room. Then another showed up carrying hot water and towels. Yet another followed on her heels with a large platter of morning-type refreshments, biscuits, sausages, and a few sweet pasties, with small pots of both hot tea and chocolate. Not ten minutes after that one left, yet another young miss arrived to ask if there was anything else he might be needing.

And lastly, Willis arrived.

Willis was a thin little man of middle years on the high side of middle, who proudly proclaimed he'd been chosen to be Duncan's valet. He had brown hair, what little hadn't receded on him, and brown eyes, his expression what one might call true haughtiness—and here Duncan had thought he'd seen the most haughty one could get in the Glade's butler, but Willis managed to appear even more proud and lofty.

Duncan wasn't so ignorant that he didn't know what a valet was for. He was just so surprised that one was in his room expecting to do for him, that Willis was already unpacking his traveling valise—which he'd had to fight with a footman to bring upstairs himself—before Duncan had a chance to tell him he wasn't needed.

And then he heard, "A skirt, m'lord?"

"That's a kilt, y'dafty mon!" Duncan fairly roared over the insult, his cheeks turning hot with color.

Willis was undisturbed by his tone, merely tsked as he moved to put the kilt away in the bureau. Duncan stared at him aghast. The insult had been bad enough, but for the little man to ignore his fury over it?

Tight lipped, Duncan ordered, "Get oout."

That did get Willis's full attention, but he merely said, "M'lord?"

To the perplexed look he was getting, Duncan explained, "I've ne'er needed a valet in m'life, and I'll no' be needing one now."

But instead of getting huffy and leaving, Willis simply tsked again and said, "It's no fault of your own where you were raised, but you're in England now and will want to do things properly, I'm sure."

"Will I now?" Duncan replied ominously, his temper on the rise again.

"Of course you will, and of course, you *do* need me. No gentleman of any consequence would even think of dressing himself."

"I'm no' a gentlemon, no' a lord, and I'll be bluidy well dressing myself. Now be gone, mon, afore I have tae toss you oout."

At that, Willis finally took him seriously and looked somewhat panicked. "You wouldn't *really* dismiss me, would you? It will reflect horribly on me."

"Just because I dinna need you?"

"But no one will believe that," Willis assured him. "No, this will be my fault alone, and prevent me from ever aspiring to such a prestigious position again. I will be quite ruined, m'lord, if I'm sent back to London."

Duncan would swear the man's lower lip just quivered. He sighed. He wasn't a mean man, just one set in his own ways. Yet he had no desire to be responsible for someone's being "quite ruined." Bedamned, he didn't *like* compromising.

"Verra well, you can see tae the pressing and cleaning o' what's tae be worn, but I'll be doing the dressing, is that clear?"

"Thank you, m'lord," Willis said, returning to his haughty and gratingly condescending tone. "And may I summon the marquis's tailor for some fittings, or do you have more trunks that will soon be arriving?"

Duncan just stared at the man. Give an Englishman an inch . . .

9

Sabrina didn't see it as such a tragedy, the revelation of her family history. But then the London *ton* was so funny, in their reaction to it, that she was more amused than not. Where people had previously looked at her with the mere curiosity reserved for any newcomer on the scene, they now gave her looks that said clearly, *You're still alive? But not for long, I'll warrant.* One silly lady had even screamed, thinking her a ghost. Sabrina could just imagine how distorted the rumors had been before they reached the screamer's ears.

Her prospects of finding a husband in London were now quite done in, of course. After all, what gentleman marrying to get himself an heir, and that was why a good many of them married, would want a wife who might not live long enough to produce that heir? Both her aunts were still living many years after the tragedies, obviously breaking the chain, but did anyone take that into account? No, that was definitely overlooked by the sophisticated London *ton.*

It did no good, really, to tell anyone the truth about her family. They would believe what they wanted to believe, and didn't the evidence support their belief? Hardly, but then the truth didn't make such juicy gossip. Much more interesting to insist that it must run in the family, the inclination to end one's life before it was ready to be ended.

Unfortunately, Sabrina's great-grandfather Richard had done just that, and his flighty wife, unable to bear up under the tragedy of it, had followed suit. That might have been the end of it, though. Their surviving daughter, Lucinda, after all, was already married at the time to William Lambert, an earl of strong constitution, and they already had two daughters themselves in Hilary and Alice. Sabrina's father, John, had yet to be born, which was why the old duke's title went to another distant branch of the family whom the Lamberts had never even met.

No one, in the family at least, was quite sure whether Lucinda jumped from that upstairs balcony or accidently fell off. Her health had declined somewhat after she bore William a son, and she'd been blue-deviled for months after John's birth, so it *was* quite possible that she had taken the same route as her parents. But whether she did or not, no one else doubted for a minute that she did, thus the scandal resurfaced and stayed around long enough to ruin Hilary and Alice's chance of a successful London Season.

It *should* have ended there. After all, there was new blood in the family now from the earl's side. And the talk of "bad blood" did die down by the time John married Elizabeth, and Sabrina came along from that union.

But then her parents had the misfortune to consume some tainted food and they both died of it before the doctor arrived. Even the dog died, having been given the scraps. And two of the kitchen maids, having had only a small taste of it, had been severely cramped as well. The doctor himself claimed it had been bad food. But it didn't take long for the rumor to start that they had taken poison—deliberately.

Hilary and Alice knew better. Their brother and his wife had loved each other and were very happy. *Their* deaths, at least, were truly accidental. But once again, no one else would believe that.

Her aunts, not surprisingly, were devastated that the scandal was running wild once again, all these years later, but then they'd had such high hopes for Sabrina, which were now quite dashed. They couldn't imagine who had been mean and spiteful enough to reintroduce that old scandal to the London gossip mills, not that it would make any difference to know who did. The damage was done. And because of it, there was really no point in staying any longer in London.

Sabrina was actually glad to be going home. London, she had found, with all its bustle and glitter, just didn't suit her at all. It was much too crowded, mostly dirty, the air more often than not thick with soot and smoke. She sorely missed the pristine cleanliness of a walk in the snow-covered countryside, and the earthy scents of animals and foliage in warmer months, rather than people and garbage.

She was glad that she had attended at least one ball, since she wasn't likely to ever find another to attend at home, and a few other parties before the gossip about her ran rampant. She at least knew what it was like now, London. Better to know than to always wonder, so the trip wasn't a complete waste of time in her mind.

And unlike her aunts, she wasn't worried that she would probably never marry now. On the contrary, she figured she would find a nice man someday, one intelligent enough to see through the rumors to the truth. So a few of her ancestors had actually killed themselves. That hardly meant that her entire family was fated to do the same. And if she didn't find anyone, well, that would be no great tragedy either, and her aunts were proof of that, too.

Ironically, their hosts, the Reids, found it necessary to travel to Yorkshire as well, since they had received notice to present themselves at Summers Glade to meet Neville Thackeray's grandson, who would soon be arriving there himself. Quite naturally, it was suggested that they all travel together. This was Lady Mary's idea. Her daughter, Ophelia, though, went beyond what could be considered good form in beseeching the Lamberts to join them at Summers Glade as well.

Alice and Hilary no doubt would have declined if they hadn't been so despondent over why they were leaving London, and not thinking clearly. They didn't even like the marquis, after all. But Ophelia admitted that she'd already invited many of her other friends to come to Summers Glade, and it was going to be quite the festive country gathering.

Sabrina's aunts were possibly seeing this as one last chance for Sabrina to catch some young gentleman's eye, so they had readily agreed. They were also anticipating the many parties that Ophelia would no doubt be having at the Glade after she was wed, which would be even more exposure for their niece. The very thought had cheered them up some small bit, so Sabrina didn't have the heart to object herself, though she at least saw the impropriety of descending on the Marquis of Birmingdale without his personal invitation.

Nor was Sabrina ignorant of Ophelia's real motives in inviting them and a slew of other people to Summers Glade, which were twofold. She had been furious, and didn't mind who knew it, that she was being dragged away from the London Season, and this was her silly way of bringing the "Season" to her. More to the point, though, she apparently felt she needed reinforcements to bolster her courage, but then she'd made it quite clear that she was terrified of the Highland barbarian whom her parents were forcing her to marry.

Though Sabrina was still disgusted over how Ophelia was going about getting rid of her fiancé, she did sympathize somewhat. It was so antiquated, after all, in this day and age, to be engaged to marry someone you'd never clapped eyes on. Her fear was understandable.

Sabrina might have sympathized even more if Ophelia had expressed a desire to marry for love instead, but that, apparently, wasn't on her list of priorities at all. She had merely been too impatient to wait and see if the marquis's grandson might suit her well enough, and besides, she aspired to a grander title than his. That there weren't a great many young dukes running around who would fit the bill of having a grander title was beside the point. She was sure she could find one, or a prince, even a king if she set her mind to it. She did think that highly of herself.

It was quite an embarrassing moment, though, facing the Glade's stern-faced butler, who had been expecting no more than three visitors but was met with eight instead—two of Ophelia's admirers had joined them on the road—and more still to come. Ophelia handled that in her typical way, however, dismissing the man as a menial.

"If *I* must stay here," she told him, "so must my friends. I am rarely without visitors, so you will just have to get used to it."

Fortunately for Ophelia, her parents were still outside and hadn't heard that haughty remark, or she would probably have got a dressing down for it. The butler's look said clearly that the marquis would hear of it, though. Ophelia no doubt hoped so. She did *not* want the marquis to like her. When either he or his grandson could end the unwanted engagement, she was determined to be unpleasant to both to speed up that ending.

At least Sabrina and her aunts wouldn't have far to travel if the worst happened and the marquis kicked them all out. Their own house, closer to the nearby small town of Oxbow, was only twenty minutes away, so it would be no hindrance to leave, even at night. They would just have to wait and see whether Lord Neville would be of a mind to pamper his soon-to-be grand-daughter-in-law.

10

Unaware of the arriving London guests, Duncan and his grandfather were at that moment upstairs meeting for the first time themselves. Duncan had insisted on waiting in Neville's sitting room for him, while Neville's valet had refused to wake him any sooner than the marquis's customary hour of arising. So Duncan had waited, nearly two hours, for the old man to bestir himself and make an appearance.

But he had finally done that, and the valet, looking red-faced on his way out, had obviously gotten a scolding for not waking Neville sooner. Not that Duncan had minded the wait, which had given him time to examine some of the possessions that Neville must consider of importance, for them to be in his personal sitting room.

The strange African artifacts on one wall suggested that Neville must have visited that continent at some point in his life, or wished he had. Another corner of the room was filled with Chinese art; around the mantel were things Egyptian. Either Neville liked to travel or he was a collector of un-usual art.

The furnishings, however, were in the same French flavor prevalent throughout the house. The desk was so dainty looking, Duncan would be afraid to use it himself, concerned that the slightest bit of weight from an elbow might send it crumbling to the floor. On it were two miniature portraits, one of which he recognized as his mother when she was a young woman, undoubt-edly painted before she'd left home to marry Donald. The other was of a child—with bright red hair.

The second picture caused Duncan to pause and simply stare at it. It *could* have been himself, he supposed, though he cer-tainly had no recollection of anyone ever being around him who could have painted it. It wasn't a pose, was a male child in play outdoors, oblivious to anyone who might have been watching him. And Duncan's hair *had* been that bright when he'd been a child, though it was nowhere near that color now, had darkened considerably as he'd aged. He saw no resemblance, though, really, other than the hair, but that could be the fault of the artist—and he was running out of reasons why it might not be his portrait, when he knew deep down that it was.

He just couldn't figure out why Neville would have it, or want it, when he'd never, not once in Duncan's entire life, tried to see him or even contact him. He'd written to Archie, but never to his only grandson, which spoke eloquently, as far as Duncan was concerned, about how Neville felt about him. He was a promised possession, and Neville probably saw him no differently from one of his art objects, to be prized and of value, but there was no sentimentality involved.

Now, seeing each other for the first time—Neville had paused in the doorway that connected to his bedroom and moved no further—they each simply stared, each surprised that the other was not what he'd been expecting.

Neville had a full head of hair, albeit

every bit of it a silvery white, and cut just below the ear in the current style. And he had aged—gracefully. There was no doubting that he was far up there in years, yet he sported very few wrinkles, and his eyes were sharply alert. With the silver goatee he wore, he had a very distinguished if Continental look, his slimness, or what could be considered frailty in his case, and his lack of height adding to it. His posture was very erect, though. In fact, this was not a man near his deathbed, as Henry had implied. Far from it. Neville looked in perfect health.

"You're bigger . . . than I expected," was the first thing Neville said.

In the same vein, Duncan replied, "You're no' as old as I was expecting—nor as sickly."

The words broke the surprised silence. Neville entered the room, his stride brisk, though he did sigh as he took the chair behind his small desk. Duncan, finding no chair in the room that looked like it wouldn't shatter if he even glanced at it, moved to stand in front of the fireplace. A bad choice, he quickly found, since the fire had been burning strongly before he even arrived, and still was, making the room uncomfortably warm, and near the fireplace, intolerably hot.

He moved to one of the windows instead and started to open it—all three in the room were closed tight.

"Please don't," Neville stopped him, and after a questioning glance from Duncan, added in a somewhat embarrassed tone, "I have been cautioned against drafts. My doctors seem to think my lungs won't withstand another bout with congestion. Regrettably, that means the rooms I frequent are kept unduly warm."

"So you have been sick then?"

"I spent the last entire winter in bed. I have fared better this year."

Duncan nodded. It had been said matter-of-factly. Neville wasn't bemoaning the fact, merely relating it. Duncan stayed near the window, where it was at least a little cooler, but not cool enough after standing next to the fire. Sweating now, he shrugged out of his jacket.

"I suppose you get that height from your father—and the hair," Neville remarked, watching him.

"I've your eyes, I'm told."

"Would you mind—coming closer so I might see them?"

The question, almost in the form of a plea, disconcerted Duncan. "Is your sight no' so good then?"

"I have spectacles," Neville replied in a grumbling tone, "I just keep misplacing them."

The new tone, reminding him of Archie, nearly had Duncan relaxing. He had to mentally remind himself that this old man wasn't the grandfather who'd raised him and who'd earned his love. This one, never a part of his life, meant nothing to him at all.

But he came forward and stood directly across from Neville's desk. And grew quite uncomfortable under the close examination Neville was giving him. Squirming came to mind, it was certainly what he felt like doing, though he managed to stand still.

"Elizabeth would be proud of you, if she could see you now."

It was a compliment of sorts, from Neville, not from his mother. It had the effect of annoying Duncan rather than flattering him.

"And how would you be knowing what

she'd feel, when you ne'er saw her again after she wed?"

The bitterness was unmistakable. Neville would have had to be deaf not to hear it, and some of his other senses might be failing him at his advanced age, but not his hearing. He stiffened. If he'd been willing to talk of the past, he changed his mind.

Abruptly he said, "Lady Ophelia and her parents will arrive today. It would be in our best interest if you would make an effort to impress her. Although she will benefit more from this marriage than you will, I have been informed that she is extremely popular with the London crowd, and has had countless other offers, so until the wedding, we will need to keep her happy. These young people today," he added in disgust, "think nothing of breaking commitments on a whim."

Duncan wondered if that last had been said just for his benefit. They might be blood related, but Neville had never made any effort to contact him, even by letter, before the time of "fulfilling the promise," and even then it was to Archie that he'd written, not to Duncan. There was no way he could know what manner of man Duncan had turned into—unless Archie had told him. He frowned to himself, wondering just what Archie *had* told Neville about him, in all those letters that had passed between them.

"I dinna break commitments—once I make them, but I've no' made one yet."

A look of surprise. "Didn't Sir Henry tell you of your engagement—?"

"He told me o' the engagement o' *your* making, which wasna my doing. D'you ken yet, Lord Neville, that 'tis a grown man you have standing here, no' a lad who needs decisions made for him? I'm here for my mother's sake. I'll wed for Archie's sake, since he seems tae want that done quickly. But I'll be picking my own bride. If your Lady Ophelia suits me, I may even wed her, but by no means am I committed tae do so until I do the committing m'self."

"I see," Neville said slowly, stiffly. "You've come here with a chip on your shoulder—"

"D'you think so? I'd call it a powerful dislike for being here m'self. Someone— you, Archie, my mother—*someone should have bluidy well told me aboot that promise of hers sooner than Sir Henry did.*"

Duncan left the room then before he could say even more that he'd regret later. He shouldn't have revealed his true feelings. He hadn't meant to, at least not so soon.

11

It wasn't surprising that Sabrina would find her way outside for a nice walk the first chance she got. She loved the seasons, all four of them, and even when it was its coldest, she could enjoy a brisk walk. Nature, at its harshest or its most beautiful, was always a marvel to her. She took pleasure in lifting her face to the rain, rather than running for cover, of feeling the wind in her hair, the sun on her cheeks. Her aunts had teased her as a child that she had fairy blood and had merely misplaced her wings.

She climbed the hill that she had sometimes stopped on in the past, when coming from the other direction during one of her walks. It was as close as she had ever come to Summers Glade before, that hill, but it had always offered a perfect view of Lord Neville's large estate. She had viewed it in each of the seasons, so knew that the dreary look of it now would change come springtime, when the stately old trees around it donned their green mantles again.

It was truly a lovely old home, and now that she'd seen the inside of it, she was quite impressed. A shame that Lord Neville didn't entertain more often, to show it off to his neighbors, who, like the Lamberts, had always been most curious about him and his home.

Of course, he really wasn't entertaining now, though he did have guests of the unexpected sort. Whether he would be entertaining them, though, was still a matter of speculation. In fact, Sabrina could return from her walk to find her aunts packing once again. That wouldn't bother her much, though she *was* looking forward to finally meeting the esteemed Lord Neville, after living so close to him all these years but never actually seeing him, even from afar.

But she was in no hurry to return and find out, either way, and reaching the top of the hill, she sat down, with no thought to the grass or dirt stains she might pick up, and simply enjoyed the view. Her aunts use to complain to their friends that Sabrina never outgrew her cloths as a child because they were always ruined by bramble tears or grassy stains long before they needed replacing due to growth.

She *had* been careless in that respect and still was, but then her appearance as perceived by others had never been high on her list of concerns. When there wasn't much to work with or improve upon, why waste time trying?

She removed her bonnet and set it aside on the ground next to her. It would have blown away if the ribbons weren't still in her hand, but it did bounce around on the ground, unnoticed by her, getting quite demolished. She had closed her eyes, to better feel the wind as it caught her hair and sent it flying in all directions about her head. She chuckled as a strand whisked across her nose, tickling.

That her eyes were closed, though, and the wind loud in her ears, wasn't the reason she didn't see or hear the rider coming and was nearly run over. He had simply come up so quickly from the other side of the hill behind her that he was upon her before either of them noticed.

It really was a close call, so close that when the horse reared up and was jerked to the side to avoid her, its hooves came down right on top of her bonnet. Not that she noticed that—yet. She was too busy rolling out of the way, which had been quicker to do than to try and find her footing under her heavy skirts.

But she wasn't the only one to do some rolling on the ground. The rider had been unseated when his horse reared up, and landing where the hill started to sharply decline, he'd found no flat purchase and so had rolled a bit before he could stop himself.

Sabrina was the first to recover, though, and get back to her feet. The man was sitting there with his legs spread wide, looking somewhat dazed, or at least he was probably wondering what had happened. The horse wandered off, snorting, but not far. He took Sabrina's bonnet with him, still stuck to his foot as it was, and was now trying to eat the silk flowers he noticed on it.

It was a big man sitting there. She took note of that first, couldn't help but note it, the thickness of his short winter coat emphasizing it across some very broad shoulders. But it was his legs she stared at. She couldn't help it, they were somewhat bare, at least the knees were, between the kilt he wore and his high boots.

A kilt in winter—how unusual. She'd seen Scotsmen in kilts before, as they passed through Oxbow on their way south or back north, but only in the summer. Most of them preferred to dress warmer for the more brisk seasons. Did he not feel the cold?

She knew who he might be, Ophelia's fiancé. The kilt and the dark red hair suggested that he was at least Scottish, and Summers Glade, the direction he'd been heading, was expecting a Scotsman. And oh, my, was Ophelia going to be surprised and likely change her mind real quick about wanting to be rid of him. How could she not, when he was so very handsome, he took even Sabrina's breath away?

He stood up, surprising her that he wasn't just big, but very tall as well. And he dusted off his kilt in such a way that some thigh became visible, causing Sabrina to blush. He hadn't noticed her yet, though, and even so, her cheeks were likely pinkened enough by the wind for a blush not to make much difference.

"Are you all right?"

He swung about to face her. "Och, so there you are. I should be asking you that. I didna see you sitting there till it was almost tae late."

She smiled at him. His brogue was light and pleasant, if his voice somewhat deep. She liked the sound of it, though, strange to her ears, but lyrical. And those eyes, so dark a blue, quite disconcerting now that they were gazing directly at her.

"So I gathered."

"I mun apologize. The beastie and I dinna get along tae well," he said, giving the horse a disgruntled glower. "But then I'm no' much of a horsemon tae begin wi', preferring tae walk if the distance isna tae far."

How coincidental. Her sentiments exactly. She could ride, and very well. She'd been taught as a child as a matter of course, a rounding out of her accomplishments. She just found sidesaddles rather uncomfortable, and besides, she had two sturdy legs that the good Lord meant her to make use of.

His mention of distance prompted her to ask, "Are you just arriving then, to Summers Glade?"

He glanced down the hill at the house, which got another one of his glowers, before he said, "Nay, just needed tae work off a wee bit o' steam, and thought the stallion there could accommodate me. Silly notion. I should've known riding would cause me more aggravation than ease."

She chuckled. It caused Duncan to take a second look at her, more closely than his first.

She was a bedraggled wee lass, with her long brown hair gone all hither and yon, but he found her lack of decorum rather appealing. She was small, but even her long coat, covering her from neck to foot, couldn't hide the very plumpness of her breasts, though it did conceal the rest of her shape. He noted two buttons were missing. He noted the prettiest lilac eyes he'd ever seen.

A thought occurred to him and he

voiced it abruptly. "Are you Lady Ophelia, by chance?"

"Good heavens, no, but you must be the Highland barbarian I've been hearing so much about."

For some reason, he didn't take offense. Perhaps because of the twinkle in her lovely eyes as she said it. She was obviously amused by the term "barbarian" used in context with him, and he was amused by her amusement.

Then, too, he'd donned the kilt, which he normally wouldn't wear in winter, to make a statement for Neville's benefit, that he preferred things Scottish to English. It could be seen as a barbaric statement, though, by others, considering the time of year, not that this paltry English cold could bother him. But that, too, was amusing, now that he was calm enough to think about it.

So he said with a bit of humor in his own tone, "Aye, that would be me."

"You're not as old as I thought you would be," she continued.

He raised an auburn brow at her, asking, "How auld was that?"

"Forty at least."

"Forty!" he roared.

Her peal of laughter was infectious. Duncan just managed to not chuckle with her and gave her what he hoped was a stern look instead.

"You were teasing me then?" he said.

"Was it obvious then?"

"There's no' many I know that brave."

She smiled at him. "I highly doubt you're the barbarian you've been reputed to be, but then I'm not the walking ghost I've been reputed to be either. Strange thing about rumors and gossip. They so rarely deal with the real facts, yet so often are taken as the literal truth."

"So Neville was expecting a barbarian, was he?" Duncan said.

She blinked at him, then laughed again. "Oh, my, I highly doubt it. He would know better, wouldn't he, since he knows you well enough, being your grandfather. No, no, it's those who haven't met you yet, but know of your coming, that might be predisposed to wonder about a Highland Scot, when so few ever come to England to prove that the Highlands of Scotland must be civilized by now, and goodness, that was quite a mouthful, wasn't it?"

Duncan had been about to growl in response. That assumption that his grandfather should know him had really rubbed him on the raw. But the rest of what she said he found so amusing, it actually put him at ease again, so much so that he felt like teasing her back, rather than seriously addressing what the Highlands were *reputed* to be.

"Must it be?" he said.

"What?"

"Civilized."

She appeared to give that some careful thought, then replied logically, "Well, it might not be quite as civilized as England, of course. But I seriously doubt it's still producing barbarians of the truly barbaric sort. Look at you, after all. Or did you forget to bring your war paint?"

He burst out laughing. He doubled over with it. He had to wipe tears from his eyes.

But when he wound down a bit, he noticed she was now frowning at him, and then she said so seriously, "You did, didn't you? You forgot it."

He fell over this time, he laughed so hard. And when he was done, he felt . . . almost normal, the bitterness that had been eating at him gone, at least for the moment. And he saw the impish grin she was now wearing, proving she'd been no more than teasing him again.

What a gem she was, this young girl, certainly not what he'd been expecting from English lasses. If the rest were like her, well, he might not find it so disagreeable to wed one after all.

12

Neville's guests—and the number had grown considerably as the day progressed—had no idea that the only reason they hadn't been summarily sent on their way was that Neville was actually relieved that he wouldn't have to deal with his grandson alone again, after their disastrous first meeting. He was hoping that a house full of young people—and he'd been informed that most of those arriving were close to Duncan's age—would entertain the boy enough that he would feel more comfortable being there.

It had been obvious that that wasn't the case, that Duncan resented this trip to England. Oddly enough, Neville had never considered that his heir might not want to *be* his heir. He wasn't quite sure how to deal with that, or make his grandson more disposed to assuming the responsibilities that would come with his inheritance.

Duncan had much to learn, but perhaps immediately was not the time to begin. Getting the marriage accomplished and out of the way might be a better start, since Duncan did seem to be agreeable to that—for *Archie's* sake.

That still infuriated Neville, that the boy was quite willing to please his Scots relative, but not his English one. To be expected, he supposed, but he still didn't like it. However, he was grateful that Archibald had gotten the boy to agree to wed. He wouldn't feel relieved himself until it was accomplished and a child conceived, since he feared that if the old Scot didn't get a new heir in Duncan's first son, as soon as Neville passed on, he would try to lure Duncan back to the Highlands.

Not an unfounded fear. His communications with Archibald MacTavish had led to one clear indication. The man was very possessive of what was his, and very stubborn and unbending in his demands.

Neville didn't like this dividing of heirs, as the Scot had proposed. Duncan *was* his only heir, no matter Elizabeth's promise that the lad would come to England to claim and administer his inheritance.

That he was also Archibald's only heir, Neville had no problem with. Managers could be hired to oversee the two large estates when Duncan needed to divide his time between one or the other. Neville's holdings were not so complicated that they needed constant supervision. It would be nice if Duncan could devote himself fully to one country, but Englishmen were long accustomed to owning properties in far-off places, as well as on the home front.

It was a moot point, however. The Scotsman clearly felt that he'd lost Duncan because of Elizabeth's promise, and so insisted on the continuation of the line that would give him a new heir. On that, at least, Neville could agree. What man wouldn't like to know that his line would continue and not die out—*before he died himself? For Duncan to produce lots of offspring would assure both men of that, but only if he got started on that producing soon.*

Neville was pleased with his choice of bride for the boy. He probably should have made an effort to meet her prior to making the commitment, but he had still been so furious at Archibald for insisting on the *most* beautiful bride to be had, as if that were the only thing of importance when choosing a bride, that when his agents had promised she was just that, he had contacted her parents posthaste.

But having met her now for the first time that afternoon, he was not displeased. Ophelia Reid was most definitely as beautiful as the reports on her had claimed. She might have been a bit on the stiff side, and had seemed somewhat haughty, but that could easily be attributed to nervousness on her part, in meeting her future in-law.

And haughty pride was not an altogether bad thing, in his opinion. Neville had been known to give that impression himself on occasion. Depending on whom he was dealing with, a certain amount of condescension could be useful. But he was sure now that Duncan, once he saw her, would be quite taken with her. And that was all that mattered, really, that the boy be happy with his bride.

Sabrina *could* have been quite correct in her assumption that Ophelia would change her opinion about Duncan MacTavish once she saw him. She very well might have if they could have met alone, and under different circumstances.

But as Fate would have it, Ophelia was surrounded by her friends and admirers when Duncan made an appearance in the drawing room where they were all gathered. Having just come in from his ride, he was still wearing the clothes he'd donned for Neville's benefit, and she saw them as a confirmation of the unfounded rumors she'd started about him. Unfortunately, so did her friends.

"Good God, he's wearing a skirt," was whispered next to her.

"That's perfectly acceptable dress in Scotland," someone tried to point out. "It's called a—"

"It's a bloody skirt. And here I'd thought the marquis's relative couldn't possibly be as barbaric as anticipated, but apparently I was wrong and he is."

Ophelia was embarrassed, a circumstance that she abhorred. She had expected to have to ridicule Duncan MacTavish in other ways, not have the rumors she'd spread about him end up being quite on the mark. Because of it, she wasn't really seeing him clearly. She saw the kilt, and the red tints in his wildly windblown dark auburn hair, and she saw nothing else except that, ironically, she'd been right.

On the one hand, she was relieved. Her parents would have to see now that a Highlander, a barbaric one at least, simply wouldn't do for her. They had heard the rumors. She'd made sure of that. But they had scoffed that they couldn't possibly be true. They wouldn't be scoffing now.

But on the other hand, it was one thing to be in control of a rumor and to have it work for your benefit, but quite another to be caught in the truth of it—and the embarrassment of it. And Ophelia hated embarrassment. Pink cheeks simply didn't suit her a'tall.

So she was quite annoyed when Duncan presented himself after his moment of observing the room from the doorway, gave her a flourishing—she saw it as exaggerated—bow, and said, "Since there canna be a lassie more bonny in all o' creation, you mun be Lady Ophelia."

She had understood him well enough, but said, "When you can manage your compliments in English, I might pay attention to them. You might try dressing properly as well, or do you Highlanders actually prefer to look like women?"

To imply that there was anything even remotely feminine about a Scottish kilt was as grave an insult as could be imagined. Duncan could have forgiven her, though, attributing it to English ignorance, if she hadn't said it for effect. He couldn't miss the effect, the titters and outright chuckles from her audience, nor her smug look when she heard it.

His embarrassment was unmistakable, though, and apparently exactly what she was hoping for. Why, he couldn't imagine, not that it mattered now. Yet what he had felt at first—thrilled, amazed, grateful even, and resigned that he'd have to be thanking his grandfather for this magnificent bride— made the blow all the worse.

He might have been truly surprised when he first saw her, and utterly dazzled by her beauty—she really was a bonny sight to behold. But at that precise moment, she could not have been more ugly in his eyes.

He said not another word to her. He turned on his heel and left the room to go in search of his grandfather, and found him immediately, since Neville was on the stairs coming down to join his guests.

Duncan didn't pause on his way up, said simply in passing, "She won't do."

Neville, shocked at first by the very finality in his tone, would have gone after Duncan to find out why. But considering their less-than-amicable relationship thus far, he decided to find out by other means.

Having been so pleased with Ophelia Reid, Neville was understandably annoyed and wanting to know what had happened to ruin more than a year's efforts in finding the perfect bride. He signaled his butler, who was standing duty in the hall below, and who had never failed him in knowing all. And this time was no different, since he was informed, verbatim, what had been said in the drawing room.

Silly chit, to not know any better than to voice her ignorance aloud. Beauty was desirable, but not when it came packaged with such stupidity. Duncan was quite right, she wouldn't do at all.

13

Duncan had ridden off, leaving Sabrina on the hill, but then he hadn't known that she would be going in the same direction as he. And she was in no hurry to follow, quite the contrary. She had sat back down and completely lost track of the time as she sorted through each and every single thing he'd said to her and preserved it for all time in her memory.

What an incredibly *exciting* afternoon for her, quite the most exciting she could ever remember having, but then she'd never before spent time, and discourse, with such a handsome man. And complicated. He hadn't *wanted* to smile or laugh with her. She'd had to make an extra effort to get him to. And she wondered, after he'd gone, what could be so bothering him to cause such a sour mood.

But he'd been smiling when he left her, and that pleased her more than she could say, that she'd lightened his mood, because she had liked him. She didn't usually make such a judgment that quickly, but in his case it was hard not to like him, his voice, his smile, his sense of humor when he allowed it loose, and of course, the look of him. He had disturbed her senses in a myriad of ways, but she still had enjoyed every moment she had spent in his presence.

But she wasn't delusional. A man like him was not for the likes of her; he was for the Ophelias of the world. A shame, a pitiful shame really, that it was so, but there you had it. Beautiful for beautiful, and for her, a nice, plain-looking man, intelligent, resourceful, kind, someone who would enjoy taking walks with her, and laughing, and sitting on a hill watching the sunset together . . .

Oh, my, the sun really was about to set. Wherever had the time got to?

Sabrina leapt to her feet and ran, nearly

all the way, to Summers Glade. She entered the house at the back, so as to encounter fewer people who might see her windblown appearance, and finding the servants' stairs, made it up to her room. Her aunt Alice was there, however, so she wasn't going to escape complete notice. But Alice had been impatiently waiting on her—and packing for her—so she really didn't spare her more than a brief glance before bringing another dress to the open valise on the bed.

She did spare the query, "Wherever have you been? We should have left hours ago with everyone else."

"Everyone else? So Lord Neville didn't like having London descend on him after all?"

Alice tsked. "Whether he did or didn't, he *was* agreeable to having a house party, then suddenly he wasn't, but no more than to be expected from that senile old coot. And there we were just getting ready to go down, when his housekeeper came round to ask us to leave. Poor woman was quite embarrassed about it, too."

Sabrina moved to help her aunt finish

the packing. "You can't blame Lord Neville, when having this gathering wasn't his idea. He no doubt feels that Ophelia and her fiancé should have some time alone together, to become acquainted—"

"Hard to do that, m'dear, when the Reids have already left to return to London."

"Left?" Sabrina frowned. "Just because the marquis declined to entertain grandly? Ophelia really wouldn't get into a snit about that, would she?"

"I've no idea. Didn't see them before they left. Hilary might have. You can ask her."

Sabrina did that, while they waited in the entryway with their baggage. The housekeeper had sent for one of Lord Neville's own vehicles, since they had no other transportation, having arrived with the Reids.

"Mary said she would write me," Hilary replied in answer to Sabrina's question. "She said she was too upset to talk of it just now, and poor dear, she did look quite upset."

"And Ophelia? Did you see her?"

"Yes," Hilary said, then in a whispered aside, "And she appeared to have finally been chastised by her father, for being so presumptuous. Quite pink, her one cheek was. I don't hold with physical discipline, but Mary's girl *has* been allowed to take on airs that *should* have been nipped in the bud long ago."

Sabrina was amazed. "Her father actually slapped her?"

Hilary nodded. "That handprint on her cheek would suggest so."

"But they didn't object when she invited us here," Sabrina pointed out.

"We hardly would have been noticed if it had only been us, but fifty-six people arrived here today, all invited by Ophelia, as if she were already the marquise and had every right to invite whomever she pleased. It's no wonder Neville put his foot down after he finally got a full head count. I would have, too, I don't mind saying, if the guests I *do* invite happen to invite fifty-six others. M'dear, that just isn't proper form."

Of course it wasn't, and Ophelia did no doubt know that. But then Sabrina had never spoken to her aunts about Ophelia's attempt to sabotage her engagement to be rid of what *had* been an unwanted fiancé. She just hadn't felt comfortable talking about it, when she so disapproved of it, and Ophelia's mother was Hilary's good friend.

This latest scheme of Ophelia's to have half the *ton* descending on Summers Glade had likely been done *just* to infuriate the marquis. But then that was before she had actually met her fiancé, and if she *had* met him by now, she was undoubtedly regretting what she had set in motion.

It was all very complicated, Ophelia's plans and means of accomplishing them. Sabrina was quite glad to be out of it. She had been raised to be straightforward. Setting up complicated schemes in the hopes that they would have a particular desired effect just wasn't her cup of tea. It had never been dull, being around Ophelia, but Sabrina was actually looking forward to a bit of dullness again.

However, she *was* hoping for one more sight of Duncan MacTavish before she left

Summers Glade, since she wasn't likely to see him again after today, at least not until the wedding, which they were sure to be invited to. With Ophelia gone back to London, he would probably be going there as well. But wherever he was in the big house, it wasn't near the entrance, and they were soon on their way home.

14

"Well, where is she? I mun admit I've been looking forward tae meeting this most bonny lassie in all o' England that ye found for the lad."

Neville bristled as the large Scotsman barged into his dining room where he'd been partaking of a solitary dinner. Neville's butler, arriving a second later, gave him a pained look, that he hadn't arrived first to give him warning of this intrusion.

"Archibald?" Neville guessed.

"Aye, and who else were ye expecting?"

"Certainly not you," Neville said disagreeably. "What the devil are you doing here?"

The Scot pulled up a chair across from Neville and stared at the butler, as if expecting him to serve him, now that he was there. But to Neville he said, "Ye didna think I'd be leaving it tae ye tae make sure the wedding goes forward in a timely manner, did ye now?"

"Duncan made no mention that you were coming," Neville pointed out.

Archie chuckled at that. "Perhaps because he didna know I was. The boy doesna do things in a relaxed manner, ye ken. Once he sets his mind on a course, he follows it straightaway. Not a bad trait tae have, but a wee bit tae fast paced for these auld bones o' mine. He would've been impatient tae hae me holding him back on the trip here, sae I decided tae follow after at a slower pace, withoout telling him. Impatience annoys him, after all, and ye wouldna hae wanted him arriving here annoyed—more'n he already was."

The last was added in an unmistakably smug tone. Neville didn't miss it and just managed to keep from grinding his teeth in his own annoyance.

"Yes, that's quite a large chip he arrived with on his shoulder. I wonder why."

Archibald snorted. "Ye'll no' be blaming me for that, mon. 'Twas no' me tha' decided he should hae the stability o' know-

ing only one home whilst growing up, 'twas
ye and his muther decided that. A good
decision, mind ye, tha' I was happy tae
agree wi', but ye could've come tae visit
him, tae let him know ye afore he was full
grown."

"After the first trip I made up there to
do that nearly killed me?"

"Och, ye English are weaklings, tae
shrivel in a wee bit o' cold," Archie said
in disgust, aware of that one time Neville
had tried to venture into the Highlands.
"But if he hasna told ye, it wasna that he
never met ye afore now that has him in
such a fash, 'tis that yer taking him from
his home and expecting him tae live
amongst strangers."

"We won't *be* strangers to him for long."

"*And* that he had nae warning that ye'd
expect him tae move here."

Neville blushed slightly, unable to dispute that accusation, and said weakly in
his defense, "Elizabeth should have told
him."

"Aye, and likely she would've if she'd
lived long enough tae, puir lass."

"You could have told him long before

now yourself," Neville added. "Why didn't you?"

Archie raised a brow at that. "When I was hoping ye'd die afore he reached his majority sae he'd ne'er have tae know at all?"

Neville's cheeks reddened fully this time, but in anger rather than embarrassment. "So sorry to disappoint you, but he would still have become the next marquis, no matter when I happen to pass on."

"Ye've *nae* other kin, no' even some distant, distant, long-forgotten cousin?"

"I was an only child," Neville said stiffly. "My father was an only child. My grandfather had two sisters, but they both died in childhood. The generations before that had brief lines, but none that have survived. Duncan is my only heir, and I still do not understand your insistence that he can't be your heir as well."

"Ye wouldna mind him living the year round in the Highlands then?" Archie said in feigned surprise. "Och, mon, ye should've said—"

"Of course he can't remain there permanently," Neville cut in impatiently. "He'll have duties here that—"

"As I thought," Archie cut in as well. "But ye ken for yerself tha' for most o' the year 'tis nae wise tae travel far in the Highlands, even for those who live there. Yet ye'd hae the lad doing it? Or are ye suggesting that his duties here would be more important than his duties in Scotland? Or mayhap yer just suggesting that he come home, tae the only home he's ever known, for only a few weeks oout o' each year, during our short summer?"

"No, what I think is that you don't have enough confidence in him to manage an empire on his own. But he's got Thackeray blood in him. Unlike you, I have little doubt that he can do just that."

"That boy can do anything he sets his mind tae," Archie all but shouted. "I'm just nae wanting tae see him kill himself trying tae spread himself tae thin, as *yer* willing tae let him do."

"So we disagree on what he's capable of, or rather, what you'll allow him to be capable of. This is beginning to sound like those ridiculous letters that passed between us. I wouldn't be a bit surprised if you would disagree and end up spiting yourself, *just* so you can disagree."

Archie actually laughed. "They dinna raise fools in the Highlands."

"I beg to differ—fools aren't raised, they are born, and they *can* be born anywhere. That you're sitting here arguing with me in my own house is proof of that."

"So yer calling me a fool now?" Archie chuckled. "Actually, sounds tae me like yer calling yerself one."

To which Neville said in crisp abruptness, "Get out, MacTavish."

"I'll be staying till the lad is wed, sae the sooner ye make sure that happens, the sooner ye'll be rid o' me. Sae when is the wedding?"

Neville gave up the idea of getting rid of his nemesis, as aware as Archibald no doubt was that Duncan wouldn't be very pleased if this grandfather of his was refused a welcome. "Your guess would be as good as mine, since he has no one at the moment that he wants to marry."

Archie shot out of his chair in a grand display of Scots temper. "He wouldna have her? I could've swore he said he'd at least meet the lass afore—"

"He did meet her."

Archie's brown eyes narrowed on Neville

at the conclusion that answer drew. "Then she wasna as bonny as you claimed she was?"

"Oh, she's definitely the most beautiful chit I've ever seen," Neville replied.

Archie sighed as he sat back down, truly disappointed. "I'd hoped the lad wouldna let his anger get in the way o' his own happiness, but apparently he needs a wee bit more time tae adjust tae these changes being forced on him."

"Whether he does or doesn't has nothing to do with his refusal of the girl. Would have done the same thing myself, after the way she insulted him. A pretty shell is all she turned out to be, with the sense of a twit, not at all what we want for the boy."

Archie made a mumbling sound, then, "So who was next on yer list of brides for him? Or did ye no' investigate more'n this one lass?"

"There are a few other possible choices, but I won't be making the same mistake again of not meeting them prior to making an offer."

"Ye've made arrangements tae bring them here, then, tae get the meeting oout o' the way?"

Neville stared up at the ceiling for a moment. He would have preferred to roll his eyes for effect, but doing so these days gave him headaches.

Calmly, though, as if explaining to a child, he said, "He only just refused the first girl this afternoon. I've barely had time to absorb the fact of all that time wasted on her, much less think of how to go about meeting the others without letting them know why—"

"Yer tae much of a recluse, mon, or ye'd ken tha' the easiest way tae bring folk t'gether is a blasted party. Throw one, a big'n, and make sure each o' yer other candidates shows up for it. The lad can then do his part and decide which he wants tae offer for."

Neville almost laughed. A party? After he'd just kicked a good portion of the *ton* out of his house, he was now to invite them back?

"A party might not be a good idea—"

"Och, yer disagreeing just tae disagree wi' me, and well I ken it. A big party is just the thing tae gather 'em all in sae the lad will be having a good selection tae choose from. If ye dinna know how tae throw one, get one o' yer society dames in here tae show ye how."

Neville flushed with color once more. "It hasn't been *that* long since I've entertained."

Archie was less restrained. When he felt like laughing, he laughed, and just now was no exception. Neville did grind his teeth a bit this time, listening to him, and longed for the days when a duel at dawn was an acceptable way to get rid of one's enemies.

"I do know how to go about it, thank you very much," he continued, tight-lipped.

"Then should ye no' get started sending oout the invitations? Ne'er put off tae t'morrow what can be accomplished t'day."

"If you don't mind, I'll finish my dinner first," Neville gritted out.

"Speaking o' dinner, yer a puir host, mon, tae nae be offering me some o' that fine-smelling beef yer eating," Archie said with a sigh, shaking his head as he stared forlornly at the food across from him on Neville's plate. "I do hope ye'll do better once yer many guests start arriving."

The insult didn't work. Neville pointed to

the door behind Archie and replied, this time with a smile, "The kitchen is that way."

Archie gave a hoot of laughter. "Ye just might be a worthy adversary after all, Thackeray, indeed ye might. Time will tell, though, but then we've some o' that tae spare now, since ye blundered on that first lass sae badly. Now, where are ye hiding m'grandson, or did ye send him off tae be eating in the kitchen as well?"

"I assume he's nursing his wounds from that viper's tongue somewhere in private. The girl did shred him to the core, or so I've been told. But please, do relieve me of your presence and go find him. You probably *are* just the thing to cheer him up just now, though personally, I can't imagine a more distressing thought."

Archibald chuckled on his way out the door. "Ye'll get used tae me, Englishmon . . . but then, ye've nae other choice, have ye?"

15

When Ophelia arrived, Sabrina was out enjoying her daily walk, so the London girl was already unpacking to settle in when Sabrina returned to learn of their unexpected guest and joined her upstairs. And she really was unexpected, and alone, without her parents.

A week had gone by since the Reids had returned to London. Hilary had not heard from Lady Mary yet, so they still didn't know what exactly had happened at Summers Glade that day when they had all been ousted.

They did know, however, couldn't help but know since it was all the entire neighborhood was talking about currently, that the Marquis of Birmingdale had decided to do some entertaining on a grand scale, after all. And it had gotten out, through the servants' grapevine, which was usually much more accurate than the *ton's* gossip mill, that the reason for the extended house party was that the marquis was shopping for a new fiancée for his grandson.

That had been a shock, to Sabrina at least. She still couldn't quite credit it, that for whatever reason, the young Highlander had rejected Ophelia after meeting her, which was the tale making the rounds. It was, of course, what Ophelia had hoped for, but still, Sabrina had been sure that once the two young people met, they would both be quite pleased to be engaged to each other. Instead, Duncan Mac-Tavish was apparently looking for a new bride now, and with the wide selection of eligible young misses invited to Summers Glade, was sure to find one in short order.

Sabrina and her aunts, of course, had not been invited to the grand party, no doubt because the old family scandal had resurfaced again and had reached even the marquis's ears, if he didn't remember it from years past. One avoided scandal at all costs when looking into matrimony; one did not marry *into* a scandal.

Summers Glade had begun filling with the elite of English aristocracy since yesterday. More than a hundred guests had already arrived, including some of those who had been ousted just last week. But then it was being touted as *the* party of the year, so not to be missed.

That was partly because so many of the *ton* were as curious as Lord Neville's own neighbors were, to finally meet the reclusive lord. Others were of a mind that you simply didn't tell a marquis no, for whatever reason. But one countess had even canceled her midseason ball so that she could come to Yorkshire instead. That alone would make the invitations highly coveted, once word of it spread.

Hilary and Alice were disappointed that Sabrina hadn't been invited, and even had a row about it. Not that they thought she might catch the eye of the future marquis, but because all the other eligible young men would be at a party that size. Sabrina was disheartened herself, but not for the same reason. She simply regretted the lost opportunity to see Duncan MacTavish again, after enjoying so much her first encounter with him.

But now here was Ophelia, back in Yorkshire, and most likely she didn't have an invitation to Summers Glade either. Once Sabrina's initial surprise subsided, she could only wonder why, and that was the first thing she inquired about, in her less-than-direct fashion, as she joined Ophelia in the room she had been given and got the greetings out of the way.

"I would have thought you would be glad to be back in London where all the excitement is," Sabrina said.

Ophelia all but snapped, "When just about *all* of London happens to be here just now?"

Sabrina raised a brow at the tone. Ophelia might be here, but apparently she didn't really want to be here, so what the devil was she doing here? Unless . . .

"You've been invited back to Summers Glade then? Have they just run out of room—?"

"Don't be obtuse," Ophelia retorted. "Of course I wouldn't be invited back there. I've come here to hide, if you really must know, and to see what can be done to rectify this appalling situation."

Sabrina was having trouble keeping up with Ophelia's thought processes. "Hide from whom? Your parents? Don't they know you've come here?"

"I swear, Sabrina, you can be annoyingly dense," Ophelia said unkindly. "My parents don't care where I go. They are most displeased with me just now. My father even slapped me. Can you believe that? *He slapped me!* For which I will never, ever forgive him."

"Then you *are* hiding from them?"

Ophelia threw herself down on the bed with a very loud sigh, indicating that she was done explaining things to people who didn't have sense enough to understand her. Sabrina didn't take offense. She'd witnessed this type of theatrics from the London girl enough to not be impressed by them, though she would allow, Ophelia didn't seem to be pretending this time. She really did seem upset.

Sabrina chose not to comment further. Silence did have a surprising effect on Ophelia. More often than not, it tended to get her to come right to the point of a discussion without any further prompting, where otherwise, she would go round and round a subject until her listeners were ready to expire from curiosity—or exasperation.

This time was no different. After a few moments, she mumbled to herself and sat up, glaring at Sabrina as if it were all her fault, whatever it was that had upset her, though she cleared up immediately just what it was.

"I'm in disgrace," she said, then on a rising note that turned into a wail, "I'm being pitied! *Pitied!* Can you believe that? No, of course you can't, because it's simply far too unbelievable."

Sabrina, wisely, said exactly what was expected. "I don't believe it."

Ophelia nodded. "It's true, though. Even my closest friends were 'poor dearing' me, before they set off for Summers Glade, official invitations in hand."

"Poor dearing" did indeed sound like pity. Carefully Sabrina asked, "But—why?"

The anger returned, shooting Ophelia off the bed for several paces around the room before she said, "That barbarian Highlander, that's why! The stupid man was supposed to agree that we wouldn't suit for matrimony. It was supposed to be a mutual decision where neither of us would have suffered any consequences for it. Instead, he got all huffy over a little minor criticism and let it be known that *he* didn't find *me* acceptable. Now everyone and their mother knows that he all but jilted me at the altar."

"But you didn't reach the altar," Sabrina calmly pointed out.

That got her another glare that said clearly, *Idiot, what difference does that make?* but aloud Ophelia said, "You still don't understand yet? I was to be congratulated for escaping a match made in hell. Instead I am the latest gossip making the rounds. Because *he* broke the engagement, everyone now thinks there must be something wrong with me. Why else wouldn't he want me, after all?"

Sabrina sighed at that point. "I guess I don't understand then. I could have sworn you had hoped he would break the engagement."

"Not *him!* My parents were supposed to end it, since they were the ones who got me into it. *He* was supposed to remain besotted until the end, no matter what I said to him. But he is too barbaric to realize the gentlemanly part he should have played. And now I don't dare show myself until this dies down—or he rectifies it."

Well, that finally explained the "hiding" part of Ophelia's visit. Sabrina couldn't imagine, though, how Duncan was supposed to rectify this situation for Ophelia, unless it was to offer some reason for breaking the engagement that would show her in a better light.

"What did you say to him that did cause him to reject you?"

"I told you, it was just a minor remark that he took undue offense over. I will admit it was rather thoughtless of me, but then I wasn't thinking clearly when he showed up in that barbaric costume of his, which served to confirm in my mind that he was everything I'd feared he would be. If he had been dressed normally, I wouldn't have been so shocked, and that first meeting would certainly have gone much differently."

Sabrina had to agree with that possible outcome. Hadn't she herself thought that surely the engaged couple would be very pleased to be engaged, once they met and got a good look at each other? But she also knew Ophelia well enough by now to realize she was stressing her own innocence a bit too much, and wondered why.

"So you're going to stay with us until the gossip settles down?"

"Goodness, no, that might take forever. I do make a wonderful target for gossip, after all. No, we're going to rectify this ourselves."

Sabrina blinked. "We?"

"Yes." Ophelia nodded. "It's the least you can do, after I befriended you in London and helped with your launch there. You simply must help me with this now."

"Well, certainly—if I can."

"You can," Ophelia assured her. "And you needn't even do much. Just arrange a meeting is all."

"A meeting with whom?"

"My ex-fiancé, of course. We're going to get him to ask me to marry him again. Then it will all seem like a silly lovers' tiff that caused the breakup, which will be quite acceptable and put an end to the gossip."

16

"You just show up at the door."

Truthfully, Sabrina was so appalled by Ophelia's newest scheme, and in particular that the girl wanted to involve her in it, that she could barely put two thoughts together. And even Ophelia's suggestions for how to go about it, she found highly distasteful.

"I didn't receive an invitation, Ophelia, any more than you did," Sabrina reminded the girl.

"But you're a neighbor. Neighbors don't need invitations to visit."

"During a party they do."

Ophelia waved a dismissive hand. "A minor point. And besides, you don't really want to enter the house, where you might be overheard by one of the guests. No, no, you want to draw him outside where you can be assured of privacy when you speak to him."

On the one hand, that sounded like something Sabrina would very much like to do, speak to Duncan MacTavish in private, that is. But on the other hand, she knew it was bad form, *really* bad form, to come visiting your neighbor when you knew he was having a party—that you hadn't been invited to. Beyond rude. Simply *not* done.

And the subject matter that she was to broach, well, that would be utterly embarrassing as well. She didn't know the first thing about matchmaking, after all, which was pretty much what Ophelia was asking of her.

Besides, all things said and done, she liked Duncan. So did she really want to see him married to a woman like Ophelia who schemed and started rumors about people whether they were true or not? Liking him, and quite aware that she had no chance whatsoever to have him herself, then yes, she would like to see him marry someone as beautiful as Ophelia was, but hopefully someone with a bit more moral fortitude and honor than the London girl had.

So she didn't really want to help Ophelia. However, she couldn't refuse outright either, when Ophelia *had* befriended her in London. She owed her some help in kind for that. But she did want one thing clarified first before she agreed to this latest scheme.

"Do you *want* to marry him now, or is this only a means to end the gossip about you?"

Ophelia seemed surprised by the question. That she had to give it some thought before answering didn't greatly reassure Sabrina, either.

But she did finally say, "Of course, I do. I told you, if I had actually noticed him when I met him, rather than just that silly kilt he was wearing, none of this would be necessary now. He *is* quite handsome, after all, which I realized after it was too late."

"There was always a possibility that he might be handsome," Sabrina pointed out.

"Not really," Ophelia disagreed, and shook her head just to stress it. "My mother knew Lord Neville from years ago, when she used to live here, and she confessed he was quite plain looking himself, which didn't offer much hope that there would be any improvement in a grandson of his. Quite ironic that the Scottish side of Duncan, which was the side I objected to, or at least I objected that he was from the far northern regions that are known to still be quite barbaric, would be the side to give him his good looks."

Sabrina was forced to accept that reasoning, not that the northern Highlands were barbaric, because who knew, after all, what they were like, when Englishmen so rarely visited there to tell about it? No, she accepted that reasoning only because she knew that people did fall in love based on mutual attraction, and if Ophelia was now attracted to Duncan, that might be all that was necessary to turn her into a good wife for him. The London girl had schemed and lied because she had felt desperate and trapped, but now she found it had all been wasted effort on her part, that she was pleased with her fiancé, or ex-fiancé at the moment, after all.

So Sabrina found herself walking to Summers Glade that afternoon, even though she'd rather be walking in any other direction. She really, really didn't want to be doing this, not just because she liked Duncan, and didn't really like Ophelia all that much, after getting to know her, but because this matchmaking thing just wasn't something she would ordinarily do. Ordinarily? *Never* was more like it. It was tampering with people's lives, trying to matchmake them, when they might end up with a disastrous marriage that she would then see as *all* her fault.

But a favor—no, a discharge of an owed debt was how she tried to see it. And the sooner she got her part out of the way, the sooner the bile in her stomach would go away.

Frazzled, that was how Duncan started feeling, once Neville's guests began arriving at Summers Glade. It was bad enough before the party began, when he had to sit through the arguing over the agenda for it. He'd swear, if his grandfathers were any younger at all, they'd be taking their fists to each other, so much did they hotly disagree on things.

But once the guests showed up, he had Archie taking him from room to room to point out the physical attributes of each lass they came across. Then he had Neville dragging him aside to point out the family histories of each girl, and which ones were more desirable socially. He'd had to put his foot down finally. There were just too many women there for him to keep track of all the information being given to him about each. So now the two old men were sending him notes, and the butler, delivering them, was becoming as frazzled as he was.

He had to wonder, what ever happened to the old tried-and-true fall-in-love-and-*then*-get-married philosophy that served so many people well? This getting married because this lass was the prettiest, or this one had the most titles in her ancestry, just didn't sit well with him.

He'd already seen the most beautiful, and so knew firsthand that prettiest did not make for best choice. Of course, Archie insisted they couldn't all be senseless twits like Ophelia Reid, and so he was still pushing for beauty rather than credentials. Neville agreed that beauty often came paired with too much vanity and overweening pride, so was still insisting on the better social status. Duncan was inclined to think they'd disagree just to disagree.

He had to admit, though, that he was being offered an abundance in the way of choices. Since he *had* agreed to get married—a moment of insanity, surely—if he couldn't find at least one lass to his liking out of the fifty or so who had been invited, then he'd be deliberately not trying. During that first day of the arrivals, and on into the next morning, he did find himself continually looking for a pair of lilac eyes, but none were to be found.

Not that he was thinking of that particular girl as a possible candidate for matrimony. He'd simply enjoyed her company, and was looking forward to a bit of her humor, which had managed to lighten his mood that day he met her, and he was definitely in need of mood lightening again.

When he began to wonder why she hadn't made an appearance, since she had seemed to be a neighbor of Neville's, having been out for a walk in the area—and who better to invite to a party than your own neighbors?—he decided to take his question to his grandfather.

It was the first time that he had actually sought out the old man since the day of his own arrival. They had spoken, of course, at meals and in passing, the stilted speech of strangers, which they really still were. But Duncan still wasn't comfortable in Neville's presence, his bitterness rising each time he saw him, and so he avoided him when he could.

He found Neville after lunch, back in his private sitting room. The old man did seem to hide out upstairs for most of each day. He'd been making an appearance at meals, and for a few hours each evening, but other than that, he left his guests to their own devices.

Too many years of solitary company, Duncan supposed, would make a large house party of the scope this one had become very intimidating, or rather, unappealing. Neville wasn't the sort to be intimidated, after all, though at his age, he didn't inspire that emotion either, at least not with his grandson. But he was the sort who wanted to just be left alone, thus the "recluse" description that Duncan had heard more than once paired with Neville's name.

He had no intention of disturbing the old man for long, in fact, got right to the point in asking about his violet-eyed neighbor.

After blinking a few times, indicating that Duncan's knock might have caught Neville nodding off for an afternoon nap, the marquis said with assurance, "There are no young women of gentry in the neighborhood, not suitable for marriage to you, that is, or I would have invited them, since they, at least, wouldn't have to abide here for the duration, but could commute back and forth. Bloody well running out of room here as it is."

Duncan dismissed the notion that the lass could have been common stock—her speech had been cultured, and she'd displayed no nervousness in dealing with a lord, as the working class tended to do, so he insisted, "She's gentry."

"Then she might have been a visitor, might even have been one of those fools who came here at the Reid girl's request and were sent packing with her. Lilac eyes, you say?" Neville shook his head. "I don't know a single person with unusual eyes like that. But if you were taken with the girl, I'll investigate and find out who she was."

Duncan shook his head. "I just enjoyed her company when I met her. She made me laugh, and I was sore in need of that at the time."

That remark had been thoughtless on Duncan's part, rather than deliberate, and now they were both embarrassed. Sighing over his own loose tongue—if he was going to get a dig in on someone, it should at least be intentional—Duncan went back downstairs.

He was disappointed, though, that the lass wouldn't be showing up as he'd thought, so he was in no hurry to rejoin the guests in one of the many rooms they were congregating in, and hearing the knock at the door, took that opportunity for delay by answering it himself. The butler, absent, was no doubt off searching for him to deliver another note. The thought almost amused him.

But he really wished he hadn't decided on this particular delay when the young man standing on the other side of the door looked him over in a rude manner and then exclaimed, "Good God, you must be the barbarian, with that hair, yes, must be indeed. Didn't expect to meet you this soon. They've put you to opening doors, have they?"

Duncan, in the process of trying to unravel the English drawl, with not all that much success, latched on to the one word he'd heard a bit too much since coming to England. And in his present mood, which was still mixed with embarrassment, he very easily could come to blows over it.

"You're calling me a barbarian, are you?"

"Me? Wouldn't think of it. Barbarically handsome, perhaps, but no, no, just what's making the rounds, don't you know, but then—perhaps you don't know? You've been the major *on-dit* for weeks now."

Duncan decided what he was hearing might as well be an unknown foreign language, yet he did grasp the "you've been the major . . ." part, he wanted clarified, "What is *'on-dit'?*"

"Gossip, dear boy, juicy gossip of the slanderous sort," he was told. "I have it on good authority—but then can there really be such a thing when dealing with rumors?—that your dear fiancée, er, well, your dear *ex*-fiancée, was the very one to start it all."

It wasn't the first time he'd heard that he had been the subject of rumors, either. Hadn't the lass on the hill mentioned something about *hearing* that he was a barbarian? With her, though, he'd been unable to take offense. With this fellow, he was having a hard time not being offended.

Nearly as tall as himself, though not quite as broad of shoulder, the man was athletically built. Wearing a traveling greatcoat merely draped over his shoulders, impeccably dressed beneath it, despite the fact that he'd been traveling and that tended to rumple even the best materials, he cut a dashing figure. Blond—Duncan was truly beginning to think most of England was—blue eyed, and in his mid-twenties, he had an air of importance about him.

Duncan wouldn't have cared if he were royalty, he still didn't like the fellow's manner, and in one of his calmer tones—though those who knew him would surely call it ominous—he asked, "What, exactly, has been said aboot me, if you dinna mind telling me?"

"Just rubbish that anyone with a whit of intelligence would dismiss, but you know how ridiculous some females can be. Take my sister there."

The fellow nodded over his shoulder at a lass with the same shade of blond hair that the gentleman sported. She was in the process of directing no fewer than four servants in the unloading of no fewer than six large trunks from the coach pulled up nearby. Very pretty girl, though.

Duncan no sooner had that thought than the fellow added, "Had to drag her here kicking and screaming, the silly chit is so sure you're going to be toting a club and wearing bearskins to dinner. Takes gossip as the literal truth, Mandy does, when it should be enjoyed for what it is, titillating fiction designed to break the inevitable boredom of a nonworking class."

"Why come, if she didna want tae come?"

"And miss this golden opportunity to meet the reclusive Neville Thackeray? Wouldn't think of it. He's only been speculated about for years and years, and most of the people I know have never even clapped eyes on him. 'Sides, the little sister there is in the market, if you know what I mean, so Mum and Dad pretty much insisted she not miss the exposure of a grand country gathering as this one is sure to be. Not that they're hoping for *you* in particular, dear boy, just that they want to keep her circulating while the Season lasts, and yours truly gets to chaperone, don't you know."

Duncan was starting to understand the fellow better now, and wishing he didn't. That "dear boy," he found particularly condescending, enough for him to remark, "If you havena noticed, I'm no' exactly a *boy,* and certainly no' a *dear* one tae you, when we havena met prior. I've laid men on the floor for implying less."

"Have you?"

This was said in a very unimpressed tone. But then the fellow began to chuckle. That in turn turned into some extended laughter. When that wound down, the Englishman continued, "A piece of advice, my friend. Learn to distinguish between a deliberate insult and what is clearly, or at least clearly intended as, no more than an affectation of speech. It might save you much angst, I'm sure, and might save a few innocent noses as well."

Feeling foolish never had been a preference of Duncan's. It usually annoyed the hell out of him instead, and now was no different. "Your own nose isna safe yet, mon. Just who are you?"

Grinning, and so obviously not taking Duncan's threat seriously, the Englishman answered, "I've a few titles, but truly deplore passing them out. Just call me Rafe, *old* chap."

That last crack got the door shut on one of the most highly sought-after young lords of the realm, heir to a dukedom, wealthy beyond measure, the most eligible bachelor of the Season and every hostess's dream come true. And yet the door was being shut on him.

Duncan would *not* have been impressed had he known all of that. He was hoping their first meeting would be their last. They were to become great friends, though. They just didn't know it yet.

17

"Why, Miss Sabrina!" Richard Jacobs exclaimed in surprise. "You've never come this far on one of your walks before. Is something amiss?"

Sabrina smiled at Lord Neville's butler to put him at ease. She knew the man well, and his family. She knew just about everyone in their small area of Yorkshire, after all, including everyone's servants, and everyone knew her. Her walks did take her everywhere, after all, and being the friendly sort she was, she would usually strike up a conversation with anyone she came across. Then, too, she had grown up here, and it was hard not to know everyone in such a small community—with the exception of Lord Neville himself.

Her embarrassment was starting to

show, however, since Jacobs would know that she wasn't there by invitation. He did so pride himself on knowing every single thing that had to do with Lord Neville, and in his position of greeting the guests, would know whom to expect.

To put *herself* at ease, she didn't get right to the point, asked instead, "How is your lovely wife faring now? Better, I hope?"

"Oh, much better, miss. And do please thank your aunt Alice again for that tea recipe. It was just the thing to soothe her cough."

Sabrina *could* have continued to chat, but felt her cheeks already heating, and before they got too bright a red, she wound up her courage. "I will be sure to do that. And no, nothing is amiss. I've just been asked to deliver a private message to Lord Duncan while I was out and about today."

She couldn't imagine why he rolled his eyes at that, until he said, "I've been charged with the same task, repeatedly, since last evening. The young lord is getting quite annoyed with me, and I can hardly blame him." And then he leaned forward to whisper, "It's his grandfathers, the both of them. They seem to be pulling him in two different directions without a moment's peace."

"His Scottish grandfather is here as well?"

"Oh my, yes, and a very . . . loud gentleman he is, too. But when they are in the same room together, Lord Neville and Lord Archibald, that is, well, they really don't like each other, if you know what I mean."

Now, that was a shame. You'd think that the grandfathers would get along splendidly, both having their grandson's best interests in mind. To Jacobs, though, she nodded, and much as she would have preferred otherwise, got the subject back on track.

"If Lord Duncan is busy, don't disturb him. I can always come back another time, since I don't think my message is of an urgent matter. But if he has a moment to spare, and it shouldn't take any longer than that, I would like to get this duty dispensed with."

"Certainly, Miss Sabrina. I'll try to locate him right now. And please step in—"

"No!" She coughed, to cover how horribly appalled she'd just sounded. "I mean, I know you have a house full of guests, and, well, the weather is so nice today, I'd prefer to wait out here."

The weather was anything but nice, was quite cloudy and looking like rain was imminent, but then anyone who knew Sabrina knew that she loved being outdoors and never missed her daily walk, no matter the weather. Rain, snow, or the hottest day in summer, she'd be out in it, so what he might see as cold and dreary weather, she might well find refreshing or even beautiful.

He nodded, and not to be rude, even left the door open as he disappeared into the house. Sabrina, afraid someone might notice her in passing, stepped well away from the door. She was hoping that Duncan would be busy; then again, she was hoping to get this over with. Contradictions in feelings really did not sit well on the stomach, and hers was protesting most vehemently with a queasiness that wouldn't go away.

Five minutes passed, then another five. She was just about positive that she would be vomiting in the bushes if she had to endure this embarrassment even one more minute, and decided it would be better for her stomach, at least, to just leave. Then she heard the footsteps behind her.

She swung about just as Duncan began to say, "The butler said you—" He stopped, surprise lighting up his features as he recognized her, then added, "You! So you *do* live around here, aye?"

"Well, yes, our cottage is just off the road on the way to Oxbow, about a twenty-minute walk from here."

" 'Our'? You're no' married, are you?"

She blinked, then grinned. "Not that I've noticed lately. I live with my two maiden aunts."

He frowned. "Are you new tae the neighborhood then, that m'grandfather wouldna know you tae invite you tae this party o' his?"

This was approaching what could be called a sticky subject, and she'd just as well not go into the details of exactly why Lord Neville wouldn't send her any invites. Duncan was proving much too inquisitive—about her—when he should be asking about her message.

So she said merely, "I've never met Lord Neville, so no, he doesn't know me."

"Well, then." He smiled at her. "Since I know you, let me extend a belated invitation—"

She held up a hand to stop him. Had she really thought she could avoid the subject?

"I fear I may have misled you. Your grandfather has never met me, but that doesn't mean he doesn't know of me, and I think I can safely say he wouldn't consider me an appropriate guest for the purpose of his party."

Bright red, her cheeks were, by the time she got all that out. But he nodded in understanding, then surprised her by saying, "So you'll come anyway, at my request, and bedamned what the auld mon has tae say aboot it."

"No, really, I couldn't. Now, you really must let me deliver my message and be on my way."

He twisted his lips a bit, as if he might argue, but then he sighed. "Verra well, what message is that?"

Now that she had to say it, the words just wouldn't come out. Her cheeks, with barely a chance to cool off, were surely scarlet now. She glanced away from him,

getting desperate, aware that he was waiting . . .

Spotting the edge of the stable off to
the side of the house, she procrastinated
after all. "It was very strange, seeing
coaches milling about a stable yard, rather
than horses, but still not as many as one
would expect to see from a gathering this
large. Have some been put out to pasture
then?"

"Put out—?" he began, but the image
her words produced, of fifty or so coaches
grazing in a pasture, had him laughing before he finished.

Sabrina couldn't find anything amusing
about what she'd said just then and took
advantage of his distraction to blurt out,
"Lady Ophelia would like an opportunity to
speak to you in private. She suggested a
meeting in the common room at the inn in
Oxbow so that she might apologize to
you."

She had managed to catch him completely unawares. In fact, he was looking
at her now as if she were daft. But as
quickly a scowl came and he bit out, "More
like insult me again."

"No, really, she has assured me she regrets whatever it was she said to you before. Will you meet her?"

"Nae."

Oddly, Sabrina felt her embarrassment subside, hearing that emphatic answer. But she wouldn't be honestly discharging her duty if she didn't at least make another effort or two on Ophelia's behalf.

So she said, "Is that an 'I'll think about it' nay or an 'I'll need more convincing' nay?"

" 'Twas a flat-oout 'ne'er tae be considered' nay."

"Oh, dear, and I'd thought that type was obsolete."

"What type?" he said in a tone beginning to sound like exasperation. "What *are* you blathering aboot now?"

"Your 'never to be considered' no. I thought everyone left a little room for changing their minds these days. Saves embarrassment, you know, if you try evasiveness instead—just in case you *do* want to change your mind later."

"Aye, but e'en more time is saved if you know your own mind and say so."

She gave up on that tack, asked instead, "Would it really be so hard on you to hear what she has to say?"

"Hard, nay. A waste o' m'time, aye."

She was blushing again, profusely, aware that she was wasting his time as well. "I'm sorry. I should have realized, with you needing to be in constant attendance here just now, that this wouldn't be a good time to bother you about this. I'll be going. G'day, Duncan MacTavish. It really was nice, seeing you again."

"Wait."

She had taken a good fifteen brisk steps, trying to escape her own embarrassment, which put her almost beyond shouting distance. She turned, not even positive that it wasn't just her hopeful imagination that had him calling her back. But indeed, he was walking toward her, and reaching her, he looked like a man about to eat sour grapes.

"I'll meet her on one condition," he said.

She was surprised enough to say, "Certainly. What condition would that be?"

"That you pack your bags and get back here afore dinner is served t'night."

Her eyes widened. "You're inviting me to dinner?"

"I'm inviting you tae the blasted party, for the duration, however bluidy long that is."

She smiled then. She couldn't help it, he sounded so aggrieved that he was compromising just to get his way.

"I, ah, don't need to pack any bags. I do live just down the road."

"You'll come then?"

"My aunts would have to come with me. I can't go to affairs like this without their chaperonage."

"Bring whomever you like—except *her*."

She nodded. "But you *will* meet her?" At his own curt nod, she added, "When?"

"In one hour. But if she's no' there on time, I'm no' waiting on her. And you'll be telling me later why you were bringing me this request o' hers."

He turned abruptly and went back into the house. Sabrina, utterly amazed at the outcome of her visit, turned to hurry home to give Ophelia the good news. Her debt was paid. She felt such relief that it was over, that she wouldn't feel obliged to do again something she'd found so abhorrent.

She was nearly halfway to the hill where she'd met Duncan when Lord Neville's butler, running after her, was finally within distance for her to hear him.

Out of breath, he more or less panted what he had to say when he reached her. "Lord Neville's coach will pick you up this evening."

"That isn't necessary," she told him. "You know we have our own coach."

"Yes, miss, but I believe the young lord wants to make *sure* you come."

She blushed. Jacobs's assumption, surely, but it still sounded rather nice.

18

Duncan couldn't believe he hadn't asked the lass for her name yet again, nor did he even realize that he hadn't until Neville asked him who she was. He was rather embarrassed at that point. He'd sought out Neville this third time, fully expecting to have an argument when he told the old man he'd invited someone to Summers Glade who wasn't gentry. But that was the conclusion he'd come to when the lass had given her reasons for why Neville wouldn't consider her for his guest list, that and that she and her aunts lived in a cottage.

It made no difference to him, her social status. He still liked her, and especially her knack for the absurd, which could so easily disperse any anger he was fretting with. And it wasn't as if he were looking to marry her, so what, really, could Neville object to? But he was deceiving himself.

He knew very well that the class of people who had been invited by Neville, lords and ladies all, might be offended by someone not of their own class being at the same gathering as they were, not in a serving capacity, but as another guest. He knew also that that would be Neville's objection, which was why he'd come expecting an argument.

But he wasn't going to get the argument he'd come for, when he couldn't even tell Neville who the lass was. He supposed he could have mentioned that she wasn't gentry, but decided to wait and let Neville discover that on his own. It was an excellent opportunity, after all, to see just how the old Englishman would react in such a situation. Duncan would find out whether he was an aristocrat of the old school who were mostly snobbish beyond belief, or if he was of the more enlightened school and realized that a title did not represent a man's worth.

But he probably should have opted for the argument, which he had hoped might relieve some of the tension he was feeling.

That tension just got worse as he approached the inn in Oxbow. He'd been distracted from it only briefly, when he'd tried to figure out just where the lass's "cottage off the road" might be, when he hadn't seen a single small dwelling, only one manor house and a few farms, on his ride there.

Perhaps she'd meant on the way to Oxbow coming from the other direction, or right on the edge of the small town—there were plenty of cottages along the narrow lanes off the main street, after all. But as a distraction, it didn't last long, not when it didn't take all that long to ride to town.

He still couldn't believe he'd agreed to speak with Ophelia Reid, when he had hoped to never lay eyes on her again. What purpose would it serve, other than to relieve the guilty conscience that *she* might be having? Any apologies from her would have little meaning to him. She had shown her true colors. There was nothing she could say to excuse the extent of her insults to him. And now he even knew, if he could believe that Rafe fellow, that she had herself started the ridiculous "barbarian" rumors about him.

She wasn't there yet. He allowed he was five minutes early himself, but for someone eager to make amends, he had expected her to be there early, to make sure she didn't miss him. Now he had to wait, and even five minutes was too long to give her, in his opinion.

He waved the innkeeper away, and waited before the large fireplace in the common room. He would have preferred a shot of whisky, but wanted to be absolutely clearheaded when dealing with this particular lass.

She entered from the back. So she had been there early, after all, and just wanted to make an "appearance"? It *was* quite an appearance. With a white fur cap about her blond head, and a powder-blue long coat of velvet, topped by a short cape trimmed in the same white fur, she cut a dazzling figure, actually, near blinding when she spotted him and cast a smile his way before walking toward him. She did that slowly, giving him ample opportunity to be mesmerized by her beauty. The white fur and the lighting combined seemed to make her glow with an ethereal beauty.

He wasn't the only one in the room who

couldn't take his eyes from her. The few patrons who were there were staring at Ophelia with their mouths dropped open. Duncan wasn't quite that bedazzled, though he did have a hard time for a moment keeping in mind that for all her beauty, this lass had a vicious streak. Impossible to tell, looking at her, but hard to miss once she opened her mouth.

She was still wearing the smile when she reached him. There had been the briefest moment when it altered and went a little stiff as she noticed his kilt. He'd worn it deliberately. If she had any sense at all, she'd realize that the kilt was his way of telling her, without words, that this meeting was pointless.

"I see you got my message," she said.

"Aye, and why was the lass the one tae deliver it?" he replied.

He hadn't meant to ask her that, had meant to bring it up later with the violet-eyed lass, so he was actually relieved that he didn't really get an answer. Don't distract her. Let her have her say and he could be gone the sooner. He needed to keep that in mind.

She shrugged. "Why not? Most people feel privileged to assist me."

He said nothing to that, but then it was hard to think of a reply when he was concentrating on not laughing. That single statement of hers said so much about her, and the irony was, she didn't even realize the impression it gave. Beyond mere condescension, beyond self-pride, it was so far into the upper reaches of vain conceit that Duncan couldn't think of an exact word to describe it, if there even was one.

His silence, though, disconcerted her, putting her on the spot, as it did, to get what she had to say said. He wondered if she even had anything in particular to say to him. An apology had been stated as the purpose for this meeting, yet did someone like Ophelia Reid even know how to apologize? Wouldn't that be an impossible concept for someone who felt she could do no wrong?

When she *still* said nothing, at least not quickly enough to suit him, he shrugged and walked away from her. He didn't consider that rude, not to her, anyway. Her insults had put her into a "not worthy of his notice" category, and that was being kind.

Were she a man, she would most definitely be considered an enemy.

But his action did prompt her to speech. "Wait! Where are you going?"

She actually sounded confused. He paused long enough to tell her, "I didna come here tae stand aboot and gawk at your beauty, lass, as everyone else in the room is doing. If you've something tae say tae me, then be saying it."

She blushed prettily. "I wanted to explain why I wasn't very cordial at our first meeting."

"So that's what the English call it? Not being very cordial? I'll have tae remember that the next time I deliberately insult someone."

"It wasn't deliberate," she tried to tell him. "I was shocked."

"Were you now?" he replied, his skepticism so obvious even a child couldn't miss it. "O'er what? That I talk like a Scotsman? That I look like one? You werena expecting either, I suppose?"

She sighed. "I wish you would try to understand. I was so sure you and I wouldn't suit."

"And that I'd be a barbarian?"

"Well, yes, I did fear that. But I realize how silly that was now. You aren't barbaric at all."

"I wouldna be sae sure o' that, lass," he replied, turning on the thick brogue just for her benefit.

"The point is, I was mistaken in my assumptions."

Duncan had a feeling that was as close as she was getting to an apology. The concept really would be too foreign for someone like her, who no doubt felt she could do no wrong, to actually mention the word "sorry."

"Verra well, so you were mistaken. Was there any other point you were wanting tae make?"

His impatience to be gone was a tangible thing, yet somehow, she didn't notice it.

"Well, actually, I thought we could start anew," she told him. "You know, simply forget about that first meeting, as if it had never occurred."

"As if we were still engaged tae wed?"

She perked up and gave him one of those brilliant smiles. "Indeed. Isn't that a grand idea?"

He had been joking. She was serious. He was now incredulous. Did she really think he could just forget the embarrassment of her insults? What she had said to him that day had been not just for him, but for the amusement of a whole room full of people. Had a man said those things, Duncan could have laid him out on the floor and been instantly satisfied. But because she was a woman, he'd had to leave with his tail tucked between his legs, something he'd never forget.

Not that that was the only reason he wouldn't marry her, and he gave her another, replying, "I dinna think I'd care tae be competing wi' m'wife for her own attention."

"Excuse me?"

He wasn't surprised that was lost on her. Self-centered people were usually the last to own up to being self-centered, but those in love with themselves, as Ophelia so obviously was, were a definite lost cause.

He'd heard her out. She hadn't even offered a real apology. As far as he was concerned, he'd given her all the time she deserved.

"Good day."

Ophelia stared after him in shock. Men didn't walk away from her unless she wanted them to. And what had happened to him groveling at her feet in his gratitude that she had changed her opinion about him?

The meeting had *not* gone as it was supposed to. She had been giving him a second chance to marry her, so why weren't they engaged again? She was beginning to suspect that he really *was* a barbarian. What other excuse could there be for his not being smart enough to realize what she'd been offering him with this meeting?

19

Ophelia didn't know yet that Sabrina had been invited to the party. She had run off so quickly to prepare herself when Sabrina told her that Duncan had agreed to see her. She hadn't even asked for the details. Nor had she seemed surprised that he had agreed. Sabrina suspected the London girl just might have taken it for granted, as highly as she thought of herself, but that was an unkind thought that she put aside.

But Sabrina realized, much too late, the horrible impropriety of her accepting an invitation, to anywhere, when she had a houseguest herself. And of course, Ophelia couldn't be left there alone. Either Hilary or Alice would have to stay with her. And that, too, was going to cause problems, when both her aunts would no doubt like to attend Neville's party, now that they had an invitation to.

Of course, Sabrina was probably worrying over nothing. Ophelia would come back with an invitation herself, perhaps even be engaged again. The thought was depressing actually, but was highly likely. Sabrina had witnessed it herself, how men behaved around Ophelia. Most were so in awe of her beauty that any sense they might possess was easily misplaced as long as they remained in her presence.

She continued to put off even telling her aunts of the invitation, so sure was she that they would all be going—right up until Ophelia returned, slamming the door on her entrance, and ran upstairs to her room, slamming that door, too. It wasn't too hard, at that point, to guess that the meeting had not gone as Ophelia had wanted it to, and Sabrina was forced to take her blunder, as she was now thinking of it, to her aunts.

Their reaction was typical of them. She had to go, of course, at least tonight. It was an opportunity they had hoped for and could not be ignored, now that it was already accepted, just because they had an unexpected guest. Were Ophelia not there, et cetera, et cetera. But she would have to explain, gently, to the young lord that she couldn't come to Summers Glade again, for the rest of the party at least, not unless their own guest decided to go home.

Sabrina found it amusing that, without actually saying so, both her aunts were obviously now hoping that Ophelia *would* go home, and the sooner the better.

"I'll stay with her," Alice offered, managing to hide at least part of her forlorn sigh, that she would miss the party herself. "And I'll let her know where you've gone, m'dear—if she asks. But is there any reason she needs to be told, which would only make her feel offended, if she doesn't notice your absence?"

This was asked of Hilary, who gave it a little thought before she replied pragmatically. "I don't see why the gel needs to be needlessly offended. And it will only be for the one night. And if it's necessary to tell her, she'll just have to understand that in Sabrina's excitement, she briefly forgot that Ophelia was visiting."

Sabrina actually had a much better excuse than that, but then she didn't think that Ophelia would want it known, what she had asked Sabrina to do, and so she hadn't told her aunts about her short career in matchmaking. But she would tell Ophelia, if she had to, that her accepting the invitation to Summers Glade had been the condition for Duncan meeting her.

No matter the outcome of that meeting, and Ophelia's dramatic door-slamming return didn't suggest it had gone as she'd hoped, Ophelia had gotten her chance only because Sabrina had agreed to attend the party. That wasn't very flattering to Ophelia, so Sabrina *would* keep it to herself if at all possible. And as her aunts were hoping, Ophelia might not even notice their absence, might well spend the rest of the evening in her room sulking. Well, one could hope . . .

Sabrina and Hilary were able to leave the cottage before Ophelia made an appearance, so they wouldn't know how Alice fared with the girl until their return later. But it didn't take long, after they arrived at Summers Glade, for them to completely forget about their houseguest.

It was such a *huge* gathering, quite larger than even those they'd attended in

London. But of the fifty or so young women whom Neville had invited, each had to have her chaperone, whether both parents, or a brother or two, or sisters, or even cousins. One invitation could easily have brought four or more guests, and indeed, it seemed well over two hundred people were in attendance.

Sabrina couldn't imagine where they all had been put for sleeping accommodations, and remarked on it to her aunt. Summers Glade was large, but fifty bedrooms, it certainly didn't have, let alone two hundred. Having been to at least one such country gathering in her youth, Hilary chuckled and said, "Just be glad we weren't asked to put up some of them, as our other neighbors were."

There were several neighbors Sabrina recognized who didn't have daughters, who she realized now had been invited just so they could be asked to open their own homes. The inn in Oxbow must also be filled to the brim for once.

"Besides," Hilary added, "it's only the most important guests that would be given rooms of their own. I remember sharing a room once with six other girls, and Father,

who accompanied Alice and me to that affair, didn't fare as well, was stuffed in with
nine other gentlemen. But when you throw
parties of this sort that go on for weeks,
there really is no other choice."

"You came."

Sabrina turned around to find Duncan
had come up behind her. She had been
smiling at her aunt and so was still smiling
as she greeted him.

"Did you think I wouldn't?"

"After the ooutcome o' that meeting you
arranged, aye, I did have m'doubts."

"What meeting would that be, m'dear?"
Hilary asked beside her.

Sabrina managed not to blush, saying
evasively, "Nothing of importance, Aunt
Hilary. And may I introduce you to Duncan
MacTavish?"

Duncan cut a bow for her aunt, very
gentlemanly. Actually, he did look quite the
gentleman tonight, formally dressed in a
midnight-blue tailed coat that brought out
the deep blue of his eyes.

"You don't look anything like your grandfather, young man," Hilary told him, adding
in her blunt way, "I consider that quite fortunate—for you."

He laughed, but another party was heard from. "Do you indeed? And who might you be, madame?"

Hilary raised a brow at the old gentleman who'd joined them. "Don't recognize me, Neville? I'm not surprised, it's been more'n twenty years."

"Is that you, Hilary Lambert?"

"Indeed."

"You've put on a bit of weight, gel," he humphed.

"And you're looking like you belong in a sickbed. So what else is new?"

Sabrina put a hand to her mouth, wishing she were about ten feet away so she could laugh in peace. Duncan, glancing between the two older people who were glowering at each other, said, "Then you *do* know the lass?"

"What lass?" Neville demanded grouchily. "You're not calling this old bird here a lass, are you?"

"I think he means my niece here, you old coot," Hilary supplied helpfully.

That brought Neville's eyes to Sabrina, who was at the moment no longer in need of laughing. Hilary's testiness could be amusing, but not when she resorted to actually insulting their host.

He hadn't seemed to notice that, however, was now staring at Sabrina with avid curiosity, and finally said, "Well, damn me, they really are lilac, aren't they? Thought the boy was exaggerating." Then, as it suddenly dawned on him, "Good God, you're a Lambert?"

Sabrina, of course, knew exactly why he was suddenly so shocked. Unfortunately, like her aunts, she sometimes was more blunt than she ought to be, and replied, "Last time I noticed, yes, and still alive, too."

He had the grace to blush. She blushed for her own reason, that she'd been less than diplomatic in her response. Duncan, seeing the blushes, frowned, said, "Excuse us," and dragged Sabrina off into the next room.

The next room was just as crowded, of course, but since it was the ballroom, which was easily the size of three large rooms combined, and had been set up with a buffet for dinner rather than for dancing tonight, he was able to find a spot off in one corner where they wouldn't be overheard. And she knew exactly why he wanted a bit of privacy. The poor man was quite confused, and understandably so.

"Would you be explaining tae me what that was all aboot?" he demanded as soon as he stopped and let go of her arm.

She winced, deliberately. "Must I?"

For answer he just stared at her, and stared, until her next wince was genuine. "Very well." She sighed. "But this story would be much more interesting if you heard it from someone else. Are you sure you wouldn't rather have your grandfather tell it? I'm sure he could exaggerate for effect. Most people do."

"Is that a wee bit o' bitterness I'm hearing, lass?" he asked.

She blinked at him, then smiled. "You've found out my secret."

"I'm still waiting tae hear it."

"But you just did."

He tapped a palm to the side of his head a couple of times, saying, "Then something mun be wrong wi' my hearing, lass, 'cause I've heard nae secret yet."

"Now, how could you forget so soon, when you only *just* said you heard my bitterness? That's my secret. The rest," she said, waving a dismissive hand, "is public knowledge, so hardly a secret."

He was staring again, quite pointedly, letting her know that her silliness wasn't going to lighten his mood this time. But just in case she wasn't sure of that, he said, "Should I remind you that I've no' been part o' this public for verra long, and any knowledge taken for granted in this area would be unknown tae me?"

"Let me give you the brief version then, since it's not really all that interesting. Lamberts, those closely related to me, that is, are known to have died not by natural means, but by their own incentive, as it were. This has given rise to the general conclusion that 'bad blood' runs in my family, and that surely I will follow this same path. Honestly, some people just can't understand why I'm still alive. Some even swear that I'm not, that surely I must be—"

"A ghost?"

"Ah, you remember my mentioning that?"

He nodded, replying, "I'm thinking I'd rather hear the long version, the one that explains why you're a wee bit bitter o'er this."

"I'm not really bitter, Duncan. Truly, sometimes I find this quite amusing, like when poor corpulent Lady Marlow shrieked to the rafters before she fainted upon seeing me. Now, everyone present might not have heard her shriek, but they surely felt it when she hit the floor. One fellow even complimented our host on having such good architecture that the floor survived that fall—the lady really was very wide of girth. Oh, go ahead, I know you want to smile."

He chuckled instead, then cut it off and tried to look serious again, he really did, but he couldn't quite manage it. She could have got him really laughing at that point with not much more effort, to where he just might forget about wanting to hear the "long version," but he'd remember eventually, and she'd just as soon get it over with, so she could enjoy her one night at Summers Glade.

"It was my great-grandfather Richard who started the scandal by killing himself. No one really knows why he did, but it was pretty obvious that he did, and his wife, unable to bear up under the tragedy of it, did the same not long after. Their only child, my grandmother, was already married at the time and had two daughters herself, the two aunts I live with. She bore up well under this double tragedy, for a while anyway. But after she gave birth once more, to my father, she, ahh, fell down some stairs. My aunts insist this was an accident, but no one else was inclined to think so, thus the 'bad blood' theory arose and took further root when my own parents died together."

"I'm sorry aboot your parents."

"So am I. I regret mostly not even knowing them, since I was too young at the time to remember them. But they didn't kill themselves. It was tainted food. Even the doctor who arrived too late to help them said so. Of course, it makes for a much better story, that they took poison together. And now, even though my aunts, from the same tree, are quite hale and hardy, with no inclination to go walking off any cliffs, I'm next in line to take the tragic plunge."

"I canna think o' anyone less likely tae take anything so seriously that they'd come e'en close tae contemplating ending it all."

"Goodness, I believe you've just called me a carefree scatterbrain."

"I did nae such thing," he snorted.

"I'm gravely insulted."

"The devil y'are."

She humphed. "Well, it was certainly a golden opportunity to say so."

He burst out laughing, loud enough that a few heads turned their way. One fellow who'd been walking around with plate in hand—Neville didn't possess two hundred chairs either, so not everyone could sit down to eat—sauntered over to them. Sabrina could almost feel Duncan stiffening and was quite annoyed that her effort to amuse him had just gone to waste.

"So here you are, and who is this?" the fellow asked. "Don't believe we've met."

He was looking to Duncan to make the introduction, but the Highlander was suddenly blushing, and Sabrina realized, belatedly, that she'd never given him her full name. Before Duncan had to admit that and be even more embarrassed, she supplied, "Sabrina Lambert."

The fellow was surprised at first, but

then seemed quite delighted. "The walking ghost? This *is* a pleasure. I was quite disappointed to have missed you in London recently. Truly wanted to meet the young lady who had everyone showing what bloody fools they are."

She smiled, realizing that she was actually meeting someone who didn't believe the rumors about her. "And you would be?"

"Raphael Locke, most definitely at your service."

"And most definitely intruding," Duncan added.

Raphael wasn't insulted, seemed instead to have expected just such a remark. "Oh, come now, old chap, you don't think you can monopolize the most interesting lady here, do you?"

"Should you no' be chaperoning your sister?" Duncan reminded him pointedly.

Raphael looked appalled. "The dear chit is surrounded by a gaggle of giggling friends. God forbid I get anywhere *near* them. Do have a heart. Besides, you should brave that bunch. You're the one shopping for a bride, after all, not I. How can you make a proper decision if you don't mingle?"

"Perhaps I've already made a decision."

"Never say so! My sister will be sooo disappointed."

"Your sister will be relieved."

"You're going to ask for her then?"

"Bedamned, go *away,* mon."

Raphael chuckled, apparently satisfied that he'd annoyed Duncan enough—for now—but he did part with, "Very well, I shall go in search of that old Scotsman who claims to be another grandfather of yours. Very amusing, what he has to say about you, and I just *love* good ammunition, don't you know."

It took quite a while for the color to leave Duncan's cheeks after Raphael Locke left them. Sabrina might have been able to put him at ease sooner, but then again, she might have made his annoyance worse, the roots being in male rivalry, which was beyond her comprehension. Besides, she was having a real hard time with the realization that she just might have been the bone of contention they'd just fought over.

In the end she decided she'd imagined it, and by then Duncan had calmed down enough to ask her, "Have you heard o' him prior tae just meeting him?"

"No, should I have?"

He shrugged, saying, "Auld Neville is delighted he's here. A duke's son, he is, apparently."

She smiled. "That would make his sister a fine catch for you then."

"D'you think so? She seems a bit scatterbrained tae me, and aye, *this* time I said it. E'en her brother agrees, but I just might marry her tae spite him."

"Oh my, you *really* don't like him, do you?"

"Och, nay, how can you think so, when m'fist is so eager tae get more friendly with his face?"

20

Sabrina was enjoying herself too much to have realized any sooner that the reason for it was that Duncan hadn't left her side. He had even eaten with her, finding them a couple of empty chairs in the music room to take their plates to. And afterward they had joined a game of cards where she had found it necessary to teach him how to play it as they went along, without letting the other two players be aware of it. Now, that had been hilarious. She hadn't laughed so much herself in a very long time.

When it did finally occur to her that as the guest of honor at the party, or at least the very reason they were even having a party, he should be dividing his time more equally among the guests, she didn't point that out to him as she should have. She was having a bout of selfishness and fully acknowledged it. And she decided that as long as she recognized it for what it was, and didn't try to delude herself, she could indulge it just this once.

Nor did she try to delude herself about why he was staying near her. He had laughed too much during the evening for her to think other than that he'd simply enjoyed her company. There was nothing romantic about it. She made him laugh. She was fun to be around.

It had been an enchanting night for her, though, the stuff of fanciful dreams. But all dreams must come to an end, and her one night at Summers Glade did as well.

When she saw her aunt looking for her, with their coats over her arm, she turned to Duncan and told him, "I must be going."

He didn't protest because he fully expected her to be there every day for the duration, and said as much. "I'll see you in the morning, then."

"No, actually, you won't."

She sighed, really regretting what she needed to tell him. He was already starting to frown, but she'd put this off all evening and couldn't any longer. It was a shame, though, it really was, that this wonderful night, for her at least, had to end like this.

"When you invited me here, well, in my original surprise I completely overlooked the fact that my aunts and I have a houseguest ourselves just now. I shouldn't even have come tonight. It's not as if I was committed before our guest showed up, and she does know that. So I can't be rude and desert her a second time."

"You didna want tae come."

She smiled at his mistaken conclusion, which was so completely illogical that she was sure even he knew it, and told him, "Nonsense. I've enjoyed myself tonight. I really would like to come again, and per-haps if our guest leaves before your house party ends, then I can—"

"Bring her along," he cut in.

"Ah, Duncan, shouldn't you ask *who* my guest is, before you make an offer like that?"

"As long as it isna Ophelia—"

He didn't continue. Her expression, which told him clearly that it was Ophelia, had him really scowling now.

He was practically growling when he got

around to adding, "Bedamned, what is *she* doing staying wi' you?"

That, at least, was easy enough to explain. "Taking advantage of the same courtesy her family extended to mine when we were recently in London."

"And running her errands, was that part o' the same courtesy?" he asked.

"No, that was settling all debts," she said, still smiling despite his testy tone. "She befriended me, Duncan, and made my first trip to London much easier than it would otherwise have been. I couldn't very well refuse her one request, even though I didn't want to do it, when I felt so obliged to her. But now I feel that debt has been paid."

"Then ignore that she's there, or leave her wi' your other aunt again, as you did t'night."

She shook her head at him. "Do you really see me being that rude to someone?"

He said nothing for a long moment, then he sighed. "Nae, I ken you wouldna do that. And I'll let you go afore you're thinking I'm a spoiled lad, wi' the way I keep behaving when I dinna get my way."

"I wouldn't think that." She grinned at him. "A Highland barbarian perhaps—"

"Begone wi' you," he shot back, but he was grinning now, too.

"Perhaps I'll see you on one of my walks again," she offered in parting.

"Aye, and perhaps you'll be getting rid o' unwanted guests sooner than later."

He walked her and her aunt to the door, and stood there a moment with the butler as they got into the waiting coach, long enough for the butler to take note of it and remark, "A nice girl, our Miss Sabrina."

Duncan turned to Mr. Jacobs. "Our? You've known her long?"

"Yes, she's lived here most of her life."

"These walks she takes, does she take them often?" Duncan asked.

"Every day, no matter the weather," Jacobs replied. "She prefers the mornings, but sometimes she'll go out again in the afternoon."

Duncan nodded, thinking about taking a walk himself tomorrow morning—until he realized that an hour or so of her company just wouldn't be enough. And both his grandfathers would have a fit if he disappeared most of the day, when he had the job of finding a wife to do.

After having enjoyed himself that evening, really enjoyed himself for the first time since he'd come to England, he went to bed that night in a very disagreeable mood.

In the coach rambling toward Cottage by the Bow, the manor house that was so named years ago when it was still part of the old ducal estate, Hilary was rambling herself about the party. Sabrina wasn't really paying attention, was still savoring her own experiences from the evening, until she heard, "He likes you."

That definitely caught her attention and didn't even need explaining, since she knew her aunt well enough to know just who she meant. "Yes, I believe he does, but not in the way you mean."

Hilary took offense on Sabrina's behalf and huffed, "And why not in that way?"

"Let's be truthful, Aunt Hilary, if you put someone like me next to someone like Ophelia or even Amanda Locke, I wouldn't even be noticed. And the crème de la crème of English aristocracy has been invited here by Lord Neville to tempt his grandson into marriage. You saw for yourself tonight, the young women in attendance weren't the same young hopefuls who descended on London this Season with us. A few of them were, but most of those that Neville invited don't need to go on the marriage block, they quite know their worth and don't need to parade it about."

"Posh, what has that to do with the fact that he likes *you?*"

"We've become friends, nothing more than that," Sabrina replied. "When he does actually choose his bride, it will be from one of the beautiful—"

"You're no wallflower, m'dear. You may like to think so, but it just ain't so."

Sabrina sighed. It was nice to hear, of course, but one of them had to be realistic, or she'd be getting a swelled head and start hoping for something that just couldn't be.

"Don't you think I'd know if a man was interested in me in *that* way? I promise you, Aunt Hilary, Duncan doesn't look at me and see me as wifely material, he sees me more as his confidante who can help advise him on which one of those young lovelies he should be picking."

"Time will tell," Hilary replied, unwilling for some reason to deviate from her hopeful speculations.

Sabrina, unwilling to argue further when she'd rather still be savoring her memories in silence, said, "Just what was that all about, the way you attacked Lord Neville tonight?"

"Why, nothing a'tall. Just pure dislike that goes *way* back."

But Hilary, being forced into the defensive, said no more for the rest of the ride home.

21

Sabrina overslept the next morning, so when Alice came in to wake her and mentioned cheerfully that she didn't have much time to get ready, that the coach was already there and waiting for them, she was too groggy yet to grasp what that meant. And Alice left her room too quickly, before Sabrina could form a coherent question or even find out what coach she'd been talking about.

She didn't hurry, though. The night before was recalled, and with a smile, she lay back on her pillow to do some more savoring, just as she'd done when she'd gone to bed last night—which was why she hadn't gotten to sleep until near dawn, and why she'd overslept.

But then Hilary poked her head around

Sabrina's door and said, "Everyone is ready, m'dear, we're just waiting on you. Do hurry."

The door closed again, and Sabrina, getting seriously curious now, threw back her covers and raced out into the corridor to catch Hilary, who was already halfway down the stairs. "Ready for what? Have I overlooked something we were supposed to do today?"

Hilary frowned. "Didn't that nitwit sister of mine tell you? She was supposed to wake you *and* tell you. Knew I should have done it m'self."

"Ah, she mentioned a coach—"

"Oh, so she did tell you." Hilary sounded disappointed, having a good excuse for an argument with Alice nipped in the bud as it were. "Well, do hurry. The coachman has been here for over an hour already, waiting."

What a dilemma that gave Sabrina. Find out what the devil was going on, or give Hilary a reason to complain to Alice all day. She opted to look out the upstairs window in her room instead, which faced the front of the house. And there was the coach in question, Lord Neville's coach again, there when it shouldn't be there.

She was appalled at the conclusion she immediately reached. Obviously Duncan had forgotten to let the coachman know that he wouldn't be needed this morning, at least not to pick her up again. And now because of that little oversight, her aunts both thought that they were all invited to Summers Glade, including Ophelia.

What else could her aunts be thinking? She was supposed to have told Duncan that she couldn't return to the party, not without their own guest, and if the coach was there, then it must be there for all of them. They could have come to no other conclusion.

She thought about getting back into bed and hiding there all day. She thought about hitting Duncan over the head with her parasol for his forgetfulness, and most surely would have if it were the time of year to carry a parasol. She thought about how angry he was going to be when Ophelia showed up at his house. But it was *his* fault, *his* oversight. So why did she feel as if it were all her fault instead? Perhaps because she knew, she just knew, that he was going to blame her somehow, simply because Ophelia was *her* guest.

She ended up hurrying in the end, and choosing one of her more becoming morning dresses, not that her appearance was going to help her in the least, would do no more than bolster her own courage, if that was possible. She was going to have to warn her aunts, and without Ophelia overhearing. She may not like the London girl all that much now, but she had no desire to hurt her by explaining that she hadn't really gotten the hoped-for invitation that she now thought she had.

They were all waiting for her, right there in the entryway, so there was no chance that Sabrina could have a private word with one of her aunts without pulling them away, which would likely draw questions from the other two. But she wasn't given a chance to even try, when Ophelia grabbed her arm and whisked her right out to the coach, so impatient was she to make her entrance.

The ride was excruciating for Sabrina, who envisioned all sorts of disastrous outcomes now. She even pictured Duncan tossing the lot of them out his door. After all, she could have prevented their showing up, could have confessed the truth. *He* wouldn't be concerned about hurting Ophelia's feelings with that truth.

It was Ophelia's impatience that did finally give Sabrina an opportunity to at least warn her aunts, when the coach arrived at Summers Glade and the London girl was the first to jump out. Sabrina caught Hilary's arm and whispered quickly, "We shouldn't be here. Duncan didn't invite her."

Hilary merely patted her arm without the least little concern and replied, "He must have changed his mind then, because the driver informed us that he was to escort us all, including any guests we might have."

That, of course, left Sabrina sitting in the coach with her mouth hanging open, so she was the last to enter the house. She didn't know what to think at that point. She would *like* to think that Duncan had compromised again, as he'd done yesterday, just so she would come to the party. But she had to be realistic. She didn't know what had happened at that meeting at the inn yesterday. Duncan could be wanting

Ophelia back now, but didn't want Ophelia to know it yet. In that case, Sabrina had given him a perfect excuse to at least get the London girl near to hand again.

It certainly didn't take long for Ophelia to desert them. She had already disappeared when Sabrina came inside, gone off to find her London friends to let them know she was back in circulation. She was accustomed to being the center of attention, no matter where she was. And the very fact that she *was* here, at her ex-fiancé's party, would totally reverse the gossip about her.

She had gotten just what she wanted. And she was back in her element, among the London *ton.* It was no wonder she was shining with an exquisite beauty today that put Sabrina, even in her best lilac morning dress, to shame.

Well, there was nothing for it but to accept it and get on with enjoying herself as best she could. Not that she would now. Today was not going to be like last night, with Duncan in constant attendance on her. It couldn't be, not with Ophelia there.

They had arrived in time for breakfast. Hilary and Alice had already eaten, but

Sabrina hadn't, and so she meandered into the breakfast room where food was being served, if not eaten. A few other guests had apparently arisen late too, or were just late eaters. Raphael Locke and his sister Amanda were among those few at the buffet tables getting their plates filled before going off in search of a chair somewhere.

"Alone at last," he said to Sabrina when he noticed her and moved to her side.

"At last?"

"Well, I was trying to figure out all last evening how I was going to get you out of the barbarian's clutches, and here you are without him in tow."

She blushed, but not on her own account. "I wish you wouldn't call him that. He's not, you know."

Raphael chuckled. "Course I know, but I have to have *something* to ride him about, don't I?"

"Why?" she asked baldly.

"Well, one, because he's so amusing when he gets annoyed with me. And two, because I like him. And three, because someone has to teach him how to roll with the punches, as it were, and I've elected myself to educate him on the intricacies of English humor."

"Goodness, and here I thought you were just being facetious," she replied, tongue in cheek.

He burst out laughing, which drew every eye in the room to them and brought his sister over as well. "And what, pray tell, can you possibly find amusing this early in the morning?" Amanda asked, smothering a yawn as she did.

"That you were apparently so tired when you dressed this morning that you forgot to have your maid button up those last few—"

The poor girl shrieked and looked mortified and immediately gave him her back with the order, "Don't just stand there, fix it!"

Raphael was silently laughing and appeared to have the intention of letting his sister stand there forever waiting to be buttoned up. Sabrina took pity on the girl and leaned forward to whisper to her, "He was joking. You are fully dressed and look lovely."

Mandy turned back around to glare at

her brother and give him a heartfelt, "You wretch," before flouncing away.

Sabrina shook her head at the man. He was very handsome—both the Locke siblings were exceptional in that regard—but he was obviously an incorrigible tease as well. Not that that was a bad thing. She did her fair share of teasing too, though with a major difference. Her teasing was done to amuse people, not to irritate them.

"What?" he complained with a smile when he saw her shaking her head at him.

"That was too bad of you," she replied.

"Perhaps," he agreed. "But it woke her up, didn't it? Can't have the girl looking like a slugabed when she's supposed to be catching a husband. Sooner she does so, the sooner I can retire from this chaperoning business."

"Ah, so it was to her benefit to get her riled?" Sabrina said.

"Course it was," he replied. "Gads, don't tell me you were thinking I'm mean-spirited. It would break my heart, it surely would."

Sabrina took a bite of her sausage wrapped in a biscuit before she pointed the remainder of it at a nearby table.

"Heart and kidney is being served over there, I believe, if you're in need of replacements."

"Ouch," he said, but he was grinning at her. "Lucky for you, m'dear, I'm not so easily discouraged. So it might take me a few extra days to convince you to marry me." He shrugged nonchalantly. "When you realize how ideally suited we are, you'll give in."

She chuckled over his new line of teasing. "We aren't the least bit suited, and well you know it."

"Course we are," he insisted. "We both come from a line of dukes."

"Ah, but my line has scandal attached to it," she reminded him.

"Ah, but *my* line eats scandal for breakfast," he countered cheerily.

"And which table are they serving that at this morning?" she asked him.

He laughed, loud enough to again draw eyes their way. Sabrina was starting to enjoy herself, but she was also starting to wonder why he was paying her such attention. It was going to cause gossip, she was sure, if he didn't move along soon. He was too well known for it not to.

But in the end she decided he was just bored and passing the time. And anyone who would actually try to link her name with his would have to be an utter idiot, so she wasn't going to worry about it.

22

"I heard it from his own sister," Edith Ward said. "He likes to champion the underdog. Who better would fit that description than Sabrina?"

"I wouldn't mind being an underdog, if it would get *his* attention," Jane remarked.

"You can't just be an underdog because you want to, dear," Edith told her. "You're too pretty."

Jane blushed, but was obviously disappointed, though at any other time she would have been thrilled by the compliment. But keeping in mind their purpose, she added, "Not that it will matter, once he notices Ophelia."

Both girls had been trying to soothe Ophelia's jealous nature, which they knew had been pricked when they had all spotted Sabrina leaving the breakfast room with the very handsome Raphael Locke by her side. The mere look of incredulity that appeared on Ophelia's face was enough to predict what would occur.

Mavis, on the other hand, was delighted by this turn of events. Actually, she had felt her world was finally righting itself when Ophelia's scheme to get rid of her fiancé had turned on her and the gossip had turned against her. She had never before witnessed such just deserts as that. So she had been utterly disappointed to see Ophelia show up at Summers Glade this morning, apparently invited, which she knew, just as the others did, would put Ophelia right back into the position of reigning queen of the Season.

The *only* good thing about her appearance, as far as Mavis was concerned, was that she would now be around to witness Sabrina's success, and that her campaign to ruin Sabrina's debut hadn't worked completely, at least not where MacTavish and Locke were concerned, apparently.

And Ophelia didn't even know who Raphael Locke was yet, had never met him. None of the girls had, prior to yesterday when he'd arrived here with his sister. Amanda, they knew, of course, and had cornered her to find out that he was her brother, *the* Locke heir, who had only just returned to England from several years abroad, which was why they'd never met him or even heard of him before.

Unfortunately, it was more than likely that once he met Ophelia, he would fall at her feet in worship just as every other silly male did, Duncan MacTavish being the only exception to that, which Mavis truly admired him for. Edith and Jane were of the same opinion, had only just been telling Ophelia about him as they brought her up to date on what had been happening, that he was the heir to a dukedom, how handsome and rich he was, how ideally suited he was for her if she was done with her ex-fiancé—when he'd appeared with Sabrina at his side. And it wasn't by accident that they just happened to leave the room at the same time. They were talking and smiling together as they went off in search of chairs to sit on while they ate.

Of course, the three girls had been there to witness Sabrina's success last night, in managing to capture Duncan MacTavish's undivided attention for most of the evening. Jane and Edith had even been having a friendly argument over which of them would try to win him for themselves, now that Ophelia was done with him, until they'd seen how enthralled he seemed to be with Sabrina.

Not that they would *ever* mention that to Ophelia, at least Jane and Edith wouldn't, and prayed she didn't hear of it elsewhere. So they were both a bit incredulous when Mavis remarked with a snort, "Underdog, my foot. I tried to tell you that Sabrina has a winning way about her, but you all scoffed. The proof is she's got the two most eligible men here vying for her attention."

That immediately brought Ophelia's narrowed blue eyes to Mavis with the demand, "What other man? Who are you talking about?"

"Why, your Duncan, of course," Mavis relished saying before Jane and Edith could stop her.

Having said it, she barely managed to hide a triumphant smile. But she then scored even better, though she didn't realize it yet. She couldn't know, after all, that Ophelia had spent the night being un-communicative with her hosts, locked up in her room, trying to figure out why Duncan hadn't behaved as he ought to have behaved yesterday at their meeting.

"Didn't Sabrina tell you how he barely left her side last night?" Mavis added.

Since Ophelia didn't even know that Sabrina had *been* here at Summers Glade last night, she was being dealt a double blow. Nor was she adept at concealing her feelings. Though she *tried* to sound non-chalant in her reply, the myriad of emotions that had crossed her features were a dead giveaway that she was anything but.

"Sabrina isn't one to reveal confidences," Ophelia pointed out.

"Nor successes, apparently. Pity," Mavis replied. "I for one would love to know what they found so amusing, that had them laughing for most of the evening."

"Imply all you want, Mavis," Edith jumped in, still trying to defuse Ophelia's temper, though even she knew it was likely a lost cause, after everything Mavis had revealed. "It doesn't mean either man would actually consider *marrying* her. Or are you forgetting her bad blood?"

"Well, who could forget *that?*" Mavis rejoined, tongue in cheek. "Especially when she appears so happy and—alive. But then it was such a silly rumor."

"Are you forgetting who started the rumor?" Jane said in Ophelia's defense.

"No, actually, I remember perfectly well who spitefully instigated its circulation again."

There it was at last, a direct insult to Ophelia. Mavis was thrilled that she'd finally had the nerve to do it. And it didn't go over Ophelia's head as she'd feared it might. The gorgeous blonde wasn't quite so gorgeous when her face was beet red with fury.

Edith gasped. Jane was too shocked for speech. Ophelia was sputtering, "Spiteful? You're . . . calling . . . me—!"

"Oh, yes, please do make a scene that will get you booted out of here for a *second* time," Mavis interrupted with a brilliant smile. "Then perhaps the rest of us can actually enjoy ourselves again."

Mavis turned to leave, aware that she'd completely severed her ties with this group, and proud of herself for finally doing so. But Edith and Jane, she had liked, at least when they weren't behaving like brainless twits around Ophelia, and so she paused long enough to tell them, "When are you two going to wake up and realize that she's no friend to you? She'd back-stab you in a second if she thought it would get her something she wants, and have not a single regret for doing so."

Mavis sauntered away with a bounce in her step and a grin on her lips. She knew she might as well pack her bags, that some atrocious rumor would start about her that very day. She just didn't care anymore.

"Well, I never," Jane huffed, unable to think of anything more appropriate to say after that shocking speech of Mavis's.

"I never either," Edith agreed.

"I'm not surprised, myself," Ophelia said, recovering nicely, if boiling inside. "She's such a liar, after all. I've caught her at it, oh, at least five times before, but was kind enough not to point out that I knew she was lying. Poor dear, I wonder if she just can't help it. Some people can't, you know."

23

"Sit down, Archibald, we have a problem."

The Scotsman took the seat across from Neville's desk in his sitting room and gave his nemesis a narrowed if skeptical look. He hadn't liked being *summoned,* as he saw it, hadn't had his breakfast yet, hadn't slept well last night, and the heat in this particular room had started him sweating the moment he entered it. More problems, he didn't need.

"We?" he questioned. "And how would *we* be having a problem when the only thing we share in common is the lad, and he's doing exactly what we asked o' him? A fine passel o' lassies ye hae gathered here, by the way, if I do say sae m'self. If I'd known ye had such an abundance o' beauties down here, I might hae come tae visit after m'dear wife passed on, and found me anither one m'self."

"Would that you had, then we might not be fighting over Duncan now," Neville grumbled.

"Who's fighting, eh? I could hae swore we were finally in agreement o'er the dividing o' heirs."

"Hardly a fitting solution, but not the point I wish to discuss either," Neville replied. "If you didn't notice last night, Duncan has done some inviting himself to this party, of one Sabrina Lambert, whom he proceeded to waste his time on the *entire* evening."

"The buxom wee lass? Nicely shaped, but no' exactly a beauty, sae dinna fash yerself o'er her, he'll pick a pretty one in the end."

Neville sighed and said in a weary tone, "I wish you wouldn't harp so much on superficial beauty. A pretty face does *not* make for an ideal wife, as was so drastically found out with the Reid girl."

"Course it does," Archie disagreed blithely. "Ye dinna hae tae listen tae a wife, can ignore them as ye please, but ye do ha' tae *look* at them every sae often, sae a pretty face does take precedent o'er an empty head."

Neville rolled his eyes, but pointed out, "Duncan must not feel the same, since he *is* showing a marked interest in this particular girl. Now, he may just enjoy her company. He admitted as much. She amuses him. If that's all it is, then there is no problem."

Archie frowned at that point. "Yer no' making sense yerself, mon. If ye dinna care if he weds a beauty or no', as *ye* keep harping, wha' *is* yer problem wi' this lass? Is she no' titled tae yer satisfaction?"

Neville sighed again. "Sabrina Lambert's looks have not a thing to do with my concern, Archibald. As it happens, I think she's quite pretty. Her eyes make all the difference, remarkable as they are."

"Pretty eyes, eh? I didna notice."

"Likely because all you look at are breasts and faces and so don't take in any of the finer details a girl might possess, let alone if she had a lick of intelligence."

Archie smiled over the sour tone. "Nae, I just havena met the lass yet tae get close enough tae see her eyes. It mun be her credentials yer objecting tae then."

"No, as it happens, her great-grandfather Richard was a duke, her grandfather an earl. Her own father would have held that title as well, if he had survived his father, but he didn't. She doesn't need a title to be quite suitable in that regard, in fact, far surpasses most of the chits in attendance. What does concern me is she comes with two cantankerous old-maid aunts—"

Archie's chuckle interrupted. "That's yer problem, no' mine, I'm pleased tae be saying. I'll be going home after the wedding."

"Thank God for that," Neville said with undisguised relief. "But she also comes with a forty-year-old scandal that I'm told is making the rounds again."

Archibald was no longer amused, sat forward to demand, "What sort o' scandal?"

"Not one that I ever gave much credence to, since I happen to have known Richard Lambert personally, knew how clumsy he was with weapons. He bloody near shot my foot off once when we were hunting together, so it was entirely possible that he shot himself by accident, rather than deliberately as the story goes. His wife, now, was a silly twit who I have little doubt did kill herself when the scandal broke that he had. She wouldn't have had the courage to dispute it, nor the courage to face the ridicule over it."

"Tha' hardly seems the stuff o' scandal tae me," Archie scoffed.

"I would agree, if that were all of it, but there was a daughter who did the same, and her son and daughter-in-law— Sabrina's own parents—who did likewise. Are you getting the point yet, Archibald? When our main concern is another heir who will continue both our lines, do we really want to take the chance that there might be any truth to this girl's sad history?"

"Does Duncan know all this?"

"You think he confides in me? I have no idea if he's aware of it, though he may have heard the gossip. Would it make a difference to him?"

Archibald frowned thoughtfully. "Likely it wouldna, and definitely no' if ye bring it up tae him."

Neville's lips tightened at the implication. "Haven't we been over this before? I know you would like to think that the boy would be stubborn and go against his own common sense just to spite me, but I give him more credit than that. However, on this marriage business, he *is* more likely to listen to you, so find out if he knows, and if he doesn't, apprise him and make clear that this chit simply won't do."

Archie actually nodded in agreement for once, though he did add hopefully, " 'Tis likely nae more than ye said, that she amuses him."

"As I *also* said, there would then be no problem, *but* the very fact that Lady Ophelia Reid is back under my roof this morning—"

Archie cut in, "The devil she is—"

Neville cut back in, *"Because* she happens to be a guest of the Lamberts at the moment, and they were invited by Duncan despite that fact. This either means he was smitten by her beauty after all—which should delight *you*—and has decided to forgive her insults and marry her anyway, or he's serious about the Lambert girl. Take your pick, Archibald. I'm pleased with neither."

"And I am?" Archie snorted. " 'Tis more likely he's going tae be surprised himself when he sees who the Lambert women hae brought wi' them. I'm guessing he didna ken who their guest was when he invited them. And that right there will get rid o' the lot o' them."

Neville actually chuckled now. "Wishful thinking doesn't get you very far, you know. Sabrina Lambert would have told him last night. She may have this unfortunate scandal attached to her family, but she's not an empty-headed twit who wouldn't realize the ramifications of bringing Duncan's ex-fiancée to a gathering arranged for the express purpose of him picking a bride."

"Och," Archie said in disgust to that as he rose to leave the room. "I'll be finding him now and finding oout for m'self what's what. Speculating wi' ye, Neville, just gives me a bluidy headache."

24

Duncan had avoided going downstairs this morning, after the decision he'd made last night. He had slept on it, or rather, tossed and turned on it for a while before sending a second message to the coachman that canceled the earlier one he'd sent, and added any guests on the Lambert premises to the man's list of pickups. He'd then gone promptly to sleep. But this morning the decision was not sitting well with him at all, was turning his disposition quite sour.

Letting Ophelia Reid back into this house was a big mistake, no matter the reason. It would be an unspoken "forgive and forget" message in her mind that wasn't at all what had been in *his* mind.

He could have figured out ways to visit with Sabrina every other day or so over the next couple of weeks of the party, without being unduly missed, and if he was missed, well, too bad. No one had told him that he had to be in attendance at Summers Glade twenty-four hours of every day. So why hadn't he done that instead?

But he knew very well why. Having Sabrina at the party meant she'd be there for up to sixteen hours each day, be available if he wanted to talk, be handy if he needed cheering, be able to advise him about this major decision in his life he was expected to make within the next couple of weeks, and just *be* there with her calming effect. He was willing to pay for that with any misconceptions it might cause with Ophelia, which he could correct easily enough. But he had overlooked how it might appear to others, after he had ended their engagement, for her to be there again.

That was brought home to him directly when Archie tracked him down in his room to demand to know if he'd changed his mind about Ophelia. That was easily answered, but then he wanted to know what his intentions were toward Sabrina, and that was much more complicated. Not that he *had* any intentions, it was just that the relationship he was enjoying with her was one that Archie wasn't likely to believe, and didn't.

"A friend?" Archie snorted. "Men make friends o' other men, they dinna make friends o' lassies."

"Why?"

"Because sex gets in the bluidy way, tha's why. And if ye tell me ye havena once thought aboot it where this wee lass is concerned, I'll call ye a liar."

Duncan didn't take offense, he was amused instead. "So call me one. Fact is, I've been tae busy laughing with the lass tae think o' aught else."

Archie, of course, snorted again. But then Duncan had known he wouldn't understand. It was such a simple concept, yet Archie couldn't see past the "natural order of things" between men and women.

He still tried to explain. "Consider this, if you will. You have a verra good friend who lives near you, perhaps e'en your best friend. You're having a party. You'd be wanting your friend there tae share what promises tae be a good time wi' you, aye?"

Archie joined in the speculation. "But m'friend is otherwise committed."

"Aye, but 'tis a minor commitment that can be got around by bringing it tae the party as well. And you know verra well you'd arrange it just that way."

"No' if the other 'commitment' was a viper-tongued lass who could well spoil the whole bluidy party, and I ken *tha'* verra well."

Duncan sighed. Now, *that* he couldn't dispute, since it was a distinct possibility. But then he grinned. At least Archie had got the point.

"Dinna worry aboot Ophelia until there is cause tae worry. And dinna worry that my intentions toward Sabrina are other than friendship. Talk tae her yourself t'day, and you'll see why she's nice tae be around. She has a way o' making you forget your troubles."

Archie's frown indicated that didn't exactly reassure him. "As long as yer no' forgetting the purpose o' this gathering o' lassies."

"I've told you I dinna object tae getting m'self a wife. 'Tis this hell-bent rushing I dinna like, and I'll tell you true, if I canna make up m'mind afore the party ends, I'll hear nae complaints o'er it. I willna pick a lass just tae be picking one."

"We dinna expect ye tae be falling instantly in love, lad," Archie replied in a grumbling tone. "That takes time tae grow on ye."

"I'm no' talking aboot love, I'm talking aboot *liking.* I have tae at least like this lass I'll be committing m'self tae. There has tae be something there tae work wi', Archie, other than indifference."

"Course there does, but ye willna be finding it if yer spending all yer time wi' *friends* instead. And how will these other lassies be seeing that, when they dinna know she's just a friend tae ye? They'll be thinking ye hae made yer choice, sae they dinna need tae put themselves forward for yer notice. Some might e'en pack up and go home."

Duncan grimaced. Trust Archie to make *his* point as well, and one he couldn't dispute.

"So I took one evening off from wife hunting, tae plain and simply enjoy m'self," Duncan said. "You begrudge me e'en that, do you?"

"Nay, as long as it was only the one evening. But this party canna go on indefinitely, lad. And ye'll no' be finding a better opportunity than this one tae make a choice. I've ne'er in m'life seen sae many fine lassies gathered in one place before. Auld Neville did verra well in his selection o' who tae invite here, making it easy for ye tae do the same. Use yer time more wisely, is all I'm asking."

Duncan agreed that he would, yet when he came downstairs a bit later, it was Sabrina he was unconsciously looking for as he passed through each room. Unfortunately, it was Ophelia he found instead, or rather, she found him, stepping into his path so he was forced to stop or rudely ignore her.

He would have done the latter without hesitation, since he'd said all he cared to say to her yesterday. If she hadn't gotten the point, that was no fault of his. But she wasn't alone, had two other girls with her, and he *was* keeping Archie's admonishments in mind.

He'd met her two companions briefly, but too briefly for him to remember their names, when he'd been introduced to more than a hundred people in the last two days. Each was rather pretty, though, so worth getting to know a little better, he supposed, and that meant not being rude just now. But he changed his mind about that abruptly with the first words out of Ophelia's mouth.

"I believe you've met my two very dear friends, Edith and Jane?"

Anyone who could call herself a good friend of hers, he didn't want to know any better. Sabrina was the exception to that, but then she had never claimed to be a friend of Ophelia's, had mentioned obligations instead.

"Indeed," he said without sparing a glance for Ophelia. Looking at her companions instead, he added before walking around them, "A pleasure, ladies, but if you'll excuse me, I havena eaten yet."

"He's awfully—" There was a pause as Jane tried to think of a word other than *rude* to describe Duncan's attitude. She settled on, "—abrupt, isn't he?" as they all watched him leave the room.

"A Scots trait, I would imagine," Ophelia said in a bored tone.

She was actually glad that he hadn't

stayed. She'd been seen talking to him. That was all she was interested in at the moment.

"Will you accept when he asks you to marry him again—that's if he doesn't take the request to your father instead this time?" Edith asked.

Ophelia pretended to give that some thought. "I haven't quite made up my mind yet. There is Lord Locke to consider now, after all."

"Of course," Jane replied. "He hasn't met you yet, but that can be rectified immediately. Sabrina could introduce you if she's still with him."

Ophelia's bored stance ended with amazing swiftness. "I don't *need* an introduction," she said tersely. "And certainly not by Sabrina. I will meet Raphael Locke when I am ready to meet him—perhaps tonight. You did say there was supposed to be dancing in the ballroom tonight?"

"We heard that mentioned, yes."

"Excellent. I do have a new ball gown for just such an occasion."

"Ah, Ophelia dear, I don't think the dancing tonight will quite be classified as a ball," Jane warned. "Things are much more informal in the country."

"Nonsense, a ball is a ball, no matter where it's held. And I do want to look my best when I meet him for the first time. A splendid new ball gown assures that."

Jane started to protest further, but a look from Edith changed her mind. Ophelia was still their friend, they still wanted to bask in her popularity, but neither of them had liked the way she had turned on Mavis, who had also been their friend. And Mavis's prediction was weighing heavily on them, since they could both see how easily it could come to pass.

So if Ophelia wanted to overdress for the evening, that was her business. If she was embarrassed by it, that was also her business. She'd been warned, but typically, no one's opinion but her own mattered to her.

25

By the time Duncan finished eating his breakfast, he was quite proud of himself. He had managed to accomplish a lot of socializing by taking his plate with him, as he'd seen others do, and making a circuit of the downstairs rooms, stopping here and there to pass out a compliment or remark on the storm that had blown in and was now battering at the windows.

If any guests had considered an outing for the day, they had now changed their minds. But then no one really cared to go out in winter, even if it weren't raining, when there were enough activities to occupy them indoors.

Card games were already in progress, some merely friendly, but most with gambling involved—a pastime the English *ton* seemed to find particular enjoyment in. Charades were being enacted in the drawing room amidst much laughter. The billiards room sported not one, but two tables which kept many of the older gentlemen busy, including Archie—Neville hadn't made an appearance yet.

A young lass was entertaining a group of ladies in the music room, a pretty girl with a touch of red in her blond hair who caught Duncan's eye. You'd have to be deaf to enjoy her singing, though, so he didn't stay long there.

He would have lingered in the drawing room, but that was where Ophelia was now holding court, which was too bad, since Amanda Locke was also there, and he had been thinking he'd get to know her a little better. Just because he didn't like her brother was no reason to discount one of the prettier lasses there. She wasn't as beautiful as Ophelia, but then it was unlikely that anyone could be. Ophelia was an oddity, too pretty and well aware of it.

He had covered all the rooms when he realized he hadn't seen Sabrina in any of them. The only two he hadn't checked were the ballroom, not used during the day, and Neville's study, also unused since it had pretty much been given over to Neville's estate manager, who'd been given leave while the house was entertaining. Sabrina's aunt who had been with her last evening was in the music room with another woman about the same age, but Sabrina wasn't with them either.

It occurred to Duncan then that Sabrina might not have come to Summers Glade. How ironic, that he would now have to suffer Ophelia's presence, yet the boon he was supposed to have for it, Sabrina's company, was going to be denied him. But why wouldn't she come herself when the rest of her household was here, even her guest?

Before he asked her aunt that very question, he checked the last two rooms. He found the study had been locked—a wise precaution, he supposed. The ballroom wasn't, but it was dark inside due to the storm, and empty as it should be; at least at a glance it seemed to be. A slight movement caught his eye, though, just as he was closing the door, and there she was, across the room, standing at the side of one of the glassed balcony doors. It was the lilac wallpaper behind her, which was about the same shade as her dress, that had blended her with the room, nearly hiding her.

Sabrina heard him approaching, and without looking, knew it was Duncan. There was something about his stride, so brisk, that was quite recognizable. Her pulse picked up a beat, an odd occurrence that happened each time he was near. She wondered why he was there. It wouldn't be for the same reason she was, she was sure.

As soon as the storm had begun, she had sought a quiet place to observe the primal magnificence of nature unleashed in full fury. She loved storms as much as she did gentle rain. While some people might grow nervous at the rumble of thunder or a whip-crack of lightning, she actually found such things soothing and would as soon be out in the midst of it.

That was impossible, at least today it was. But the next best thing was to watch, and the balcony doors with their glass panes gave her an unobstructed view of the terrace and beyond, and the empty ballroom gave her the privacy to enjoy that view alone.

But she didn't mind that she was being disturbed by Duncan; in fact, it was rather nice that she could share the view with him.

"It's beautiful, isn't it?" she said when his step stopped next to her.

She thought she'd have to explain what she meant, but knew he understood when he replied, "Would you like a closer look at it?"

She glanced at him and smiled, but shook her head sadly. "My aunts would disapprove of a wet, bedraggled look, particularly so close to the luncheon hour when I wouldn't have time to go home and change."

He smiled back, but took her hand in his and, opening the balcony door, pulled her outside with him into the rain. He stopped there on the terrace and lifted his face to the sky, savoring the elements as she might have done.

God help her, in that moment she fell completely in love with him.

Duncan thought he must be mad, to have given in to that impulse—until he looked down at Sabrina. There was such joy in her expression, such delight, that it made her radiantly lovely. Even though her hair had quickly soaked and was stringy about her face, for a brief moment he was completely mesmerized, by her incredible eyes, a raindrop on one lash before it slid to her cheek, another rivulet pooling in one dimple before dividing and rushing over her perky little chin, the suppleness of her lips when she smiled that drew his eyes to her mouth . . .

He cupped her adorable face in his hands and kissed her. It was another impulse, but one he couldn't regret once begun. The rain was stingingly cold, but he didn't feel the cold, felt only the heat of her lips, and the steamy heat where their bodies touched. She was ambrosia to taste, a fresh breath of summer in the bleakness of winter.

Thunder rumbled distantly and he drew her instinctively closer. Lightning flashed and he parted her lips, his tongue thrusting inside. For a time there was no one else in existence, just the two of them and the elements, and the passion that had burst upon them.

When Duncan came to his senses, he was assailed with guilt, embarrassment, and something else, which he didn't recognize immediately as fear. He could blame Archie for having set him to thinking about Sabrina as a woman, rather than just as a friend, and he would blame him if this impulse ended up costing him her friendship.

He took his hands from her and stepped back. He was too upset now to look at her, wanted only to escape before she said something that would sever their relationship, yet he had to apologize first, couldn't leave her thinking that he was the barbarian he was reputed to be.

"That was—it shouldna—" Duncan groaned inwardly. When had he ever been so bloody tongue-tied before? "I'm sorry, lass. I dinna ken why I did that, but it willna happen again, I promise you."

26

It was quite a while before Sabrina came out of the daze Duncan's kiss had left her in. She was shivering, had been for some time, but was only now aware of it. She didn't go back inside, though, to get warm. She walked around to the stable to see if she could find the coachman who had brought them.

He was there, fortunately, and agreed to take her home so she could change her clothes. Her aunts wouldn't have to know that she had gotten soaked, so she wouldn't have to explain why. She was in no condition to explain anything when she couldn't fathom what had happened herself.

Duncan had kissed her, thrilled her to her depths, then swore it would never happen again. What was she to make of that? That it was an accident, a spur-of-the-moment thing that shouldn't have happened and likely wouldn't have if they had been anywhere other than standing in the middle of a violent storm? Storms soothed her, but they apparently excited him, Mother Nature in her finest fury. Yes, there was something primitive in that, she supposed, something that might incite a man's passions.

She wished he hadn't done it. Knowing how wonderful and exciting it was, being kissed by him, wasn't going to help her peace of mind any. Not that it mattered compared to the other thing she had discovered, that she had actually fallen in love with him.

She wasn't surprised, really. There had been vague hints that it was happening, which she had tried to ignore. But actually admitting it . . . She knew it was going to make her miserable, loving Duncan. How could it not when she could never hope to have him for herself, when she would have to watch him marry someone else? And not from afar. She was his neighbor! She would see him often, him and his wife, and then him and his wife and their children.

She was late for lunch, not that it mattered since it was being served over the course of many hours, like breakfast, so not everyone was trying to crowd the tables at the same time. It still wouldn't have mattered either way, since she had no appetite now, had too much emotion churning around inside her to tolerate any food.

She joined her aunts in the drawing room. They'd already eaten and there was only a brief inquiry about her new day gown, which she covered nicely by simply saying the other had needed changing, without giving a reason. They accepted that, drawing their own conclusions as she'd figured they would, which kept her from having to lie about it. But then they had news to impart and were eager to impart it.

Alice beat Hilary in that, saying, "Ophelia has decided to stay here rather than with us, and has already sent for her things."

Sabrina's surprise wasn't that Ophelia would want to stay here, now that she'd been invited, but that she could. "They actually still have room here?"

"No, none a'tall, but she has friends here that offered to make room for her in the room they're sharing."

Hilary got her own thoughts in on the matter by adding, "Can't see why she'd want to be crowded in with a bunch of other gels when she could have a room to herself only ten minutes away."

Sabrina could and offered, "Being in residence, she's less likely to miss anything that occurs."

She didn't add that Ophelia would probably prefer crowds because they gave her the audience she seemed to constantly crave. That was an unkind thought best kept to herself. But staying at Summers Glade would also put a thorough end to any of the gossip about Ophelia, if any still lingered after her appearance today.

Alice pretty much confirmed that by saying, "It's being assumed she was invited back, so no hard feelings between her family and the Thackerays, even speculation that young Duncan has changed his mind and will propose again. D'you think we ought to point out that she's only here because *you* were invited, and she was our guest at the time?"

Sabrina sighed inwardly. She could frankly care less what turn the gossip took where Ophelia was concerned, but she didn't want to be responsible for influencing whichever direction it went.

"I think if Lord Neville wants it known that she's not here by his invitation, then he'll let it be known. It's not up to us to correct any false assumptions in that regard. Let everyone think what they like. You know as well as I that they will anyway."

That was a touchy subject that Sabrina immediately regretted mentioning, so she quickly added, "I heard there is to be dancing tonight. Has that been confirmed?"

"Indeed it has," Alice replied. "But there's no need to rush home to break the ball gowns out of storage. It will be quite informal."

"It has to be," Hilary pointed out. "At gatherings this large, it's almost impossible to set anything to a schedule, where everyone would need to prepare at the same time. Can you just imagine eight women in the same room, with eight ball gowns laid out, and eight maids trying to dress their ladies all at once? Can't be done, not without mass confusion and tempers flaring."

Sabrina did imagine it and smiled. "I don't know, the flaring tempers might be amusing to witness."

"Have you met Lord Archibald MacTavish yet, m'dear?" Alice asked next.

"No, but I've heard he's here," Sabrina replied. "Have you?"

"Not yet, though we were hoping to today."

"*She* was hoping to," Hilary corrected her sister. "She has the silly notion that the widower MacTavish could use a new wife himself."

Sabrina raised a teasing brow. "Why, Aunt Alice, are you thinking of getting married?"

Alice blushed and humphed in her sister's direction. "Certainly not. It merely occurred to me that with his grandson moving to England, he'll be alone up in those Highlands of his now."

"We don't know what his home is like," Hilary argued back. "It could be filled to the brim with other relatives of his, for all we know."

"Actually, it's rather empty, according to Duncan," Alice said, smirking at Hilary in triumph that she had that information.

Sabrina decided to nip their bickering in the bud before it got seriously started by satisfying her own curiosity. "You spoke to Duncan?" she asked Alice.

"Yes, just after lunch, though not for long. Poor boy seemed rather upset about something. He did ask where you had got to, and I couldn't answer him. I presume this was when you went home to change?"

"Possibly," Sabrina replied uncomfortably, and even more uncomfortably, tried to sound nonchalant in asking, "Did he say if he was looking for me for a reason, or merely wondered where I was?"

"No, but it's all right for you to seek him out to find out," Alice said.

"Yes," Hilary confirmed. "It's quite acceptable for you to do that in a gathering like this. You *are* his neighbor, after all."

Sabrina gave both of her aunts a narrow look, aware of what they were doing. "If it's important, I'm sure he'll find me. But in the meantime, stop imagining there is more there than there is. He sees me merely as a friend, something *neighbors* tend to do."

As they watched Sabrina leave the room, Alice said, "She stressed that rather nicely, didn't she?"

"Yes, rather overstressed it, actually. He likes her, you know."

"I thought as much, but apparently she doesn't," Alice said, frowning thoughtfully.

"Can you blame her for being less than confident after the disaster London turned out to be?"

"It wasn't a disaster, merely a—"

"Disaster."

"I swear, Hilary, could you *not* disagree with me for once, when we *do* happen to be in agreement about Duncan MacTavish? If Sabrina thinks he only wants to be friends with her, then she's not going to notice any hints to the contrary that will come from him. We need to convince her that she has a chance at a fine match here."

27

Ophelia wasn't overly embarrassed to be the only woman there that evening wearing a ball gown. She would have changed her clothes, however, if she'd noticed it in time, rather than after she was already halfway into the ballroom. She'd been too busy trying to locate Raphael Locke, though, to see what everyone else was wearing.

But she ignored it after her initial surprise and momentary discomfort. She knew how splendid she looked, after all, and that was all that mattered. She would merely shine even brighter compared to the other women there, which was fine by her and as it should be.

She didn't see the Locke heir yet, but she did see that Mavis was still there, and was exceedingly annoyed by it. The hateful bitch should have left Summers Glade already, but apparently being labeled a lying, backstabbing traitor to her friends wasn't enough to shame her into going. Ophelia would have to think of something else to send her running home in tears.

When she did finally spot Raphael Locke, it was to see him standing with Sabrina—*again? How intolerable! What* did he and Duncan find so interesting about that girl? It certainly couldn't be her looks. *Amusing,* Mavis had said. What nonsense. It was more likely they were getting something from her that they shouldn't be, yes, that *must* be it. And who would have thought the little country mouse would have loose morals? But why not? It wasn't as if she had any hope of ever marrying, so she wouldn't really care if she got a sordid reputation, now would she?

Ophelia strolled near them, hoping no gentlemen would stop her along the way. She was in luck, for once, and arrived without anyone trailing behind her. She offered Sabrina a brief smile before giving Lord Locke a demure look that she knew was exceptionally flattering, since she had practiced it enough before her mirror.

"I don't believe I've had the pleasure," Ophelia said. "Would you do the honors, Sabrina?"

"Certainly," Sabrina said, grinning impishly. "Lady Ophelia, may I present to you Raphael Locke, scion of the Locke family, from a long line of dukes and sure to carry on that line someday—if some woman doesn't shoot him first for his outlandish flirting."

Lord Locke, instead of being insulted as Ophelia would have expected him to be, laughed. But what else could he do, without being rude? Yet he must be mortified over that bizarre introduction. Whatever could have prompted Sabrina to say something so ridiculous?

"I don't believe a word of it," Ophelia offered, gaining his attention again.

"Oh, it's quite true, the 'flirting' part, at least. I object to the 'outlandish' part, though, 'deed I do. My flirting is quite refined, I'll have you know."

He was being kind. How nice of him. He should have put Sabrina in her place instead, as Ophelia would have. She turned to do just that, but Sabrina chose to leave at that moment, and since that was what Ophelia had been hoping she would do, she held her tongue.

"If you'll excuse me," Sabrina said. "I believe my aunts are in need of rescuing."

Raphael, who'd met her aunts earlier, saw them across the room and protested, "From whom? They are standing there alone together."

Sabrina chuckled. "Exactly. If you knew them better, you'd know that they frequently need rescuing—from each other. Even in a gathering like this where they should just be enjoying themselves, not five minutes can pass that they won't start arguing about something. Doesn't matter what. Pick any subject, and they'll disagree over it."

"Well, if you must play the angel of arbitration, then you must," he said with an exaggerated forlorn sigh. "But do keep in mind that I haven't forgotten how skillfully you evaded my request to dance. You can be sure that I'll mention it again later."

Sabrina still left them, though she did so now with a blush on her cheeks. Ophelia snorted to herself, would have done so aloud if it weren't such an indelicate sound. They wouldn't be dancing together later if she had anything to do about it, she promised herself.

But she was alone now with Raphael Locke, and far enough from any of the other guests that they wouldn't be over-heard. And he was finally behaving as he should, his blue eyes now taking in every inch of her in a slow, thorough examination. She wasn't the least bit embarrassed by it, was quite used to being stared at, even methodically as he was doing, had in fact expected it much sooner.

"You really are exquisitely beautiful," Raphael told her at last, not in awe, though, more in belated surprise. "But then you probably hear that so often that it has little or no meaning to you."

That was true, but hardly circumspect to say so, so she demurred, "On the contrary, a lady can never hear such compliments too often, particularly from such a hand-some gentleman as yourself."

For some reason, her own compliment made him tense and his look turn wary. She found out why when he said baldly, "Don't look here for another conquest, m'dear. The men in my family do the pursuing, they do not tolerate being pursued by marriage-minded females."

She could have taken offense easily enough, but that wouldn't suit her purpose. "Why, Lord Locke, whatever can you mean? Surely you aren't implying that you think I want to marry you, just because I find you handsome? I find many men handsome, and if they compliment me, I might return the compliment as I just did with you. Perfectly innocent, I assure you, with no hidden motives."

"Excellent," he replied jauntily. "Glad to hear it, 'deed I am."

He *should* have been embarrassed now over his mistake, but he wasn't. Instead, he was smiling in a way that implied he was skeptical. Well, no matter. She *would* marry him. She made the decision right then and there. He was young and very handsome, and the dukedom and wealth that he would inherit would suit her well enough. But she wouldn't tolerate his association with Sabrina any longer, sordid or otherwise, and would nip that in the bud right now.

"You shouldn't be so obvious, you

know," she said to him in a conspiratorial whisper.

"Obvious? Pray tell about what?"

"That you've been bedding Sabrina. Or don't you care that her reputation is in danger?"

His reaction wasn't what she anticipated at all. Any other man would have immediately assured her that there was nothing between him and Sabrina. Whether there was or wasn't, that would have been the gentlemanly response. And then henceforth, he'd make sure to avoid Sabrina if only to support his claim. Either way, he wouldn't be hovering over the girl again.

Instead, Raphael Locke took a step back from Ophelia, gave her an incredulous look as color slowly climbed his cheeks, and in what was apparent anger, actually started to walk away from her without any response at all. He changed his mind, though, swung about, and the anger was most definitely there—and turned on her.

"Good God, what an appalling rumormonger you are," he said in an amazed tone. "I had heard that it was so, but hadn't believed that any female could be quite as spiteful as you, but apparently it's true. But I warn you, Lady Ophelia, if you attempt to spread that particular rumor about Sabrina, which isn't the least bit true, I will ruin you myself. Do you understand? I will see to it that you are never accepted again in polite society. Your superficial beauty will not save you, m'dear, I promise you it won't."

Now he did walk away, back stiff, fury contained—he hadn't once raised his voice—and left *her* in shock. The very idea that he would talk to her like that, her, *and* threaten her, just to protect a nobody like Sabrina, she simply couldn't comprehend it. Well, she wouldn't have him now. The stupid man had quite ruined his chances.

And that left Duncan MacTavish.

Ophelia sighed inwardly. She didn't really want to marry him, but he wasn't as bad as she had feared. He *was* different, with his brogue, his red hair, his unpredictability, but he was handsome enough, and every other woman there seemed to find him a fine catch, which made all the difference as far as she was concerned.

But dealing with that Scot again and his denseness—he hadn't even grasped that she was apologizing to him yesterday—as well as his offended pride, was going to be a lesson in patience for her. Yet he *did* want her back. That was obvious, at least to her, or she wouldn't be here now. He was just pretending otherwise, nursing his grudge, she supposed, and probably quite at wits' end, trying to figure out how to get her back without it appearing that he was willing to forgive her.

She could help in that regard by pretending that the incident was forgotten as far as she was concerned. It might be more amusing to let him flounder about, no more than he deserved for not immediately forgiving her, but there were all these other young hopefuls in attendance who needed to realize that they didn't stand a chance with him, now that she was here. She didn't want to see any more simpering looks and eyes batting his way than she already had.

As for Sabrina garnering Duncan's attention as she'd apparently done last night, he was obviously just trying to make

Ophelia jealous, since he knew she'd hear about it, which she did. As if Sabrina could. So absurd. But at least Ophelia had figured out what he was up to now, and she knew just how to counter such nonsense.

28

Now that the guests at Summers Glade had been in residence for several days, and Duncan had been introduced, and in some cases reintroduced, to all of them, they were no longer wary of him as being the "outsider" in their midst. The simple passing of a few days acquaintance had elevated him into being "one of them."

This began a phenomenon that he discovered late that day. It was now increasingly difficult for him to pass from room to room, or even just across the hall, without being stopped by guests who wanted to chat with him. He found he *much* preferred it when he'd been the "stranger" and most of them were leery of approaching him.

The phenomenon continued into the evening. He had tried to get to the ballroom sooner, where he expected to find Sabrina and could attempt to correct the blunder he'd made with her on the terrace that afternoon. But not all the guests were interested in dancing, however informal it was, and so many of them were still spread out in the other rooms. And they thought nothing of dragging him into the drawing room to settle an argument, or into another room to join what they considered a discussion he shouldn't miss.

Unwilling to be outright rude, which he was striving not to be, Duncan had been detained again and again, so it was several hours into the evening before he did finally escape long enough to slip into the ballroom. But it didn't end there as he'd hoped.

His eyes went right to Sabrina on the far side of the room, passing over Ophelia without really noticing her, though *she* noticed his oversight. But there was quite a trail of people between them, each determined to stop him to say something, so that he was actually annoyed by the time he reached Sabrina and his tone a bit surly in his greeting.

But insightful as she usually was, she

took one look at him and laughed, guessing, "You're not used to being so popular, are you?"

" 'Tis no' that, lass. In the Highlands we dinna talk just tae hear ourselves talk as these English do, we talk o' real concerns."

"I understand," she replied, still grinning. "It must have been difficult for you, the conversations you and I have had, which were for the most part quite frivolous."

He blushed to his roots and tried to quickly amend, "I dinna mean tae imply—"

"Duncan, stop that," she chided gently. "You should know by now when I'm teasing."

He sighed. She was right. He should have known. But then he'd been expecting a more reserved attitude from her after what had passed between them on the terrace, possibly even anger. Yet, now that he thought of it, it was almost impossible to imagine Sabrina angry, truly angry, with raised voice, flashing eyes—that would be something to behold, violet eyes filled with hot passion . . .

He glanced away from her so she wouldn't see what his own thoughts were doing to him. Unfortunately, his eyes did light on Ophelia this time, and he couldn't miss the smile she was sending him as she started his way.

It didn't take much for him to realize that standing with Sabrina, who knew Ophelia quite well, gave the blond girl an excuse to join them. This had him quickly moving off in another direction.

"I'll be back, lass," was all he tossed at Sabrina before he hurried off.

It was more than an hour later before he managed to work his way back to Sabrina. He'd realized after the fact that running from Ophelia because he couldn't tolerate her wasn't going to work, when she was going to be in the house every day. He was simply going to have to make it clear to her to stay away from him, since trying to ignore her didn't seem to get that message across.

"It seems I owe you several apologies now," he told Sabrina as he joined her near the refreshment table.

"Only several?" she replied, lifting a brow. "I can count at least seven."

It was the odd number she used, and her straight face, that made him think she was serious for once. "Och, what else have I done?"

"Well, one, you haven't asked me to dance yet. Two, you should apologize for thinking you have anything to apologize for, when you don't. Three, you shouldn't look so surprised when someone is pulling your leg, because they might get the idea that you're in need of a lesson in the art of silliness and walk off with it."

"Walk off wi' what?" he asked in exasperation after trying to follow her strange trail of thoughts.

"Your leg, of course."

It was because she was *still* looking at him so seriously that his laughter, when it burst out, was so loud and sudden. Not that he cared at the moment if he was drawing eyes their way. Once again she had managed to put him at complete ease, to more or less wash away all his aggravations of the day as if they'd never been.

"One o' these days I'll be asking you for the other four things I was tae apologize for."

"Oh, good, I just love having extra time to be creative in my endeavors. I can be really, really silly when I put my mind to it, you know."

He grinned at her and stressed, *"But I'll still be apologizing for leaving you tae your own devices this afternoon, when I should have taken you home m'self for a dry change o' clothes. There's nae excuse for such thoughtlessness on my part. I went back tae the ballroom when I realized it, but you were already gone."*

"And now who's being silly? It's not as if I had to go to London to change. Easy enough to find my way home when I live just around the corner, more or less. Is that why you were upset today?" At his own raised brow, she added, "My aunts mentioned that they sensed you were."

"Och, well, that among other things. Wi' both o' my granddas hoping I'll find a wife afore this party ends, I'm feeling a wee bit o' pressure. Disappoint them, or disappoint m'self in a hasty decision, makes for nae winners. Neville, I dinna care if I disappoint, but he's o' the same mind as Archie on this, and I do care if I disappoint him. Archie, however, is being foolish in what he wants, but you canna tell an auld stubborn Scot that."

"That's quite a predicament," Sabrina replied, her lips pursed thoughtfully. "Perhaps if you weren't trying so hard to make this important decision of yours, it might get much easier for you."

"And the sun managed tae shine all day as well, I noticed," he countered.

Since it had in fact rained most of the day, she scolded lightly, "Don't be so skeptical, when it really does work occasionally. In my own case, I have found that if I don't worry a problem to death, the answer will sometimes just come to me of a sudden. Not always, of course, that would be too simple, but often enough that I do try not to worry about it when a problem first presents itself. A few predicaments do have a way of correcting themselves with no help from you a'tall. Would that they all did," she ended with a smile.

"You're a might young tae be so philosophical, lass."

"You think so?" she said in wide-eyed innocence. "When that's a child's logic I just gave you, that most adults tend to forget once they become adults?"

He chuckled. She was such a treasure, this friend of his. And she looked especially lovely tonight in her simple blue frock with her eyes sparkling with laughter. She had mentioned dancing in jest, but he *did* want to dance with her, and he realized why. He wanted to touch her.

Duncan sighed inwardly. He had to stop these kinds of thoughts. She wasn't interested in him that way, had never once looked at him with other than camaraderie. She considered him a friend. A fine friend he would be if he pounced on her every chance he got.

He was going to frighten her away if he didn't get control of this sudden attraction he was finding to her. Much as he might like to steal another kiss or two from her, he would much rather have her friendship, which he was finding he valued beyond measure.

But he *could* dance with her. Even she would think nothing of it, probably did expect him to at least ask her for a twirl about the floor. One dance, and then he would get back to the matter of finding a wife.

29

"Will you marry me, Sabrina?"

She imagined that he had waited until they were twirling about the dance floor before springing that shocking question on her so she wouldn't just walk off and ignore it as it deserved. She did miss a step and almost tripped them both. And she didn't find him amusing. Marriage was nothing to tease about, really, at least not in such a direct way.

"Don't be absurd," she finally told him. "You know very well that you and I wouldn't suit. Nor would your family approve, as if I need to point that out, when you know it very well."

"If those are your only objections, then we can set a date for the wedding."

She rolled her eyes at him. He was joking. She just wished she could find it a matter for joking as well. Not that she wouldn't have been exceptionally flattered if she thought he was serious. But she was realistic, knew she wasn't a prime catch like he was, even if she didn't have a scandal attached to her name. But she did come packaged with an old scandal, and most families, particularly those that prided themselves on having pristine ancestry, would summarily cross her off a list of possibilities for their heirs.

And besides, she had decided that very afternoon that she was never going to marry, after coming to the heartbreaking conclusion that she loved a man she could never have. Marrying someone else just wouldn't be fair to the man in question, even if that man was Raphael Locke, who might deserve it for treating this subject so frivolously.

"Why won't you believe me?" Raphael asked after her silence continued.

"I'm not blind, Rafe," she said uncomfortably.

He ignored the reference to her looks, said instead, "You're wonderful, is what you are. I'd much rather marry someone I truly enjoy being with than some snooty chit who spends all her time primping in front of a mirror."

She laughed. "Well, I'd have to admit mirrors and I don't get along too well. But if I *did* believe you, my answer would have to be no."

"Why?"

How to explain without really explaining? She decided not to try, to turn the tables on him instead.

"You aren't the least bit devastated by my refusal, which proves you don't love me."

"Well, no, but I like you well enough, and I've no doubt love would blossom in no time a'tall."

She snorted at him. "Now, why would you hope for such an occurrence, rather than wait for it to happen first and then proceed in a more natural order? Why would you even want to get married as young as you are, when you don't have to, and love isn't involved?"

He gave her a wounded look. "You don't think you could learn to love me?"

"When I haven't given you the least indication that I'm interested, might you not conclude that my interest lies elsewhere?"

"Aha! Are we going to confess now that we love someone else?"

She blinked at him. He seemed too triumphant by half with that conclusion.

"Is that what this is all about? You're looking for a grand confession that—"

"Now, now, don't say something we will both regret. No, I'm hoping two people I like will wake up and see what's in front of them before it's too late."

There was a serious side to Raphael Locke, and she was seeing it now. It actually made him much more attractive than his usual attitude of jocularity, but she only barely noticed that.

"And which two people are those?" she asked, her eyes narrowing on him suspiciously.

"You, of course, and that dunderhead Highlander," he replied simply.

Sabrina blushed furiously. Good God, how could he possibly have guessed her feelings when she had only just discovered them herself? Was she obvious about it? Staring at Duncan too long, perhaps? Looking at him in a way she shouldn't?

She was mortified to think she might be. Or was it only because she had spent so much time with Duncan the other night, and that had been taken note of? If that was the case, then Raphael was only guessing, and she wasn't about to give him yet another reason to exclaim, *Aha!*

"You are mistaken," she said succinctly. "Duncan and I are just friends."

He didn't exactly snort, but it was definitely a similar sound of skepticism that he made. That he made no comment, though, and the silence continued, forced her to elaborate. He was obviously still harboring false assumptions—at least where Duncan was concerned. Her own feelings hardly counted when they weren't returned.

"I can't imagine where you got this silly idea from," she said. "Duncan even discusses with me his dilemma in needing to pick a wife from among those in attendance here. I was going to recommend your sister to him. That should please you, since, as you say, you like him."

Raphael chuckled now. "Trouble is, I do like him, so I would *not* wish my sister on him, who would drive him batty within a month."

She frowned at him. "Bosh. You adore your sister. How can you not, when she's so charming? Perhaps it's your constant teasing of her that causes her to act in such a way that might cause someone to go batty."

He smiled. "Perhaps, but hardly the point. He might be dancing with her now." He paused to take a moment to spot the other couple in the crowd on the dance floor. "But take it from a man who would recognize the signs, m'dear. He isn't the least bit interested in my little sister."

"And what, pray tell, makes you think he's interested in me that way?"

"Possibly because he looks for you when you're not with him. Possibly because he's already sent a couple scowls my way since I've been dancing with you. Possibly because Lady Ophelia is here when she shouldn't be here, but she's here because he couldn't stand it that you wouldn't be here unless she was."

Sabrina stared at him blankly for a moment until that last long sentence unjumbled itself enough to make sense in her mind. She then sighed.

"You misunderstand completely Duncan's reactions, but then of course you would, since you aren't aware of all the circumstances involved."

"Which would be?"

"Basically, the effect I have on some people. I'm quite aware of it. In fact, I work at it diligently."

He was frowning now. "What *are* you talking about? What effect?"

"I put people at ease, Rafe. Whatever is bothering them, aggravation, frustration, real anger, et cetera, I'm able to tease them out of it with simple silliness or a laugh or two. It really is amazing, how beneficial a little thing like laughter is. But in Duncan's case, he's been overset with all of the negative emotions since coming here, since he really didn't want to come here. And both his grandfathers have been causing him extra frustration in insisting he get this marriage business over with quickly. And to be truthful . . ." She whispered now. "I don't think he likes Lord Neville a'tall. I wouldn't presume to ask why, but from certain remarks he's made, I have gathered as much."

"And your point in all of that?"

She rolled her eyes at him. "Wretch, you

got the point very well. He's constantly angry or frustrated or whatever, and I'm able to make him forget his troubles for a bit, that's all. Now, wouldn't you often seek out someone who was able to help you forget for a while that you're facing the guillotine in the morning?"

He laughed at that point. "Touché. Indeed, I'd package you up and take you home with me."

Sabrina grinned. "Well, Duncan doesn't have to go that far, since I live in the neighborhood. He knows very well he can always come visiting when he needs cheering up."

"That's assuming he thinks you'll always be available, but what if you marry and move out of the neighborhood? D'you think he's considered that?"

"Why would he, when it's very likely I'll follow in my aunts' footsteps and never marry?"

"Good God, what a waste!" he said in exaggeration, then seriously, "You don't *really* think that a silly scandal like yours is would stop someone from marrying you if he really wants to marry you, do you?"

"Actually, I know it will, and you know it will, when the object of most marriages is to continue the line with heirs, and if my particular scandal is believed, then I won't last long enough to beget heirs."

Raphael's snort was most definitely a snort this time. "You know very well you have no intention of ever kicking the bucket intentionally, and anyone with any sense a'tall would know it as well, when you are obviously so very full of laughter and joy of life. There isn't a melancholic bone in your little body, m'dear."

She gave him a wide-eyed look. "Well, no, there isn't, but where did you get the idea that anyone has any sense—aside from the two of us, of course?"

He laughed heartily. "Gads, I suppose when you look at it that way, you're quite right. Of course, if you *were* to agree to marry me—not to actually do so, mind you, but just to, well, to pretend, so to speak— what do you think Duncan's reaction would be?"

"I think he'd be the first to congratulate me and wish me happy, if that's what he thinks I want."

Raphael tsked. "I disagree. I think he'll discover some serious jealousy, if he hasn't already figured out that's why he can't stand seeing me dance with you. Care to give it a try to find out?"

"You are being ridiculous again and decidedly single-minded. Friends can be jealous of friends, you know, or haven't you ever experienced that when your best friend ignores you a bit and is seen having fun with other friends? Jealously does *not* always involve love. Far from it. Envy takes many different forms."

"Yes, yes," he said in exasperation. "But why don't we try it anyway? It won't hurt your reputation a'tall, nor mine, for you to announce later that you've changed your mind and don't want to marry me."

"Well, there is the point that some other young man might take notice of me here and *seriously* ask me to marry him, but won't if I'm pretending to be engaged to you. Not that I expect any such thing to happen, but if it did, I'd be losing my chance because of this silly nonsense."

He sighed as he led her off the dance floor. "Think about it, Sabrina. You know it won't do any harm, and you might be happily surprised by the results."

30

Think about it? Sabrina had trouble thinking about anything else during the next hour. What if Raphael was right and Duncan just hadn't figured out yet that he was falling in love with her? That kiss he had treated her to could even support that contention. He had been embarrassed and upset about it, yet why had he kissed her if there was nothing but friendship between them?

But when rational thoughts finally intruded, she knew she wouldn't do it, what Raphael was suggesting. It would be pure deceit just for Duncan's benefit, and she couldn't do that to him. Besides, it might have sounded logical, the way Raphael had put it, but anything could sound logical if twisted just right. That she might *want* to believe it was sheer foolishness on her part. Playing "what ifs" had never been part of her realistic nature.

And then she put the thought completely away, after her talk with Ophelia.

"Have you noticed how he's trying to make me jealous?" Ophelia purred in her ear. "I think it's rather silly myself, but you can't tell a man that, nor get him to admit that's what he's doing."

The remark, coming as it did from out of nowhere as Ophelia stepped up behind her, confounded Sabrina for a moment. She wasn't usually so dense, but having just been wrestling with the subject of jealousy that had been introduced by Raphael Locke, hearing it now from an entirely different direction actually did confuse her briefly.

She wished she could have retracted her, "Who?" though, as soon as she uttered it, since her confusion did clear before Ophelia gave her the very obvious answer. And she would have preferred, greatly preferred, not to have the conversation that followed.

"Why, Duncan, of course," Ophelia said, then in surprise, "You look surprised."

Sabrina wasn't, but apparently Ophelia

had expected her to be, and went on as if she really had looked surprised. "Don't tell me you thought the attention he has been giving you was because he might actually be interested in you?" She added a chuckle here. "My dear, I thought you of all people would know better."

"I haven't thought any such thing," Sabrina replied, her tone more defensive than she would have liked. "Duncan and I are merely friends."

"You might think so, but that just shows how naive you are. I assure you, it's all a pretense on his part that he hopes I'll notice."

That stung, making Sabrina wonder if that wasn't Ophelia's intention. Sabrina might not be desirable for a wife, but she did like to think she was worthy of friendship. Yet the blond girl was implying that Duncan wouldn't have become friends with her without this ulterior motive.

"Friendship would hardly make you jealous, Ophelia—or would it?"

"Certainly it wouldn't," Ophelia replied impatiently. "But he's hoping I'll think it's more than that, or haven't you got the point yet?"

"No, I guess I missed the point," Sabrina said dryly. "I thought it was about jealousy."

Ophelia actually blushed, but she was decidedly single-minded and got right back to stressing her *point.* "I was just trying to save you some unpleasant grief, my dear, in case you misunderstood the attention he's given you. But if you were only thinking it's friendship, then you won't be hurt when he marries me."

"No, of course not," Sabrina was forced to say. Though she would have liked to add, *I'll merely pity him,* she managed to restrain herself.

"Good," Ophelia replied, and then with a thoughtful frown, "I suppose I should warn Amanda Locke as well. He's doing the same thing with her, if you haven't noticed. And she, at least, would naturally assume his interest is real, rather than contrived for my benefit."

Sabrina was getting rather tired of these subtle insults of Ophelia's, which weren't very subtle to anyone with a modicum of intelligence. She was familiar, by now, with Ophelia's tactics, but for the girl to blatantly use them on her, as if she were too dense or simply too trusting to realize she was being deliberately insulted . . .

"I am well aware of my 'deficiencies,' " she said stiffly. "I am also aware that Amanda Locke doesn't have any. With all due respect, Ophelia, Duncan's interest in Amanda could be quite genuine."

Ophelia laughed, a sound full of grating confidence. "Certainly it could, but it's not."

"You simply can't know that for sure, Ophelia," Sabrina pointed out.

Ophelia merely tsked and said, "You are *so* naive, but then you weren't at the inn the other day to see just how much he regrets breaking our engagement. It was so obvious in his every word and action. But I'm sure he will rectify that shortly. He just has this wounded pride of his to deal with first, because of those unfortunate insults I dealt him, and nothing short of punishing me will do, before we can make up. And the silly man has decided that making me jealous will suffice. It's not working, but as long as he thinks it is, he'll be satisfied, I suppose."

A lump was rising in Sabrina's throat, making it difficult to reply, "Then you think that Duncan will ask you to marry him again?"

"I know he will. I don't know why men feel they have to 'get even' when their pride is involved, but they do, and Duncan is no different. But it's just a matter of time, Sabrina, before we're engaged again."

"Are you sure you aren't the one that's harboring false expectations?"

Sabrina couldn't believe she said it. This was Ophelia Reid, after all, the reigning queen of the Season, the most beautiful and desirable debutante to join the marriage mart in a decade, possibly centuries. So she wasn't surprised that Ophelia would be offended.

Her temerity got her a glare and the terse reply, "You have to experience the pursuit before you can understand the nuances of it. Now, how to explain to someone who has never experienced it? Well, one, there was the passionate kiss he gave me at the inn before he stormed out. He obviously didn't want to reveal his feelings quite that dramatically, but simply couldn't help himself. And he's lucky no one witnessed it, or I could have been quite compromised and he would then have been forced to marry me. I don't want that any more than he would, so I've told no one about it—except you, since you are being so obtuse I see no other recourse than to mention it."

It was probably Sabrina's own embarrassment that was causing her some anger, and not very familiar with that emotion, she didn't think before saying, "You could simply spare me this *lesson.* I assure you, I can go on quite blissfully being ignorant of these—nuances."

"Not at all," Ophelia purred. "I really don't mind educating you, my dear. There is also the fact that I am constantly catching Duncan staring at me when he thinks I don't know it."

"Hardly conclusive—"

"I wasn't finished," Ophelia all but snapped, then coughed and continued in her falsely sweet tone, "That, coupled with the kiss he all but forced on me, is really all that was necessary to ascertain his real feelings toward me. But then there is also this campaign of his to make me jealous. Now do you understand why I know he wants me back? He broke our engagement in the heat of the moment. Not that I blame him, when it *was* what I was trying to achieve at the time. He regrets that, but his pride won't let him immediately rectify it, thus these silly pretenses in the meantime."

"I would say the only pretense being enacted around here, Ophelia, is your pretense of friendship with me. And if anyone should be warned, it is you. Duncan has kissed me as well, but I didn't presume it meant anything. I've been told he stares at me also, but I'm not silly enough to think that means anything either. His interest in Amanda Locke is probably quite genuine, and if anyone would make him a fine wife, it would be she. Now, you don't like me, you've made that abundantly clear, so do spare me these 'friendly' chats in the future. In fact, Ophelia, just stay the hell away from me, thank you very much."

31

Sabrina had never in her life done anything so . . . so foreign to her nature as she had that evening. It was the unfamiliar anger, still present, that had her seeking her coat and leaving Summers Glade without even telling her aunts, sending them only a curt message to be delivered by Mr. Jacobs. But it was the mortification that followed, which she felt clear to her bones, that had her running all the way home without waiting for the coach to be brought around.

She simply couldn't believe she had said those things to Ophelia. Delivering unkindness for unkindness was never the answer, no matter how satisfying it might be. Yes, Ophelia had deserved every word, but was that any excuse to compromise her own principles and nature?

She could have just walked away. That simple rudeness would have sufficed to get her point across, that she was fed up with Ophelia and wouldn't tolerate any more of her spitefulness. But no, she'd had to let the anger she'd experienced take control of her, and stoop to Ophelia's level instead.

She would prefer not to ever go back to Summers Glade, at least not as long as Ophelia was still there, but she didn't know what excuse she could give her aunts not to. The truth was considered, then rejected. Hilary would blame herself, after all, because Ophelia's mother was her friend. She might also feel bound to inform Lady Mary about her daughter's horrid behavior, then would feel guilty about that as well. Sabrina could at least spare her aunt all those awful emotions by simply keeping the incident to herself.

She really wished she could ignore Ophelia's conclusions and believe Raphael's instead, but she couldn't. There had been nothing exceptionally passionate about the kiss Duncan had given her, other than the violent storm that had raged about them when it occurred. His kiss had been gentle, sweet, surprising, wonderful, at least for her, but there had been no great passion involved that she'd noticed. Yet he'd kissed Ophelia passionately, even though he didn't want to. That had been implied, that it had been forced out of him, and that spoke volumes about his true feelings.

She didn't doubt for a minute that Ophelia's main contention was true. He wanted her back, he was just too angry yet to admit it. How could he not? Ophelia was just too beautiful for any man not to want her for himself. Sabrina did *not,* however, think that he was just using her to make Ophelia jealous. Amanda, perhaps, but not her. Their friendship was genuine. It had to be. She couldn't be that wrong about him—or her own self-worth.

And then the painful emotions arrived, with her acceptance that the man she loved, loved someone else, and someone who wasn't even worthy of him. She had known she would experience it eventually, but this soon?

Quite naturally, the tears came next, and so many of them that she was soon running aimlessly, without really seeing where she was going. When she nearly tripped on a root, she took a moment to clear her sight and found that she'd turned herself around in a circle and was almost back at Summers Glade. Which was why the coach leaving the mansion just then was able to come across her rather quickly.

"What the devil are you doing?" she heard before Duncan jumped down from the driver's seat and thrust her inside the coach.

There was no light inside. He'd taken the first vehicle that he'd come across that had horses already harnessed to it, the one that would have taken her and her aunts home at the end of the evening, and was kept ready for that.

So he couldn't see her tears when he followed her inside out of the cold, and his next question sounded just as angry as the first. "What happened back there tae send you running from the house?"

"Nothing."

"Nothing? When you were so upset you couldna e'en wait for your driver?"

"I like to walk—"

"You were running!"

"It's cold—"

"You'll be giving me the truth, lass, and

nae more excuses. I saw you talking tae Ophelia. What did she say tae you tae upset you so?"

"Duncan, I just want to go home. If you don't want me walking, then take me home."

He must have heard the quaver in her voice this time, now that he'd let her say more than a few words without interrupting her, because his finger came to her cheek to find the suspected tears there and then he was gathering her in his arms, almost crushing her in his own upset.

"I'm sorry, lass," he mumbled. "You dinna have tae talk aboot it if you dinna want tae. Och, I'm such an insensitive brute."

He wasn't that at all, was in fact trying to make amends by wiping the tears from her eyes and cheeks with his own lips. And such a natural progression, when he began kissing her instead. She certainly didn't object. She couldn't imagine herself ever objecting to Duncan's kisses, whether they were given in sympathy or friendship or . . .

Passion, like anger, was an amazing emotion in how quickly it could arrive and—take over. The pitch darkness heightened the other senses, especially touch, and combined, what was felt on the surface and what was felt internally were too powerful to resist.

Sabrina didn't even try. She knew very well what could happen, what *was* happening, and was in a unique position to not care. She could ignore the right or wrong of it because she had already decided to never marry, yet here was the man she loved offering her a small glimpse of what marriage to him could be like. Of course she wouldn't refuse. She would accept anything he was willing to give her of himself, including these few stolen moments of passion that were her dreams come true.

There was an element of unreality, though, of doubt that something so wonderful could be real; it must be a dream instead. But a dream or otherwise, it was still not to be refused, was to be savored to the fullest extent, and Sabrina did just that.

Her hair was already in wild disarray from running, making it easy for Duncan to thread his fingers along her scalp to position her for the depth of his kisses. His tongue was teasing and bold by turns, playing with her senses, inciting her to join the play, and then as suddenly ravaging, scorching in intensity, and she met that, too, awed and thrilled by each new sensation as it arrived to tantalize her.

Breathing was becoming difficult until she realized she was too busy enjoying herself to think of anything so mundane as breathing. She kept it in mind thereafter, or tried to, though her occasional gasps suggested otherwise. It did get easier, though, when his mouth moved on to her neck, only that started a new set of sensations that had her catching her breath again in shivering delight.

Her coat was parted—she had never bothered to fasten it, merely tugged it on before bolting out the door of the mansion—as his mouth worked a bit lower. Tall as he was, though, he was having a bit of trouble bending to reach what he wanted, so she wasn't all that surprised when he moved off the seat to kneel before her.

His kisses now followed the square neckline of her day dress, the depth very circumspect in comparison to an evening gown. This was nowhere near her breasts, yet she was thrilled beyond measure, never having been kissed on her chest before, never having been kissed much in any way before.

Her hands rested on his shoulders, moved hesitantly into his hair, rested on his shoulders again—she really wasn't sure what to do with them, when what she would like to do was pull him closer and closer to her.

It was growing rather warm in the coach. She noticed it at about the same moment that he did, since he began removing her coat and then his own, and she could only nod mentally in approval. It didn't really help much, though, with her long sleeves and the thick material of her dress, so she gave another mental nod a while later when her gown came off as well—and his shirt.

Oh, my, what she wouldn't have given for a candle just then, or the moon's appearance, any kind of light really, but there was none. Viewing the bare chests on statues, which was as close as she'd ever come to seeing one, just wasn't the same as experiencing the warm male skin under her fingers, which she craved to see as well as touch.

She had to wonder if he felt the same way, because he seemed to be trying to imagine what she looked like by touch alone, since he was touching her everywhere. The length and breadth of her arms, over her shoulders, around her neck—down her chest.

Her gasp was merely in surprise when both his hands covered her breasts. There was still the thin material of her chemise between them, yet there might as well have been nothing, so hot were his palms, so firm was his grip. And when his mouth came back to claim hers as he began to knead the plump mounds, a surge of heat shot deep within her, coiled, spread, and escaped in a long moan of pleasure. And yet that was nothing in comparison to the intensity of sensations that followed as he laid her down on the seat and continued to educate her in the delights of amour.

The coach was large and luxurious, but then it would be, being the vehicle that carried the marquis's coat of arms. The seats were wide, plushly comfortable in soft velvet and thick padding, the windows tightly sealed against the cold, like a small room in a house—with narrow beds. It still wasn't where she would have chosen to lose her virginity, but there really was no choice involved for either of them. What was happening was a matter for the moment, not for careful thought, or it might not be happening.

And deep down, she was afraid he was going to stop, afraid that at any moment he would come to his senses as he had after that kiss on the terrace, or that she would awake from the dream if it was a dream. This fear lent a very real urgency to the emotions that were churning around in her. She wanted to slowly savor, and yet she wanted to hurry so that she *could* experience it all.

If he had simply said, "I'm going to make love to you," she could have relaxed and enjoyed every moment of it. But she suspected that this impulse of his was just that, an impulse, and thus could be terminated at any time if thought did intrude. She wished she knew how to prevent that, but in her innocence, she had no idea how to make him hurry other than to say so, and that was out of the question, any words from her probably the very thing that would shatter the magical moment and bring reality crashing back upon them.

His hands continued to shape an image of her for his mind, or so it seemed, spanning her waist, her hips, sliding down each thigh. On the return path, her petticoats caught on the backs of his hands and rose to her hips, but she barely noticed that, when she could now feel the heat of his palms directly on her skin. He shaped and molded her thighs, her calves, behind her knees, lifting, moving, even removed her shoes and massaged her feet. He was leaving no part of her unexamined and was very bold in his touch, with none of the hesitancy that she felt in returning his caresses.

She wondered if it was a Highland trait, that boldness. But no, she was being silly. Englishmen, she supposed, could be as bold, and yet some were so painfully correct in their etiquette that she imagined they might ask for permission before kissing or touching a knee or . . .

It just happened, before she even realized or guessed where he was going to touch her next. Suddenly his hand was just there, cupped firmly at the apex of her legs, his palm pressing, rubbing, and he was kissing her deeply again, capturing her gasps. Expecting a protest perhaps? Oh, no, no protest over what she was feeling now, no indeed, just amazement over yet another new sensation, when she thought she must have felt everything possible by then.

Still he wouldn't hurry. Still she wanted him to, so she rejoiced when he finally joined her on the seat again and filled her senses with his overwhelming presence. The heady male scent of him, so different from a life of rosewater, powder, and sweet spices in a household of just women. The hard texture of his skin, muscles that wouldn't give, coarse hair that tickled on his chest, the very expanse of him that made her feel so small and feminine. And his weight as he slowly covered her skin with his, the velvety thickness filling her, the . . .

She cried out, not so much from the sudden thrust of pain, but from the surprise of it. And he was immediately making amends, raining kisses on her face, swearing that it couldn't be helped, but that it would never hurt again.

She believed him, of course, because the pain was already gone, leaving her to experience only the fullness deep inside her, and those other sensations again when he started moving, the pleasant ones, swiftly taking over, as swiftly growing in intensity, tantalizing, enthralling, rushing her to a soaring peak that was so shockingly exquisite she could barely take in the full beauty of it.

He was kissing her tenderly now. He had climaxed, too, though she hadn't noticed, so overwhelmed had she been by her own experience. She thought she might become embarrassed, now that it was over, but no, she just felt a tremendous lassitude that might have put her fast to sleep if he weren't still keeping her attention with his kisses.

He helped her dress, which was fortunate, because she could barely keep her eyes open now. The long day was catching up to her, and the many turns it had taken. It had been the most unusual, amazing, shocking, and finally wonderful day of her life, yet she could barely stay awake to savor it.

Duncan made no excuse this time for what he'd done. In fact, he didn't say much of anything about it, other than, "We'll talk in the morning," before he left her alone in the coach so he could drive her home, which only took a few minutes, so she managed to stay awake for it.

He did walk her to her door, though, and he gave her one last gentle kiss and the admonishment to get some sleep. Her aunts weren't home yet, probably wouldn't be for another few hours, since the party would go on for at least that much longer. Sleep? She was probably asleep before her head touched her pillow, because she was never to recall getting into her bed that night.

32

Sabrina woke with a smile, still savoring her dream. It had to be a dream, making love with Duncan MacTavish. Anything that wonderful, yet that unlikely, couldn't have been real. She continued to think so until she noticed her clothes in a pile on the floor, and on top of the pile, her petticoat spotted with blood.

She sat down then in amazed wonder and continued to sit there on her bed in a near daze, remembering, and experiencing such incredulous delight, such utter . . . happiness. She might have spent the entire day in her euphoric stupor if the rap on her door hadn't signaled the arrival of the maid she shared with Hilary and Alice, causing her to make a mad dash to hide her petticoats before the door opened.

She couldn't imagine how she managed to get through dressing and meeting her aunts downstairs without letting on that her life had changed or that she was so happy she could barely stand it. She wanted to share that happiness, to confess everything that had happened, but of course, she couldn't. They might understand. They might get as excited as she was and expect an immediate announcement of marriage. And therein was why she would say nothing.

Duncan hadn't asked her to marry him, though he did say they would talk this morning, which implied that he would. She *did* expect him to now, which was one reason she was so deliriously happy, but she would also make it clear to him that he wasn't obligated to. If it had been just an impulse on his part, she wasn't going to force him to marry her by letting others know about it. She wouldn't regret it either way. How could she, when she loved him? But if he was going to ask her to marry him, it had to be for the right reasons, not because her aunts would demand it.

She couldn't wait to get to Summers Glade to see Duncan this morning, and

hurried her aunts out the door to the waiting coach. It was a bit disconcerting,
though, to sit in that particular vehicle with
the memories she now had of what had
happened in it, and if her cheeks got a
little red on the ride, at least her aunts
didn't notice.

They arrived in time for breakfast, which
Hilary and Alice both promptly went off to
have. Sabrina, hoping to find Duncan first,
declined to join them. However, she ran
into Raphael instead, who was determined
to detain her.

She supposed she ought to tell him that
he'd been right, at least partially. Duncan
hadn't needed "waking up" as Rafe had
suggested, he'd merely needed opportunity, and she had certainly provided that
in her mad dash from the mansion last
night, which had prompted him to follow
her. It just went to show why young women
needed chaperones, when being alone
with a man they were attracted to presented temptation in its purest form, which
could very easily be impossible to resist.

But distracted as she was in searching
the crowd in the drawing room for Duncan,
she was only half listening to Raphael,

though she did vaguely recognize the dryness of his tone and the distinct edge of disgust in it.

"The theme of this gathering has changed to one of celebration," he said. "Course, it would depend on the individual, and come to think of it, I doubt either camp would have much reason to celebrate. Any fool madly in love with the ice queen won't feel like celebrating, though they certainly ought to, since they've been saved from a fate worse than death, they just don't know it yet. And any young lady who fancied she had a chance with our esteemed newcomer, yourself included, m'dear, will now be sadly disappointed."

That last remark did manage to get Sabrina's attention, enough to ask, "What *are* you talking about?"

"I'm talking about happy tidings that don't make a bit of bloody sense."

"Well, thank you kindly for not making sense in explaining what doesn't make sense."

"Don't mind me, Sabrina. I'd just prefer *not* to be the one to break the news to you," he said with a sigh just before he walked off.

"Well, that was certainly enlightening," Sabrina mumbled to herself.

She considered going after him for a better explanation, at least one that made sense, when she saw Hilary charge into the room, spot her, and march to her side to say, "I don't believe it!"

Sabrina recognized the signs that Hilary was about to have a ranting fit, and by habit, tried to abate that. "I don't either," she agreed with an emphatic nod, but then with a grin, "What is it we don't believe?"

"Don't bother trying those tactics on me, dear, this is just too incredulous to shrug off. And I was *so* sure this time that I had the right of it. Just goes to show that speculating should be left to the London stockbrokers."

Sabrina blinked. Had her aunt just made a joke, or was she serious? "You bought stock in something?"

Hilary made a snorting sound. "I'm not talking about stock, I'm talking about the vagaries of romance. I know that *you* maintained you were only friends, but *I* was certain there was more to it—"

"Wait a minute," Sabrina interrupted in amused exasperation. "How did I get involved in this? Which of my friends are you talking about?"

Hilary frowned at her. "Don't tell me you haven't heard yet? It was announced last night right after Alice and I left, apparently, which is why we didn't hear about it until just now. You, of course, had gone home with your headache, but surely someone has told you by now? It's all anyone is talking about this morning."

This was starting to sound exactly like the nonsensical conversation Sabrina had just had with Raphael, enough to start a premonition of dread. "What announcement was made?"

"That the ex-engaged couple have made up from the tiff that caused them to get unengaged in the first place, and are happily engaged again."

The color drained from Sabrina's face. The moment of dizziness that caused had her reaching for Hilary's arm to steady herself. Hilary didn't notice; she continued to expound on her disbelief.

"It just doesn't make sense to me, indeed it don't. Why go to all this trouble and the expense of this gathering, get all these young women here for the boy to make a choice from, if he knew all along that it was no more'n a tiff they'd had that could be repaired?"

"If who knew?"

"Neville, of course. I hope he realizes how much disappointment his announcement has caused. Celebrate indeed. It's a bloody tragedy."

Tragedy, no. Shock, yes. Unexpected, not really, merely forgotten for a short time, that it was the more likely outcome. So Ophelia had been right all along, and unfortunately, so had Sabrina. Last night with her and Duncan had merely been an impulse for him, an opportunity a healthy male wouldn't pass up, and she certainly hadn't tried to prevent it from happening. Nor could she regret it even now.

What hurt, though, what was devastating to her, was that he went from making love with her directly to making amends with Ophelia and asking *her* to marry him. A little time in between, even if only a week, would have lessened the blow. But apparently his making love to Sabrina had been the catalyst that made him realize where his true feelings lay.

Ophelia entered the room just then and

was met with halfhearted congratulations from a few people, though she didn't seem to notice, was radiating with triumph. Raphael had been correct in one thing, at least—no one really felt like celebrating this particular engagement. The young men there, with the exception of Raphael, who seemed to really not like her, were no doubt disappointed, if not brokenhearted, that Ophelia was officially unavailable again. And there was at least one female with shattered hopes . . .

Sabrina really couldn't bear to listen to Ophelia gloat, yet knew she would if given the chance. And she suspected the only way to avoid that was to leave, and very quickly, before the London girl noticed her.

"I'm not feeling too well, Aunt Hilary."

"Don't blame you a'tall, m'dear. Feeling rather sick to my stomach myself. Shall we go home?"

"Yes, please."

33

The pounding on the door finally woke Duncan, enough to growl that he'd help whoever it was to roast himself over some hot coals if he didn't take his pounding somewhere else. The person outside didn't. He opened the door instead. Duncan didn't notice, sitting there in the middle of his bed trying to hold his head together, since it truly felt like it was coming apart.

"You don't look too good, old chap. Imbibe a bit too much while celebrating last night?"

Duncan opened one very bloodshot eye, pinned Raphael Locke with it, and said, "I'll have tae find a vat o' oil tae boil. Hot coals just willna do it for you."

Raphael chuckled and pulled up a chair next to the bed. Duncan, seeing that his unwelcome visitor wasn't getting the message that he was unwelcome, groaned and buried his head under his pillow.

Unfortunately, though Rafe's voice was now muffled, it was still heard. "I know why *I* would be sick unto death this dreary morning, all things considered, but what's your excuse? Since you've changed your mind about marrying Ophelia—"

"Why the devil would I do that?"

"Possibly because she's so beautiful she takes your breath away?"

Duncan sat back up with a snort. "What an Englishmon may find fashionably beautiful, a Highlander might find pale and sickly. A Scotsmon would want his lass tae have a sturdy constitution and enough meat on her bones tae wi'stand a northern winter. D'you ken that Ophelia would ne'er survive in the north country, that she'd wilt at the first sign o' bad weather? And bad weather is a constant there, no' the exception. I would have realized that, e'en if she hadna turned me again' her wi' her vicious tongue."

"But you will be living in England now, won't you, so what's the difference?"

"If I thought I'd ne'er see the homeland again, I'd wither and die m'self."

"Then how is it, old chap, that you happen to be engaged to her again?"

It was there on the tip of Duncan's tongue, an automatic answer, but this being the second time Rafe was implying that Duncan had changed his mind about Ophelia, it jarred a vague memory of why he had gotten falling-down drunk last night. And that stirred another, even more elusive memory of both his grandfathers confronting him with the news that he now had to marry Ophelia, and he was too drunk to care at that point. Had he really told them that? That he didn't care?

Trying to remember it all was stabbing even worse pains through his head, so he finally gave up and replied, "No' by my choice, I assure you."

"Ah, so it's like that, is it?" Raphael said, disgust and disappointment mixed equally in his tone. "Somehow I thought you would have a bit more of an independent nature, rather than jumping to do the old man's bidding."

"When did it become your bluidy concern, what the hell I do?"

"When I decided to take you under my wing, of course," Raphael replied.

"Take your wing elsewhere, I'm no' wanting it."

Raphael chuckled. "Too late. I don't abandon my friends just because they turn out to be absolute imbeciles."

"Your last warning, *friend.* If you dinna get oout o' here and let me die in peace—"

"Now, now, don't make threats you cannot possibly carry out in your present condition."

A good point, Duncan realized belatedly, so he simply gave up trying to oust the fellow and opted to bury his head again under his pillow. Ignoring whatever else Raphael had to say would get his point across, he hoped. Amazingly, he even managed to fall back asleep for a bit, which was a blessing, considering how much pain he was in.

When he woke the second time, he had no idea how much later in the day it was, but at least his head wasn't pounding so viciously now. But if he thought Raphael Locke would be long gone, he was much mistaken. The Englishman was still sitting in the chair next to the bed, reading from a book he must have pulled from the small shelf of books in the room. They weren't Duncan's books, had just been there as part of the room's decor when he'd moved in.

"What time is it?" Duncan mumbled as he sat up, very cautiously, so as not to start the hammers pounding in his head again.

"Not too late," Raphael replied, setting the book aside. "I would imagine there's time for you to still catch luncheon, if you hurry."

The very thought of food turned Duncan's complexion nearly green. Not a moment later, he was racing toward the chamber pot and throwing up a good deal of the poisons in his system. Another blessing. He actually felt much better when he crawled back to the bed.

"You're still here?" Duncan groused, seeing Raphael still sitting there with his fingers steepled in front of his mouth, calmly watching him.

"Do you always sleep fully clothed?" Raphael countered, ignoring the question put to him.

"Only when I dinna recall going tae bed."

"Ah, yes, that would be a good excuse, I suppose," was replied dryly.

"*Why* are you still here?"

"Curiosity, of course. I confess I simply don't understand what happened yesterday, or how you could turn into such a fool overnight. It's going to be rather difficult to get rid of me, old chap, until you fess up."

"If I could remember what happened yesterday, I might oblige you, but since I canna . . ."

"Now, that excuse just won't do, indeed it won't. Once you're feeling up to stuff again, it will all come back to you. I'll wait."

"Then do your waiting elsewhere, if you dinna mind," Duncan said.

"And let you hide from the truth even longer? No, no, my presence will stimulate your memory, I'm sure, if for no other reason than telling me all will satisfy my curiosity and send me on my way."

If Duncan didn't think his head would regret it, he would make an effort to toss Raphael out of the room. Instead he lay back, closed his eyes, and tried to recall the events of the night before. Slowly his memory started to clear.

"That's quite a blush, old chap," Raphael remarked with a chuckle. "Course, looks much better than that green tinge you were wearing."

Duncan's blush deepened. He would have given anything to be alone just then, to explore more fully what he was remembering, but with his unwanted guest sitting there awaiting details, some of which he would *not* be given, he gave a mental sigh and put those particular memories away for later.

"She made her cry. I was infuriated aboot that, knowing firsthand how vicious her tongue can be, and wanted tae know what had been said."

"I can imagine who it is that has the vicious tongue, but who is it that she made cry?"

This was asked with a narrow-eyed look that indicated Raphael's protective instincts had been aroused, enough for Duncan to reply, "It wasna your sister, 'twas Sabrina. And I tried tae get from her what had happened, but wi' nae luck. She was tae upset tae e'en discuss it. So I went

tae confront the cause. I recall I was furious by the time I found her, since she
wasna easy tae find. I was finally directed
tae her room by a maid. I figured she had
gone there to fetch something, since the
hour was still early, the party still in full progress, and if we were tae have heated
words, better upstairs where nae one was
likely tae hear. Ne'er once did I think she
had gone up tae retire for the night."

"Why do I get the appalling feeling that
you found her in bed?"

"It wasna that bad, though it might as
well have been. She was in her underthings, petticoats and the like. I barely
noticed—" Raphael's snort caused a
pause, then the insistence, "I swear tae
you, I was tae angry to really *see* her, and
even when I did take notice, how revealing
is a womon's underthings, eh? No' much
bluidy different than some evening gowns
I've seen. 'Tis nae more'n the fact they be
'underthings' that make them inappropriate
for the male eye tae behold."

"Yes, yes, semantics," Raphael said impatiently. "Get to the meat of your story."

"I'm nae telling you a story, mon, merely
what happened tae cause me tae compro-

mise the lass, e'en though I didna get any-where near her."

"Oh, Gawd, is *that* what happened? You let her bamboozle you into marrying her simply because you mischanced to see her in her underwear? Have you no sense a'tall to realize that no bloody harm was done by it, because she'd never mention it to anyone? I cannot believe she managed to hook you by one of the oldest tricks—"

"You might try shutting up long enough tae hear that's no' what happened," Duncan cut in. "She was as horrified and angry as I was over the outcome. I wish I could put the blame on her, but I canna."

"Don't believe it for a minute," Raphael scoffed. "Of course she would pretend out-rage. Gloating wouldn't have gone over well, would have in fact told you plainly that you'd fallen into her trap."

Duncan frowned, trying to remember more of what had occurred in those few minutes he had spent with Ophelia in her room. Mostly, all he could remember was how angry he'd been, which was nothing compared to how angry he'd been when he stormed out of there and went off to get drunk.

He had banged on the door loud enough that she was annoyed when she finally yanked it open and snapped, "What!?" before she even saw who was standing there. She'd then showed surprise that it was he, then immediately after that, worry that someone might see him there. She had in fact told him to go away and had even closed the door on him.

Fool that he was, instead of realizing that that simply was not a good time to confront her, he'd defied that closed door and entered her room, shutting the door behind him. She had come to the door with a robe held in front of her, had tossed it aside afterward, thinking she was alone again. Still, it didn't occur to him how inappropriate it was for him to be in her room when she was only half dressed. His anger had brought him there, and his anger was clouding his mind to what should have been clear danger signals.

What he did recognize was the very second she mistook his reason for being there. If he wasn't noticing that she was barely dressed, and he didn't really notice that yet, *she* apparently wasn't noticing his anger.

She gave him a coy look and said in a chiding tone, "This could have waited until tomorrow, but I understand impatience well enough. Do be quick about it, though, before one of the other girls I share this room with decides to make an early night of it, too, as I have. I'll even make it easy for you. My answer is yes."

" 'Yes' is no' the answer I'm here for," Duncan growled at her.

She frowned, then jumped to a different conclusion. "It's not? Don't tell me you're here for yet another apology first? Honestly, I don't know how else to say I'm sorry for our unfortunate first meeting. There, I've even said it again. *Now* can we get on with making amends and—"

"Nae, all I'm wanting tae hear from you, lass, is what you did or said tae upset Sabrina so much that she was in tears from it."

"Sabrina?" she gasped, then became furious herself. "You're here to question me about *Sabrina?* Just get out! I have nothing to say about that horrid girl."

"You'll be telling me—"

"What? How she insulted me? How she upset me so much that I came up here to lament it in private before anyone noticed *my* tears? *She's* upset? If she's upset, it's because she's sorry she was so nasty to me. There's your answer. Now—"

That was when the door opened again. And the young lady standing there, shocked at first, then embarrassed, and finally with a chuckle, apologized for intruding and closed the door again on them.

The appalling outcome still didn't penetrate Duncan immediately, not until he heard Ophelia shriek, "Now look what you've done! You couldn't just leave when I told you to, no, now you've utterly compromised me so that we *have* to marry. Of all people to show up here, it had to be her. I don't believe it! My worst enemy."

"There's nae way—"

"Don't even think of not fixing this, Duncan MacTavish. You can try to convince Mavis to say nothing of what she just saw, but she'll never agree. And even if she did agree, she'd be lying. She despises me. Didn't you see the delighted gleam in her eye, that she now has the means to ruin me? Our engagement will have to be announced immediately."

Much as he would like to think it was all a plot that he could somehow get out of, he had brought it all on himself by his own impatience. He could have waited until the morning to confront her. He could have got the hell out of there as soon as he realized she'd been preparing herself for bed. He could have gone after her enemy and at least made an effort to assure her silence, instead of believing Ophelia that nothing would silence the girl, because he didn't doubt for a second that Ophelia did indeed have such enemies who would love to see her ruined. Instead he had gone off to try to wipe the whole appalling situation from his mind with drink, and had succeeded so well that he still only had a vague recollection of both of his grandfathers in his room telling him that he would be marrying Ophelia Reid after all.

As for what Raphael was trying to insinuate, he had to set him straight. "You dinna ken, mon, she had nae prior warning that I would be seeking her oot, so there is nae way she could've planned any trap.

It wasna her doing, o' that I am positive. I brought the whole thing on m'self wi' my temper and impatience, and so being, I canna let her face ruination o'er it, when I am ultimately tae blame. I couldna live wi' m'self if I did that."

"Damn, you *would* have to have honor above and beyond, wouldn't you?" Raphael said in a mildly disgusted tone, but finally he did take himself off.

34

Sabrina stared out her bedroom window at the coach sitting in front of the manor. She wasn't really surprised that she cried each time she saw it there. Not much, just a few more tears to add to all the others she had shed over the last days. And the coach still came every day and waited several hours before it returned to Summers Glade, even though the driver had been told not to bother.

The party hadn't wound down apparently, was going to continue right up to the wedding, which had been scheduled for the middle of next week. Supposedly Neville felt that since he already had a house full of guests, why bother sending out invitations to a wedding when they could just have it while they already had the guests for it?

That was the prevailing thought in the neighborhood, of those gossiping about it. Sabrina didn't hear any of this firsthand, but her aunts kept her apprised, since they were still receiving visitors even if she wasn't. She in fact kept to her room, refusing to leave it. She wouldn't come down to speak with Duncan when he showed up the day after The Announcement. She wouldn't see him yesterday either, when he came again. And she certainly refused to receive Ophelia when she came to visit, and no doubt gloat, later in the afternoon.

But after three days of tears and misery, and agonizing over what could have happened to so thoroughly topple her brief happiness, Sabrina had reached a point of being numb. This was a blessing of sorts. Dead feelings didn't hurt. She supposed eventually she would manage to put it all behind her and get back to being herself, to just acknowledge the heartache occasionally with a sigh. But right now, the numbness at least let her come out of hiding.

It was rotten timing, however, that her first foray downstairs should lead her to the drawing room where she expected to find at least one of her aunts. She found Ophelia there instead, alone, having just been let in by the maid, who'd gone off to let someone know she was there.

Incredibly, Sabrina felt nothing, not even dread that common courtesy demanded she at least acknowledge Ophelia. Her numbness was holding up splendidly.

"Feeling better?" Ophelia asked with feigned concern when she saw her standing there in the doorway.

"Better?"

"When I came to call yesterday, Lady Alice said you were under the weather and had taken to your bed. I would have visited you in your room, offered to even, but she was sure you were sleeping."

"Oh, that," Sabrina replied with a dismissive wave of her hand. "Nothing that a bit of rest didn't fix up. And what brings you to our door? Isn't the party still in progress at Summers Glade?"

"Yes indeed, though the amount of guests have thinned out considerably," Ophelia said with a touch of annoyance.

"I suppose a lot of the other ladies felt they would be wasting their time to stay any longer."

Sabrina wasn't surprised. Most of the young women who had been invited were on the marriage block this Season, and with the bachelor they had come there to win now taken, they would need to get on with the search, which would take them back to London and the round of parties there.

An uncomfortable silence followed. This stilted courtesy just didn't go over well after such bilious feelings had been raised at their last meeting. Neither of them liked each other. That had been made abundantly clear.

Ophelia broke the silence with a long sigh. "I'd like to apologize," she said with a slight blush and a lowering of her eyes. "I realize I was a bit spiteful the other night at the party, and that's what caused you to, well, to lose your temper with me. I'd like to explain why—"

"Don't bother," Sabrina interrupted blandly. "It really doesn't matter."

"Perhaps not to you, but I have been regretting the harsh words that passed between us," Ophelia insisted. "We are friends, after all."

Sabrina might have snorted if she weren't protected by her numbness. But in point of fact, they had never been friends of any sort.

Ophelia had introduced Sabrina to her own acquaintances, but what choice did she have when Sabrina had been a guest in her house? None. Ophelia had done so grudgingly, Sabrina realized now, not because she wanted to, but because she had to. And the only time she had called upon their supposed "friendship" was when she had wanted something from Sabrina and felt it owed to her.

But Ophelia, typically, ignored Sabrina's lack of interest and got on with what she intended to say. "You see, I wasn't as confident as I pretended to be that night. I don't know why—actually, it was probably that Duncan's campaign to try to make me jealous was working. But whatever the reason, I was starting to have doubts, and that made me a bit cross, which unfortunately I took out on you. I'm not used to doubting myself, after all, and then to find how silly it was of me to do so. I should have known better. Why, just after that was when he gave up the pretense himself and we got engaged again."

That particular remark caused a definite crack in Sabrina's numbness. *Just* after? Before he happened upon Sabrina on the road?

"When was this?" she asked.

"What does it matter—?"

"When!?"

Ophelia blinked at the sharpness of Sabrina's tone, but after a moment of thought, replied, "Why, right after you left. I was upset and retired. Duncan must have seen me go upstairs, because he followed and insisted—insisted, mind you—that we get engaged again. So forceful, those Scots. I suppose he simply couldn't stand the pretense anymore, but more likely he ran out of patience. The sooner we get engaged again, the sooner we can marry, was probably what he had finally come to realize. And he's so passionate," she added with a slight blush. "I have the feeling he would have bedded me right then and there if we weren't interrupted."

Sabrina had to sit down after hearing

that. The shock she was experiencing was as bad as the morning when she'd found out about The Announcement—actually, it was worse. If Ophelia could be believed, then Duncan's passions had been aroused by *her,* and unable to satisfy them due to an interruption, he'd then found Sabrina alone, before his passion had abated, and took advantage of the convenience that gave him. It had had nothing to do with her personally. As dark as it was in that coach that night, he could easily have pretended to himself that she was the one he really wanted.

Unfortunately, all things considered, Sabrina did believe Ophelia. If she were a little prettier, or Ophelia a little less so, then she might have had doubts. But she couldn't deceive herself on this particular point. Ophelia would win hands down as a matter of choice for any man.

The question was, could she blame Duncan for taking what she so freely gave, when he was already engaged to another? Wouldn't any man do as he had done? No, she couldn't blame him. Besides, she still loved him. She wished she didn't, but that was something that just wouldn't go away.

Not that whether she blamed him was going to make a difference to anything. He was still going to marry Ophelia. Her heart was still going to break a little bit more the day he did.

Ophelia was going on as if her words hadn't caused any damage. "I'm so glad we got this straightened out and are friends again. Edith and Jane have deserted me, you know. They've promised to return for the wedding next week, but I really doubt they will find the time once they get back into the London whirl—I know I wouldn't. But without them there, it's so boring. You really must come again to Summers Glade, Sabrina, if just to keep me company."

Fortunately, Sabrina was saved from having to explain why that was out of the question when Alice finally arrived, took one look at her pale, drawn expression, and ushered her off to bed again, as if that really was where she had spent the last three days.

"Relapse" and "Shouldn't have come down yet" were muttered by Alice for Ophelia's benefit, not that Sabrina needed an excuse to head back to her room.

Ophelia could think whatever she liked, as far as she was concerned. But hopefully the London girl had said all she had wanted to say and wouldn't come calling again.

35

Ophelia was working herself into a snit on the short ride back to Summers Glade. She had accomplished what she'd wanted to, got that silly business of apologizing out of the way, so that things could be back to normal with Sabrina. She hoped she had managed to succeed in at least that, because she really was getting bored at Summers Glade, and Sabrina could alleviate that quite nicely.

There simply weren't enough of the London crowd left at the mansion to keep her amused. Duncan even ignored her, still in a huff, she supposed, because they'd had to get engaged again. Too bad for him. She hadn't instigated his entrapment, he'd done that all on his own, though she couldn't deny it had worked out wonderfully in her favor.

She never would have thought he'd do anything so rash, though, as to enter her bedchamber. That was *so* inappropriate, even if she hadn't been half dressed. But she really had thought he was there to patch things up between them, so she could forgive him for his impetuosity. Then to find he was only there because of Sabrina. That was really the last straw, particularly after the country girl had shown her true colors earlier, that she wasn't miss "sweet and smiles" after all, but could be quite a nasty little shrew.

But his mention of Sabrina had reminded Ophelia of her earlier conversation with her. And she'd recalled, specifically, having spoken of a situation that would lead to her being compromised, a false one, but regardless, the current one hadn't been fabricated at all.

Ironically, she never would have thought of it, if not for that earlier mention. But having it recalled, she had then been trying to think how she could keep Duncan there after he was done with his rant, at least until one of the other girls showed up, when Mavis of all people opened the door. It had been too perfect. Ophelia really couldn't have planned it better if she had planned it herself. And she'd had to do nothing to accomplish it, which was even more ironic. Duncan had brought the whole thing down on his own head.

And it had been a simple matter, after he stormed off, to locate Lord Neville and point out to him the bare facts. He was old school. He didn't need convincing that Duncan had compromised her beyond repair; that was plain enough. He *had* made an effort to find Mavis, though, but fortunately, with no luck, so he'd been forced to make the announcement of his grandson's engagement that very night.

Edith and Jane had left the next afternoon, just as many of the other young ladies had, along with their escorts. Ophelia actually had the bedroom that she'd been sharing with eight others to herself now.

Mavis had left that very night, which was why Lord Neville had been unable to find her. She no doubt didn't want to take the chance that she would be browbeaten by the marquis or Duncan into keeping her mouth shut about what she'd seen, when she had no intention of keeping her mouth shut. Why else leave immediately, without even packing her bags? She'd simply collected her cousin who had escorted her there, called for their carriage, and left. But then Ophelia would have done the same thing if she had such a juicy morsel of gossip to share, so she understood perfectly.

Announcing the engagement, *before* that gossip could be passed around, totally deflated it. Lovers' trysts would be snickered at but forgiven for an engaged couple, whereas it was complete ruination for the woman if there was no engagement involved. So Mavis had nothing to gain now by spreading the tale. She had no doubt thought she'd get some revenge out of it, but had instead helped Ophelia get what she wanted. It was too funny.

But now, on the way back to Summers Glade, Ophelia couldn't help thinking she might have made matters worse with Sabrina, and that's why she was annoyed with herself when she shouldn't be. She was *not* going to feel guilty about lying to Sabrina. The chit had deserved it, for trying to steal Duncan from her. But she did want Sabrina to be her friend again, so she probably should have tried to find out why the timing of her confrontation with Duncan had seemed so important to her, instead of lying about it.

When she returned to the mansion, she found a summons from Lord Neville. She didn't know how long he had been waiting on her, since she hadn't been there to receive the summons, but she went straightaway now to his sitting room, where she was directed.

She had been expecting a talk with him much sooner than this, but he, too, had been ignoring her since the announcement. Yet an apology was in order. After all, she was the innocent party in this, and would have been seriously wronged if she didn't want to marry Duncan, but was now forced to because he'd compromised her. Fortunately, she did want to marry him, but that didn't need to be mentioned until after she had the apology owed her.

She was quite mistaken, however, in the reason for this meeting. She no sooner sat down in the chair across from Lord Neville's desk than he stated in a hard tone, "Aside from the fact that your parents have been informed of what occurred and will be arriving shortly, we have a few matters that I feel need immediate discussion."

"Certainly," Ophelia replied with some misgiving, since his tone implied she probably wasn't going to like this discussion as she'd thought.

"I have been informed, by a number of different sources, that you have a bad habit of starting gossip and rumors."

She took immediate offense. He was going to give her a scolding when they weren't even related yet?

"Everyone gossips, Lord Neville," Ophelia pointed out stiffly.

"Not everyone, but those who do don't usually do so with malicious intent. I am merely letting you know, Lady Ophelia, that this sort of behavior won't be tolerated. Once you marry into this family, you will conduct yourself in a manner that is above reproach."

She was shocked *and* insulted now. Malicious? Her? The very idea. She might find it necessary to put people in their place occasionally, she might have to exact revenge occasionally, too, but maliciously? Hardly.

But he was no doubt referring to her

campaign to make Duncan a laughingstock so that she could get out of an engagement she hadn't wanted at the time. That incident, he would take personally. But she hadn't been malicious about it, and it hadn't actually hurt Duncan in the least. It had merely been a means to an end.

"If you find my behavior objectionable, sir, simply say so, but don't accuse me of something that—"

"My dear girl," he interrupted calmly. "If you have been listening, you would have heard that I *do* find your behavior objectionable. The very fact that I have had numerous people point out to me your habits speaks for itself. *You* are being gossiped about, and that is unacceptable. Sit down!" he barked when she stood up indignantly.

Ophelia dropped back into her chair. Her cheeks were now burning. If he weren't such a high personage, she would have marched out of there immediately. It was only that that kept her there. It certainly wasn't that he frightened her with his harsh tones and quelling looks.

"Do not misunderstand," he continued in that calm, if implacable, tone. "This conversation would have taken place previously if Duncan hadn't refused to marry you after first meeting you. You need to understand that marrying into this family entails a great responsibility on your part that you may not have been trained for or were expecting."

"I am the daughter of an earl," she replied haughtily. "I assure you my education was not lacking."

The look he gave her was entirely too skeptical to soothe her ruffled feathers, and in fact he continued in the same vein. "Your parents have lived in London for most of your life, so the education you received may not have been the one that will serve you here. This is a working estate. As the future marquise, you will have specific duties that will take up a great deal of your time and bring you into contact with a wide assortment of individuals from chimney sweeps to vicars to the queen herself. But no matter who you will have to deal with, you will conduct yourself as befitting the Marquise of Birmingdale."

"What sort of work?" she asked, frowning.

"The normal duties associated with an estate this size. I assume you have at least been trained in the running of a large household? My secretary will instruct you in the actual estate duties, which will be in addition to your household duties. Suffice it to say, you will have very little time for leisure, entertaining—or gossip."

"No entertaining?" she asked incredulously.

He couldn't be serious. She associated a peer of his stature with lavish entertainments on a regular basis. The ladies of his rank in London were the premier hostesses of the city, their invitations highly sought after. Of course she had envisioned taking her place among them, *and* being the queen of the lot.

But he was serious, or certainly sounded so as he explained further, "We are not in the habit of entertaining here, far from it. This current gathering was a rare exception for a specific purpose. It won't be repeated. Nor do we keep a house in London, which would be a frivolous expense, when we never go to London."

"I have family in London," she reminded him. "Of course I will vis—"

"Your family can visit here," he cut in. "I was quite serious when I said you wouldn't find time to travel or entertain. Nor will Duncan, not that he would want to. You will need to readjust your thinking in that regard. Consider yourself country now."

She knew what he meant by that, unfortunately. The gentry who lived on their country estates, rather than just visiting them from time to time, rarely left them. They shunned London. They didn't participate in the gay London Season. They more or less gave up any claim to sophistication and became *country.* They gained new interests; weather, crops, market prices. The London *ton,* at least those of her circle, scorned such nobles and likened them to the working class.

Ophelia pinched herself, hoping she was just having a nightmare. She wasn't. And this was *not* what she had taken for granted when she had decided that Duncan would do for her after all. His future title and good looks were not worth the horror that Lord Neville had just described.

But she realized, with growing despair, that she was now stuck with Duncan whether she liked it or not, and simply because she had made an enemy of Mavis.

If Mavis were still her friend, she would agree to never say anything about that scene she had walked in on. Of course she would agree, particularly after she was assured that nothing had really happened.

Ophelia wasn't *really* compromised beyond repair. It wasn't as if she and Duncan had actually made love. But Mavis would never agree to silence. Why would she, when she despised Ophelia? And the only thing keeping her quiet now was the engagement and forthcoming wedding. To end that, a second time, was out of the question, since it would give Mavis free rein to spread her sordid gossip.

"You don't look very well," Neville said, breaking into her chaotic thoughts.

"I don't believe I am," Ophelia replied miserably. "If you will excuse me?"

She didn't wait for his permission. In fact, she nearly ran out of the room.

36

The door slammed shut on Ophelia's exit from Neville's sitting room, making him wince at the unexpected sound. But then he leaned back in his chair with a thoughtful look, wondering if he hadn't overdone it a bit with the girl.

"Having second thoughts, are ye?" Archibald asked when he poked his head around the large reading chair by the window where he had sat unnoticed, at least by Ophelia.

"Second, third, and fourth is more like it," Neville said in a tired tone.

"Och, dinna fash yerself, mon. If yer thinking she's the innocent in all this, yer dead wrong. She did *something* tae enrage the lad, or he wouldna hae taken his anger *tae* her, throwing caution tae the winds."

"Did he ever tell you what that was, or at least what started it all?"

Archibald sighed as he changed chairs, putting himself on the other side of Neville's desk. "He willna speak o' that night, no' e'en tae me. Believe me, I've asked, but he just gets angry again each time it's mentioned. He blames himself, and his temper, for the whole mess. And it's breaking m'heart tae see him sae miserable."

"You think I like this any better?" Neville asked. "You were the one who claimed it didn't matter what the girl was made of, as long as she was beautiful. You see now that it does matter?"

"Ye dinna need tae belabor the point," Archie grouched. "Why d'ye think I suggested ye hae that talk wi' her? She was looking tae bluidy pleased wi' the results o' this fiasco. Now she isna, and if anyone can figure a way oout o' this, it'll be a schemer like her. And ye did nae more'n tell her the truth, or did ye embellish a wee bit?"

"Embellish, no. Overstressed a bit, indeed. Of course, I already knew she would never fit in here. Knew that after first meeting her, which is why I was so glad Duncan was able to see past her pretty face." Neville sighed at that point. "I just don't think that what was said here today is going to make any difference. There simply *is* no way to get out of this. The girl *can't* break the engagement even if she does now wish she could. Her reputation will be shredded beyond repair if that little incident in her bedroom ever gets out. She knows that as well as we do."

"But ye've heard nothing yet aboot it. The lass who walked in and saw them together in the bedroom, wherever she went, hasna spread any gossip aboot it. Did ye consider she just may no' be the type tae spread gossip? Even though she might hate Ophelia and relish her downfall as the lass claimed was the case, her scruples may prevent her from getting revenge in such a despicable way."

"That isn't something that can be left to chance, Archibald, and well you know it. Whether Mavis Newbolt would have started the scandal or not is redundant. We had to assume the worst and take the steps to prevent it, which we did. We've heard nothing because it's passé gossip now, due to the announced engagement. What would have been shocking, now might only raise a brow or two. The engagement completely took the scandal out of the equation."

"And ye've still had nae luck finding this lass?" Archie asked.

Neville ran a hand through his white hair in frustration. "Completely disappeared, and now her parents as well."

Archibald frowned, hearing that, and speculated, "Are they merely afeared o' ye?"

Neville snorted. "I wish that were the case, but no. Lord Newbolt is the type of man who doesn't like to be questioned—about anything, and most particularly when he doesn't have the answers. I've been informed that he was quite livid when my man showed up at his door for the fourth time, refused to speak to him again, and soon after, took him and his wife out of London so they wouldn't be bothered further. If they did know where their daughter went when she left here, they aren't about to say so. My guess is that she hasn't let them know where she is, and that is one reason Lord Newbolt blew up about it."

"Och, why in the bluidy hell does this hae tae be sae difficult? How hard can it be tae track down one wee lass? Are yer hirelings utter incompetents?"

Neville ignored the last question, remarking, "It could simply be coincidence that we haven't found her yet. But I'm beginning to think otherwise, that she's gone into hiding instead. If she has, then we had better start turning our discussions into how to keep our future great-grandchildren away from the influence of their mother."

Archibald waved that aside. "Ye'll simply send them tae me sooner than ye planned tae. She'll no' be wanting tae come tae the Highlands, believe me."

"That is *not* an option," Neville growled.

"Sae we're back to bickering amongst ourselves, are we?" Archibald shot back.

"Not at all," Neville replied stiffly. "I'm merely pointing out that Duncan's children *will* be English, *will* learn a love for this country, *will* sound like Englishmen before you get your hands on them."

"Dinna insult me more'n ye hae tae, mon, or I may be thinking ye dinna like me anymore," Archie remarked with a chuckle.

Neville scowled at him. "I'm glad you got the point, though how you can find anything amusing about this situation baffles me."

"The situation is no' the least bit amusing, but ye are when ye take on yer English airs. Now, dinna get all up in arms again, mon. We are on the same side in no' wanting the Reid lass in the family. Sae why do we no' just delay the bluidy wedding until the other lass can be found?"

Neville was back to sighing. "Because the same outcome applies. If the girl is sitting on the scandal because it will do her little good to spread it just now, with the wedding pending, then what do you think she will do with the information she has if she suspects the engagement is just a farce? She might start spreading the tale then, and that will guarantee an immediate wedding."

"D'ye ken who it is we're trying tae protect here, tae the detriment o' yer family and mine?"

"If you are suggesting that we let Ophelia Reid take her own chances, and throw her to the wolves, so to speak, I have considered that, since she does hardly deserve our efforts to protect her after what she did—at least in my own opinion. I even alluded to it with Duncan, though indirectly. Now, tell me, what do you suppose his reaction was, when he considers himself responsible?"

It was Archie's turn to sigh. "He's a good lad, Duncan is. E'en hating her, he'd nae see her harmed through a fault o' his. Sae that still leaves us searching for the Newbolt lass, or hoping Lady Ophelia herself can think o' something tae get oout o' marrying Duncan, now ye've given her good incentive tae work on it."

"You may think she's devious enough to come up with something, but I'm not counting on it, and will double efforts to find Mavis instead. Believe me, if I *can* find her, I will do whatever is necessary to gain her silence—pay her off, threaten her, plead with her, whatever it takes. But I have to find her first, and our time is running out."

37

With his wedding fast approaching, Duncan was finding it almost impossible to talk to anyone at Summers Glade without snapping at them, so he made an effort to avoid the remaining guests as much as possible. Fortunately, he was no longer the ''main attraction'' and thus didn't need to be in constant attendance anymore. This let him escape, which was how he saw it, for long periods each day, without causing too much comment about it when he returned.

His grandfathers, the both of them, pretty much left him alone now. They had what they wanted—a bride, though neither seemed all that happy with the one he'd ended up with. Perhaps they found it as galling as he did, that she was the very last woman he would have chosen—if he had had a choice.

He had never felt so trapped, and despondent, in his life. Not even finding out that he had to come to England to live with a grandfather he didn't know, or care to know, had affected him this adversely. That had enraged him. This having to marry a woman he didn't even like, and knew he never would, was eating him up inside with hopelessness.

He needed cheering. He needed Sabrina. But he was beginning to think he'd never see her again, and that was adding greatly to his misery.

He was afraid he'd lost her friendship, that she was deliberately avoiding him because she despised him now. And he couldn't even blame her. He'd taken advantage of her when she was greatly upset and most likely not thinking clearly. In reflection, she could hate him now for that. Worse, he'd gone from making love to her to getting engaged to another woman. He couldn't imagine what she thought about that, but it couldn't be to his good. Yet he'd been unable to explain—because she wouldn't see him.

He'd gone to her house, he'd left notes. He'd been told she was indisposed, which could mean any number of things, including simply "go away." And though she was reputed to enjoy walking so much that she took long walks every day, sometimes twice a day, he hadn't found her once out in the countryside. And he'd certainly tried to come across her. He traversed the road to Oxbow more than once each day, passing by Cottage by the Bow. He sat for hours on the hill where he first met her, hoping she'd take that path again. But not once did he see her, even from a distance.

And then there she was, walking down the road far ahead of him, the winter wind whipping at her hair, bundled up in her thick coat, which hid her nicely rounded curves. He set his horse into a gallop to reach her. He kicked up dust when he did. He wanted to draw her into his arms and never let go of her, yet he found himself shouting down at her instead, all his frustration and worry and dread pouring out at her.

"You're oout in this cold when you've been sick? Or have you no' really been sick? Why the devil would you no' see me when I came tae call on you?"

She gave him a strange look. She opened her mouth to reply, closed it, opened it again, closed it yet again, tightly this time, and walked on. Walked on?

He stared after her incredulously. But it gave him a moment to realize just how accusing he had sounded, and that anyone, even someone as carefree and effervescent as Sabrina was, or usually was, might take offense at it.

He sighed and cantered after her. "Wait up, lass." She didn't. "At least talk tae me."

She stopped, said simply, "We shouldn't be seen talking together, Duncan."

"Why?"

"You're engaged now. You have no business calling on other women—or detaining them on the road. If witnessed, it might give the wrong impression and get back to Ophelia, and we wouldn't want that, would we?"

She walked away again, which infuriated him enough that he overlooked the bitterness he'd just heard in her tone. "Bedamned what she thinks," he growled. "I'll call on my friends if I choose tae, or are we nae longer friends?"

That brought her marching back, but only to say, "Ophelia won't allow you to have women friends, Duncan, or aren't you aware of how jealous she is, or the bile she can spew because of it?"

"Is *that* what happened that night tae upset you? She turned her vicious tongue on you?"

She sighed at that point. "Not really. I was upset because I lost my own temper with her and stooped to her level of nastiness. That just isn't *me,* and I was appalled that I let my own tongue run away with me."

Sabrina lost her temper? He couldn't imagine it either, but he sure would have liked to see it. On second thought, no, he wouldn't. This stiff reservation she was showing him right now was bad enough, and he didn't like it one bit.

He dismounted and came to stand in front of her. "At least your outburst had nae dire consequences, lass. Try losing your temper and having it ruin the rest o' your life."

He said it so forlornly that she would

have had to be completely indifferent to him not to ask, "Ruined how? What did you do?"

"I was angry that you had been upset enough tae send you running pell-mell oout into the night. That it happened after you talked tae Ophelia told me the cause for it."

"But she wasn't really why I was so upset. Her subtle insults don't usually bother me. It was my own behavior that shocked me."

"Aye, but you wouldna say what had occurred when I asked you that night," he reminded her. "And by the time I returned tae Summers Glade, I was determined tae get the answer from the source. My anger built when I couldna find her. When I did finally locate her, I didna care that it was in an inappropriate place."

"Where?"

"Her bedroom."

There were a dozen things that Sabrina could have said just then to lessen the impact of what she was hearing, but all that came out was, "Oh."

"E'en that would have made nae difference if someone hadna come upon us there."

"Who?"

"Mavis Newbolt is her name. Ophelia claimed this lass hates her and would relish spreading the tale. My only hope is that isna so. But the lass has taken herself off and canna be found tae verify whether or no' she would make a scandal o' where she found us."

"Are you saying this is why you're engaged to Ophelia again?"

"Why else, lass?" he said. "You dinna think I *want* tae marry her?"

"And this occurred *after* you . . . took me home?"

"Aye."

Sabrina glanced away from him. He heard what sounded suspiciously like a growl, but coming from her, doubted it. When she looked at him again, a long moment later, she was without expression and her tone was matter-of-fact.

"Ophelia lies about many things, but how Mavis feels about her isn't one of them. She brought it on herself, though. They used to be friends, but only just recently had a falling out. It happened at

Summers Glade, actually, but the result was, Ophelia tried her hardest to blacken Mavis's name."

"How well d'you know this Mavis? Would she want tae get back at Ophelia, e'en if it meant hurting someone else tae do it?"

"I'm sorry, Duncan, but I don't know her well enough to say. I liked her. She seemed quite nice—at least when she wasn't around Ophelia. When she was, she became rather catty and snide in her remarks. But then Ophelia seems to have that effect on a lot of people, bringing out the worst in them. It's an amazing quality, that."

"Nae, what's amazing is that it would be assumed that I compromised her, merely because o' where we were seen t'gether, when I've ne'er touched her. And there doesna seem tae be any way tae get oout o' marrying her, unless . . ."

"Unless?"

He turned around, wondering why he'd even thought of it, much less mentioned it, when it would be indirectly using her just to save himself. Not that the outcome wouldn't be infinitely more desirable, but it would still be taking advantage of her—again.

"Never mind," he mumbled. " 'Twas a wayward thought best left unsaid."

"I would think you would want to explore every option—if you really don't want to marry her."

She'd said it rather stiffly, which had him turning back to her and countering defensively, "You dinna think I have? It stands oout plainly in my mind that I havena really compromised her, but I *have* compromised you. If I should be forced tae marry anyone, it should be you—och, that didna sound the way I meant it."

Her voice went from stiff to much stiffer, even though she allowed, "However you meant it, it's not an option, Duncan, because it wouldn't alter the fact that Ophelia would be ruined if it gets out that you were in her bedroom alone with her. Doesn't matter that you've never touched her. A scandal is just that, and I know firsthand how detrimental one can be. Perception is everything where scandal is concerned, with truth and fact having little to do with it. And much as I have come to *not* like

Ophelia, I will not be a party to her ruination, indirectly or otherwise."

She walked off yet again after that. Duncan didn't try to stop her this time. The uplift in spirits he had hoped to get from an encounter with her hadn't occurred. If anything, he felt worse now. That she had seemed as down in spirits as he was the cause.

38

It was raining, hard enough to conceal most of the view outside. Duncan stood at the drawing room window watching the downpour, and wondering if Sabrina was watching it, too. She liked the rain, liked storms, liked anything to do with nature apparently, no matter the time of year. He remembered the joy in her expression when he'd taken her out onto that terrace in the rain . . .

"You can't keep avoiding me."

It was distinctly jarring, hearing that particular voice behind him, even though he'd had warning that Ophelia might be approaching him, had seen her reflection in the window. The rain had darkened the late afternoon enough to cause the lamps to be turned on in the house, but he would probably have seen her reflection even without the light behind him, since she seemed to glow with her own internal light, her white-blond hair and pale skin only partly responsible.

He didn't turn around. He really *didn't* want to have a conversation with her, of any sort, but least of all on the subject of avoiding her. He simply hadn't decided yet how to deal with her.

He could tell her the truth, that he could barely tolerate her, but that would no doubt lead to their living estranged once they wed, which, all things considered, sounded like an ideal arrangement—for him anyway. Or he could try to get along with her, to make the best of an unwanted marriage. He wasn't sure he *could* do that, but he could at least try. However, she was bound to sense, sooner or later, his true feelings, and that would probably lead back to an estranged relationship anyway, so why bother?

But he had the answer to that. He would make an effort for Archie. Archie wanted him to marry and supply him with new heirs. He wouldn't be getting those heirs as he expected, but Duncan had plenty of time to make him see reason on that point. Yet he wouldn't be getting the heirs at all if Duncan couldn't manage to bed his own wife.

"How will it look to people?"

She was still there? Duncan sighed inwardly and turned about to face Ophelia.

"As if we dinna really want tae get married?"

He surprised himself in giving her that answer. It simply came out, despite the internal debate he had just been having with himself. So much for any pretenses. Yet he preferred the truth, and perhaps they could work around it and try to get along anyway.

That thought had him wondering if it was possible for Ophelia to change her ways, or if she was too far gone in her self-absorption. Did he even want to try to change her? Her answer suggested it would be a lost cause.

"Well, I don't want to marry you," she said in a huffy tone. "Not anymore anyway, since talking to your grandfather pointed out how tedious it will be living here. But you—there's no reason for you to keep pretending, Duncan. You know you won't mind being married to me at all. You, no doubt, only object to how we got engaged again."

He wasn't rendered exactly speechless, but it did take a moment for him to get past his amazement enough to reply, "Did it e'er occur tae you, Ophelia, that outward appearances might no' be what everyone finds important, that some men might prefer sterling qualities in the lass they marry, rather than a pretty face?"

She stared at him blankly for a moment, but then she laughed in a condescending way and informed him, "I've had hundreds of marriage proposals to prove otherwise, and most of them from men who barely knew me. What does that tell you about what men prefer?"

"It tells me they've convinced you into thinking that your beauty is all that matters. And you would have been in line for a rude awakening had you married one o' them, when they finally did get tae know you. I'm going tae be honest wi' you, lass. I dinna like your ways, dinna like the spite you're capable of, dinna like the way you treat people, as if nae one matters but yourself."

"If you think—"

He interrupted her indignant reply, saying in as calm a tone as he could muster, "Be quiet a moment, and let me tell you why I'm telling you this. If we have tae marry, and it doesna look as if anything is going tae save us from it, then we will have only tae choices thereafter, tae live in peace wi' each other, or make our own hell. But the only way we'll manage the peace is if you can change your ways. D'you think you can do that, lass?"

"There is *nothing* wrong with the way I behave," she insisted.

He sighed. "If you willna e'en recognize that your haughty airs and spiteful tendencies are reprehensible tae me, then we've nothing further tae discuss."

"One little insult I give you, and that makes me spiteful? Do you even care to know why I insulted you? Does it matter to you that I didn't want to marry you, that I was furious that I had been engaged to you without even being asked if I wanted to be engaged to you? I simply wanted out of that engagement. What was so wrong with that?"

"You had other options," he told her. "The most obvious being that you could have told me how you felt and we could have amicably ended the engagement."

"You must be joking. I knew very well that once you saw me, nothing would have stopped you from marrying me—unless you were provoked into breaking it off in a moment of rage, which you did."

He saw her reasoning—up to a point. He had thought himself incredibly lucky when he first laid eyes on her. He had been immediately smitten by her beauty just as other men no doubt were. Had she told him then that she didn't want to marry him, he might well have tried to change her mind about it—at least until he got to know her and discovered that she simply wasn't a likable person. So honesty on her part might not have made any difference.

But instead of honesty, she'd tried to manipulate him with her insults, and succeeded at it. And that wasn't even the extent of her scheme . . .

"Spreading rumors tae blacken my name was tae this same end?"

"Don't be silly," she said in a chiding tone. "That wasn't for your benefit at all, was to show my parents that you weren't the ideal husband for me that they were so sure you were, so I could convince them to break the engagement themselves. That didn't work, however. They were set on the match no matter what. But let's not pretend that you were hurt by it, nor was there any chance that you would be *unless* the rumors turned out to be true. It only took people having a chance to meet you to see that the rumors were groundless."

He shook his head at her. "D'you no' ken how despicable all o' that scheming is? When a little simple honesty would have—?"

"Done nothing," she interrupted, her tone now bitter. "I *did* try that, Duncan. I told my parents from the beginning that I didn't want to marry a man I'd never even met. Now you tell me something, and you be honest about it. How did *you* feel about being engaged to a woman you'd never met before?" She sighed then. "Never mind, you obviously didn't mind, since you went along with it."

He flushed with embarrassed heat, because that wasn't exactly true. His reaction to having a wife chosen for him had been the same as hers, or at least what she was claiming hers had been.

He was forced to admit, "Actually, lass, I didna know aboot it until a few days afore I got here. I'm auld enough tae be picking m'own wife, you ken. Neville was mistaken in thinking he could do it for me. I would have broken the engagement, but I was asked tae at least meet you first, which I did."

She blushed now as well and complained defensively, "Well, how was I to know that? But since you seem to admire honesty so much, tell me, would you have broken it if I hadn't insulted you?"

Having only just considered that, his reply was quick. "Nae, at least, no' immediately. You are a beauty, lass, there's nae denying that. But it wouldna have taken verra long for me tae see what's beneath the surface and no' like what's there. Now there's nae choice in the matter, and I've learned that e'en that is indirectly your doing because you deliberately made an enemy o' that lass who saw us t'gether. Had it been anyone but her, we wouldna be in this fix now."

"Hardly," she shot back. "Buying silence is a tricky business that is never a sure thing."

Duncan rolled his eyes toward the ceiling. "No' everyone needs tae be bought off, lass. Some people, believe it or no', would actually understand and wouldna want tae see either o' us hurt or ruined due tae one innocent meeting that might have been misconstrued."

"You put too much trust in human nature," she scoffed at him.

"And you dinna put enough. So we're back tae where we started, stuck wi' each other. And I'm still wanting tae know if you can change your ways. Can you stop making enemies of others simply because you dinna like something they say or do? Can you stop the scheming and vindictive retaliations? Can you stop lying just tae suit your needs or—"

"Oh, stop," she cut him off dryly. "Why don't I just stop breathing?"

"Sarcasm isna going tae help here."

"That wasn't sarcasm," she retorted. "You obviously are too high-minded for my own tastes, Duncan, so why don't we just admit we aren't suited for each other and never will be. I thought I wouldn't mind marrying you, after I met you, but I have since changed my mind, particularly after speaking with Lord Neville and having it outlined in detail what a drudgery it will be, living here. Believe me, I want out of this engagement as much as you do. I'd even beg, *beg,* mind you, Mavis at this point to keep her mouth shut. But I know it wouldn't do any good. She hates me, probably always did."

"Why?" he countered. "Unless you did something tae cause it."

"Don't be naive. I did nothing but be born with these looks, which cause envy and jealousy in other women, which leads to animosity of the worst sort. They try to hide it, but aren't always successful. Mavis, like so many others, just pretended to be my friend because I'm *popular,* the 'one to be around.' You think I don't know it, that I'm used that way. You think it's easy to shrug that off?"

"I think that if I didna suspect that you brought most o' that hate upon yourself, I might pity you."

"Don't you dare!" she snapped. "And if you want out of this horrid situation that, need I remind you, *you* caused with your bloody temper, then do something about it! I can't go traipsing about the country trying to find Mavis, but *you* can. So stop moping about here doing nothing, and get us both out of this."

She flounced off, leaving him back where he started, with little hope for his future. Find the Newbolt lass himself, when he wasn't familiar with this country and wouldn't know where to even begin looking? Yet Ophelia was right. He had been moping. He'd let the situation get him so deep into misery that he couldn't see any way to crawl out of it. Yet just because he was sure he didn't have even a small chance in hell of success was no reason not to search for that small chance.

His only *real* hope was that there were men out there looking for her, men accustomed to tracking down people, or so his grandfather had assured him. That wasn't enough to really sustain him, though, not when his wedding day was just around the corner.

39

Having made the decision to search for Mavis Newbolt himself, it was quickly brought home to Duncan how futile it was going to be when he began gathering information before he left Summers Glade, and counted up the many addresses involved that were spread all across the country. Ironically, Ophelia had supplied most of those addresses, including those of Mavis's close friends, who would hopefully all be in London, because even they had other addresses in other towns, any one of which Mavis might be visiting.

Knowing full well that he wouldn't be able to get to every residence in the few days he had left, he needed to decide which ones might gain him the most information the quickest, or if he got lucky,

Mavis herself. Since it wasn't a decision he could easily make, though, when he didn't know any of the people involved, he sought out someone who was sure to know more than he.

He found Raphael easily enough; in fact, the duke's son had been looking for him as well, or implied as much when he said, "You'll be devastated, I know, to be tendered my adieu, but all good things—or bad, as it were, must come to an end. And yes, I'm sure you need an interpretation for that, so in other words, I'm about to take myself back to London. This place has become much too depressing. You'd think a funeral were pending, rather than a wedding."

"I canna argue that," Duncan replied. "I'm leaving for London myself and wanted to ask—"

"Flying the coop, are you?" Rafe cut in. "My, my, didn't think you'd take that route."

Duncan bristled, but needing the man's opinion, kept that to himself. "Nor am I. I'm going tae search for Mavis Newbolt, the lass that holds the scandal in her hands. She's the only one who can get me out o' this mess."

"Search as in she's gone missing?"

Duncan nodded. "She didna return home as expected after leaving here, and her parents got so annoyed with the inquiries made aboot her that they left their London residence as well. Neville has people still looking, but they're no' having any luck."

"Sounds like she doesn't want to be found," Raphael speculated.

"I'm aware o' that, yet someone must know where she might have gone tae ground. I've the addresses o' her friends and will be—"

"No doubt wasting your time," Raphael cut in again. "If she's hiding, though I can't imagine why, she won't let her friends know where she is."

Duncan sighed. "I dinna suppose you know anything aboot the lass that might point tae where she could have gone when she left?"

"Me? I've never met the chit, but as it happens, I do know her cousin John Newbolt, who was apparently her escort here.

If it were me, I'd be looking for him, since he's the one she left here with."

"He's gone missing as well, at least I'm told he hasna returned home either."

Raphael raised a golden brow at that, but then shook his head and mumbled, more to himself, "No, they are first cousins, they wouldn't—never mind. At least your grandfather's people are being thorough, to have looked for him. You should find that reassuring."

Duncan nodded, though it was little con-solation, when those men hadn't produced results yet. "Auld Neville is sparing nae ex-pense in this matter, according tae m'grandda Archie."

Raphael chuckled. "No, he wouldn't. I imagine the thought of Ophelia as his granddaughter-in-law has quite horrified him, now he knows what mischief she's capable of."

"I wouldna know," Duncan replied with a shrug. "I talk tae him as little as possible m'self."

"What ho!" Rafe chuckled. "Intimidated, eh? Can't say as I blame you—"

"Och, dinna be running off on another tangent. I simply dinna like him."

"Your own grandfather? Why?"

Instead of answering that, which was none of Raphael's business, Duncan asked, "I dinna suppose you might know where this cousin could be found?"

Raphael got the point, and after a thoughtful frown, said, "Don't know him well, just in passing since we belong to the same club, but you know how men will talk—and brag, when there aren't any women around. I've heard he keeps a place in Manchester just for his mistresses, a property he won in a card game. This isn't unusual, having a place just for your mistress. Many married men do the same. But in this case it struck me funny, since John still lives at home with his mother, and this property in Manchester is the only one he personally owns. You'd think he would have moved into it himself, now wouldn't you, rather than put his mistresses there. Particularly when it's so bloody far from London where his mother lives."

"But it'd be inappropriate for him tae take his cousin there, aye?"

"Course it would—unless the place was presently empty." Raphael shrugged. "Only mentioned it because if I had a young cousin who asked me to take her somewhere that she could hide, as it were, and I had a house that no one in my family was aware of, that would be where I might take her—*if it was currently without an occupant. Especially since it's not that far from here, but is far from London.*"

"Would you be having the address?"

"Did I say I knew him well?"

Duncan sighed again, but thought to ask, "How big is this town then?"

Raphael laughed. "Much too big to be hoping someone on a corner might direct you where you want to go. It's a bloody city, old chap, not a little town or village."

Duncan could have wrung the man's neck at that point, for getting his hopes up, then shooting them down again. His expression probably said that was what he was thinking, because Raphael took at least one step back.

But then he grinned cheekily and said, "I could get you out of this mess."

"E'en if that were true, which I'm doubting, why would you?"

"Gads, you needn't look so suspicious. No ulterior motives, I assure you. I'm just aware that there is another you would prefer to marry."

Knowing just how frequently Raphael tended to mention his young sister, Amanda, and that he would probably like to get out of the chore of chaperoning her about, which would only be accomplished by her own marriage, Duncan didn't doubt that was who he was referring to.

So he assured him, "You're wrong, mon. I dinna want tae marry her."

"No? Well, knock me over, I really think you mean it." And then with a sigh of his own, "Very well, so I was wrong. But I'm still willing to help."

"How?"

"By asking Ophelia to marry me instead, of course. I'm probably the only one she *would* throw you over for."

Duncan couldn't restrain a snort. "That's a bluidy high opinion you have o' yourself, mon, likely tae rival her own opinion o' herself."

Raphael chuckled. "Hardly. We're talking titles here, which is all she's really interested in, that and the wealth that comes with them. Don't make the mistake of thinking it's actually you she wants. And the title I will be inheriting does happen to be a bit more lofty than yours."

"E'en if it might work, which it willna, I couldna ask you tae make such a sacrifice."

"What sacrifice? I'm not talking about actually marrying her," Raphael said with a shudder. "Merely asking her, doing the engaged thing for a bit, then breaking it off. I'll even do the gentlemanly part and let her do the breaking. Save face and all of that. Then no one's hurt, you escape this fate worse than death, I get back to my usual pursuits of debauchery and the like, and everyone's happy."

"Except Ophelia, who still has this enemy o' hers who can at any time ruin her wi' the information she has," Duncan pointed out. "What is tae stop Mavis from spreading her tale if Ophelia doesna marry me? Getting her engaged tae you won't prevent that, will merely turn the tale into the full-blown scandal we're trying tae avoid."

Raphael frowned, having momentarily overlooked that wrinkle. "Well, hell, you really are in a fix then, aren't you? So what are you waiting for? Come to think of it, I haven't been to Manchester in a while my-self. Think I'll join you. Two of us can cover much more area than you can alone. For that matter, let your grandfather know, so he can send his people there as well."

Much as Duncan hated to admit it, and he still didn't like the roundabout way Raphael said things, the man was turning out to be likable after all.

40

Sabrina was getting on with her life. She found that if she could keep Duncan out of her mind, she could even laugh again when she felt like it. Of course, it didn't take much for a spurt of tears to sneak up on her either, but for the most part, she managed to appear her old self as she went about her normal routines.

There had been one exception when poor Robert Willison had stopped to talk to her on her trek through Oxbow and had been treated to one of her spurts. He'd been *so* upset when she burst into tears in front of him that he'd gone off to fetch three of his neighbors to help.

By the time everyone converged on her, though, she had her emotions back in hand and had blamed the tears on a speck of dust that was bothering her eye, and reminded her audience that a good cry was the best way to wash one's eyes. They'd looked at her as if she were daft, but then, people often did look at her that way when she got into one of her silly moods, so that was nothing out of the ordinary.

Her aunts had decided she was "recovered" as well, though it had never been discussed just what her malady was. They knew it had to do with Duncan, but by unspoken agreement, they weren't going to badger her about it. It did come up occasionally, though. How could it not when Duncan's wedding was still the major topic of the neighborhood, and so it was hard not to mention it?

But they were back to thinking of other gentlemen who might "do" for her, and just last night when they were gathered in the parlor together after dinner, Alice mentioned a newcomer to the neighborhood.

"Sir Albert Shinwell is his name. He's building a manor house on the other side of Oxbow near that lovely meadow there. I heard he's just come into an unexpected inheritance, and decided on Oxbow for his country retreat."

Hilary nodded, adding, "People do tend to spend a lot of money when it's new money. Odd, that, but it happens all the time."

"I've heard he's also building in Bath and in Portsmouth. Sounds like it was quite a big inheritance."

"He's not married, nor ever has been," Hilary put in. "That has been confirmed."

"And he's young," Alice thought to add. "Not quite thirty yet."

Sabrina had no trouble figuring out where the conversation was heading by then. "I'll get around to meeting him, just do *not* bring him here to meet me."

"We wouldn't do that, dear, at least I wouldn't," Hilary assured her.

"Which implies I would?" Alice huffed. "I'm not so insensitive to not realize that our gel is not happy over the big wedding next week."

"No, just insensitive enough to mention it," Hilary shot back with a snort.

Sabrina stood up to get their attention off of bickering before they seriously got into it, and back on her. "It's all right. You don't have to tiptoe around me on this subject. It's true, like Aunt Hilary, I thought something more than just friendship might be occurring between Duncan and me, but I was mistaken. I *will* get over it. It was more a surprise than anything else, his reengagement to Ophelia, which I am recovered from. Really, I am fine."

She left them before she belied that statement with a quivering lip, but the two sisters looked at each other and both knew better.

"She's lying." Hilary sighed. "She's still quite devastated."

"I know." Alice's sigh was a bit louder. "I'd like to take a club to—"

"So would I," Hilary cut in. "But what would that help? It's not as if any gel would have a hope of competing with someone like Ophelia, not even one as wonderful as our Sabrina, when men can be such blind idiots."

Alice might have giggled at that, if they both weren't rather despondent over the subject themselves. "Not that it signifies, but it's just as well, if you ask me. I wasn't looking forward to being condescended to by that old coot Neville again, if we actually ended up related to him by marriage. He made his sentiments perfectly clear, back when the scandal first broke in our day, that he wanted nothing more to do with our family."

"I'm not so sure it was just that," Hilary replied thoughtfully. "He made a remark to me at the party that led me to think it was more that he was disgusted over what our grandfather did, rather than that a scandal had come of it. He was chummy with him, after all. At least, they used to go hunting together all the time."

"What remark?"

"He asked me if idiocy still ran in the family," Hilary replied.

Alice flushed with heated ire that was reflected in her tone as she blustered, "Why, that hypocrite! Who was it let his daughter go off and marry a Highlander, then bemoaned that fact forever after? *That* was idiocy."

Hilary shook her head. "That was a circumstance that couldn't be helped after she went and fell in love with the man. What he should have done was kept them from meeting in the first place."

"You snubbed him, I hope," Alice replied, still indignant.

"Of course. But after thinking about it, I was sure he was merely referring to Grandfather shooting himself, which, you'll have to admit, has been our own opinion from time to time."

"Oh, well, all water under the bridge, as it were," Alice said, then went on to a new complaint. "But you never should have encouraged Sabrina into thinking she had a chance with young Duncan. It's not as if Neville would have allowed a match between them."

"Encourage how?" Hilary glared at her sister. "I have eyes, you know. It was quite obvious the boy was taken with her, though as it turns out, it was merely her friendship that he cherished," she added with a sigh.

"Can't blame him for that," Alice replied. "She is a joy to be around."

"Of course she is. However, you're wrong in thinking Neville would have objected due to the scandal. He wouldn't have liked it, but from what I've gathered, he just wants a new heir, and quickly. With such haste involved, they can't exactly afford to be hoity-toity about it."

"Sure they can," Alice disagreed. "That was the point of the gathering. Duncan had more gels to choose from than he needed, and look what happened. He ended up choosing the very one that Neville wanted for him."

"But did he choose her?"

"What do you mean?"

"You know Mary Petty's daughter who is an upstairs maid at Summers Glade? I spoke with her this morning at the cobbler's. She says her daughter told her that no one at Summers Glade is happy about the upcoming wedding, least of all the bride and the groom."

"Neither of them?"

"That's what she said."

"Well, that doesn't make sense. Why are they getting married then?"

Hilary just raised a supercilious brow that had Alice snorting. "Nonsense. Not a breath of scandal has been hinted at—"

"Exactly," Hilary cut in with a smirk. "Forced marriages usually occur to nip a scandal in the bud *before* it has a chance to get started."

"A groundless assumption in this case," Alice noted. "You are merely guessing."

"Common sense—"

Alice cut in, "Who says you have any?"

"Humph, talking to you is like talking to a doorknob," Hilary complained.

"Implying?"

"That you can turn the knob, but you still haven't sense enough to open the door."

"Or more than enough sense to know that there is nothing on the other side of the door worth seeing," Alice shot back triumphantly.

Hilary conceded. That was a rather nice comeback, after all, and though she'd never say so, she was proud of her sister for thinking of it.

41

This morning when Sabrina passed through Oxbow on her typical walking route, she had four encounters that pretty much convinced her to give up her old routines, at least for a while. It was one thing to get on with her life if she could avoid thinking about Duncan, but quite another when people inadvertently thrust him into her thoughts. Unfortunately, Duncan, still so new to the neighborhood, was going to be a major topic for a good long time. Sir Albert was also getting his share of gossip now, but Duncan, in line for such a lofty title, was still of more interest.

The first two encounters each told her that Duncan had gone off to London, most likely to buy his bride a special wedding gift. The third encounter, with old Mrs. Spode, was only slightly different.

Mrs. Spode was a cantankerous old lady, one of Sabrina's aunts' more amusing friends, and she scoffed at the "wedding gift" assumption, whispering to Sabrina that the young lord was more likely off on a last bit of oat sowing in London before the nuptials, especially since Lord Locke, a known rake, had gone with him.

"Now I ask you, would Lord Locke know where to find wedding gifts, or would he know where to find ladies of ill repute? The latter, of course. If the young lord comes back with a gift, it will be one of those unmentionable diseases." And the old girl had cackled at her own wit.

Sabrina did *not* encourage that conversation, in fact, left Mrs. Spode in what might be considered very rude haste. But before she could get out of town completely, she had her fourth encounter.

This one was the worst, with Duncan's grandfather. Not Neville. Him, she probably could have managed quite nicely—if she could have gotten past the shock of finding him in Oxbow. But it was the Scots grandfather who hailed her as he came out of

Oxbow's combination inn and tavern, the grandfather she hadn't actually met yet, though he seemed to know her well enough to call her by name.

"Yer Duncan's friend Sabrina, aye?" At her nod, he continued, "I had been meaning tae meet ye at Summers Glade, but ye stopped visiting. I'd wondered at that. Most o' the other lassies hied it back tae London when they didna win the lad, which was understandable. But ye now—I didna think ye were there for that."

"I wasn't."

"Then why did ye stop coming?"

The direct question, and in such an accusing tone, caused a blush. Unfortunately, Archibald noticed it and interpreted it correctly.

"Sae, 'tis like that, is it? Ye've let yerself feel more for the lad than friendship?"

To admit that, to him in particular, was almost a guarantee that it would get back to Duncan, which, under the circumstances, was the very last thing she wanted. Lying, though, which she abhorred doing but had no choice but to do in this case, caused an even worse blush.

"That isn't the case a'tall. Duncan is

charming, I like him a lot, but really, just as a friend."

His expression was skeptical, even though he went along with her assertion by saying, "Och, I'm glad tae be hearing that. No' that ye arena a sweet lass, I'm sure, but ye ken auld Neville was worried aboot the amount o' time the lad was giving tae ye, and Duncan did assure us o' that same thing, that ye are merely a friend, albeit a verra good friend. I'd hazard e'en tae say yer his *best* friend just now, which is why I found it strange that ye'd desert him in his—"

"Excuse me?" she cut in, her voice quite stiff now, but because of that "worried about the amount of time" remark, which, of course had to do with her scandal, rather than his last accusation. "How have I deserted him? Just because I was feeling a bit under the weather and kept to my bed for a few days doesn't mean I have deserted him. And I have spoken to him since the engagement."

"Ah, well, I didna know that," he replied, and then uncomfortably, "Did he, ah, mention tae ye aboot the, er . . . silliness that led tae his—"

He coughed, giving up trying to ask her what had been confided to her, without actually mentioning what might have been confided. She almost laughed over his difficulty, though it wouldn't have been with much humor, when the subject was still so painful.

But she did take pity on him and admitted, "If you mean did Duncan tell me that he didn't actually ask Ophelia to marry him, and mentioned to me what led to their renewed engagement, yes, he did."

Archibald sighed in relief. "Then I can speak freely. Good, I dinna like pussyfooting around a subject. This is why I was concerned wi' yer absence, lass, ye ken? He's in need o' friends just now. I hope ye were able tae cheer him a wee bit when ye spoke tae him?"

Cheer him? That had been a very painful encounter with Duncan that day on the road. Hearing that he was forced to marry Ophelia was almost as bad as thinking he wanted to. But then she had two very different accounts on their relationship from the both of them. Ophelia was known to lie, so her assertion that Duncan was still passionate for her might have been fabrication, and yet, what if Duncan's assertion that he didn't want Ophelia was the lie instead?

He *had* reminded her that the only real compromising had been done to her. Had that been his intent all along? Had he asked Ophelia to marry him in a moment of passion and quickly regretted it as soon as he left her? Then used Sabrina to give him a way to get out of it?

She didn't want to believe that of him, yet it could have happened exactly that way. Why would Ophelia lie about the time that he'd asked her to marry him, after all? Just because Sabrina had been unable to hide that the answer was extremely important to her?

She was deluding herself, though, trying to see him in a bad light in hope that it would kill her love for him. It just didn't work. She *didn't* really think he had lied to her. But even if he had, there'd been no doubting that he was now miserable over whatever he'd done.

She had wanted to cheer him up that day. The urge had been strong. But how could she cheer up anyone when she was so miserable herself?

Archibald's question, though, she decided to simply avoid altogether, and did so by mentioning, "I heard just today that Duncan has gone to London. Perhaps the trip will take his mind off of—"

"Nae, he's gone searching for the Newbolt lass, sae his mind will be on nothing else."

She was surprised and hopeful, hearing that. "He knows where to look then?"

"No' really," he said, disappointing her. "He didna like sitting aboot doing nothing while Neville's people searched, sae he's gone hisself. No' that he's likely tae find her, and he knows it. There's just no' enough time afore the wedding."

"I suppose not." She managed to keep from sighing.

"I wanted tae simply postpone it m'self, but Neville seems tae think that any prevaricating on our part will start the scandal brewing."

"Then you must hope he gets lucky."

"A slim hope. But if he does manage tae get oout o' this predicament and is back tae looking for a bride, I've a feeling he will be asking ye tae wed."

Sabrina blinked. "Me?"

"Aye, but it would be for the wrong reasons, ye ken? He wants ye near tae hand is all. He showed how far he's willing tae go tae hae ye near, by bringing ye tae the gathering, e'en though it brought Ophelia as well. He'd move ye intae Summers Glade if it werena inappropriate. I'm thinking he'd marry ye just tae get ye there permanently. He values yer friendship that much. But it is only that. Dinna let him fool ye intae thinking there's more tae his feelings. Ye'd both sorely regret it if ye do."

Sabrina prayed she could hold back her emotions for just another few moments, until she could escape from this unwanted conversation. She'd heard the first time what Archibald had said, that Duncan had assured him that she was just a friend. She had put it from her mind when he said it, because to think about it was to rip her heart apart yet again. Yet he'd just thrust it into the open once more, where she couldn't possibly ignore it now. A friend. She was only a friend. She'd never be more than a friend.

"You are creating worries over something that has little chance of ever occurring, when the wedding is only two days away."

"True." He sighed. "And m'apologies, lass, for feeling a need tae warn ye—just in case. Ye will come tae the wedding, aye?"

Sit there and watch Duncan and Ophelia be joined forever more? No way in hell, which had her lying yet again, though evasively this time.

"I'm sure everyone who receives an invitation will be in attendance. Now I really must get home. My aunts didn't expect me to be gone this long and will begin to worry . . ."

She didn't hear his second sigh as she hurried off. Archibald was already regretting what he'd said to her. He didn't doubt any of it, he just realized, belatedly, that he had put the cart before the horse. There'd been no reason to warn her of anything, when Duncan was likely to marry the other girl. If he was saved from that, then that would have been the time to do any warning, not beforehand.

42

The letter arrived the next afternoon. It completely confounded Sabrina. She really did think it was a joke. It was just too farcical. If someone of consequence was going to be ransomed, why for only forty pounds? Forty thousand pounds, she might have taken seriously, even just several thousand, but a mere forty pounds, and such an odd number at that? It had to be a joke.

Unfortunately, she couldn't just ignore it. She wasn't even sure that the person who signed the letter was actually that person. If it was a joke, then it wouldn't be the real person who'd sent it. But she had no other correspondence from that individual to compare it with. So on the far-fetched chance that the letter was legitimate, she had to act on it.

She showed the letter to her aunts, of course. The sender might have requested that she tell no one, but she couldn't just leave home without letting them know why.

They both agreed it had to be a joke, and one in very poor taste. But they were certainly eager for a little adventure, even if it was only a waste of time, and thus their coachman was summoned from Oxbow where he lived and the three of them set off late that afternoon.

They knew they couldn't actually go all the way with her, because of the instructions that only Sabrina was to show up with the money. But they pointed out that she couldn't travel alone, and they did want to be nearby to find out soonest who had perpetuated the joke.

Sabrina didn't see it as an adventure, but she did see it as a good excuse for why she wouldn't be at the wedding tomorrow morning, since it was highly doubtful that they would return in time for it. Even if they turned right about after confirming that the letter was just a farce, they wouldn't get back home until very late at night, or rather the wee hours of the morning, thus she'd be sleeping through the latter hours—and right through the wedding.

They arrived after dark, which was why they had trouble finding the address given in the letter. There weren't many people out and about at that time of the evening whom they could ask, and they were twice given wrong directions from the few who were. It was near midnight when they did finally locate the residence.

Alice and Hilary were going to wait in the coach, close to hand. The letter stressed that Sabrina must come alone so no one would get hurt, but they absolutely refused to just leave her there. And she was to scream very loudly if she needed help. Mickie, their coachman, had been apprised of their task and had brought along a pistol as well as a very nasty-looking club. For that matter, Sabrina's aunts each had a weapon as well. She had managed to keep from laughing when she'd seen them tuck the very small pair of matching pistols, one each, into their reticules before they left home.

All the precautions were silly in her opinion, though. She fully expected to find the house vacant, or another letter waiting for her on the porch laughing at her foolishness in coming there. The utter darkness inside the dwelling supported that contention. Not a single light, not even a dull one, showed at any of the windows. And it was a nice looking house, two stories in height, not overly large, but no small cottage either. Hardly the setting one would imagine for nefarious deeds like holding people captive for ransom.

There was no letter on the porch. She tried the front door, but it was locked. As it should be for an empty house, she told herself. She thought about going around to the back to see if there was another door that might be open, but figured she'd probably trip on something in the dark, and besides, she wasn't exactly trying to keep the fact that she was there a secret. So she knocked on the door, quite briskly. The sooner it was confirmed that no one was in the house, the sooner she and her aunts could return home.

The door opened. That was Sabrina's first surprise. The second was being yanked inside and hearing the door close behind her. It was still utterly dark, but she

could hear a lot of breathing and feet shuf-
fling. And then there was light when a
cover was removed from a lantern. The
lantern had yet another cover on it, thinner,
though, so it wasn't very bright, just bright
enough to see by.

She was surrounded, literally, by four
men. She had to turn about to have a look
at them all. She wasn't impressed, though
she had to admit that the letter she had
received might not be a joke after all.

They were a ragtag bunch, clothes in ill
repair, three of them so skinny she had to
wonder if they might not be used to eating
on a regular basis. They were unkempt,
dirty even, which suggested baths might
be as irregular as meals. Their ages could
have ranged anywhere from younger than
her to her aunts' age—it was hard to tell
under all the filth.

The fourth man was a bit different, at
least he had made an effort to look pre-
sentable. He was clean, in his mid-twenties, his hair slicked back and long enough
to be clubbed at the neck. His clothes
were in better repair, too, though they
weren't good quality to begin with. And he
didn't look like he was starving, cut a fine

figure, actually. He was also the only one out of the four who *wasn't* pointing a pistol at her. Those other three weapons, quickly noted, was why she remained silent for the moment.

She supposed they could be criminals, though if they were, they obviously weren't very successful at it. Actually, the guns alone suggested they were up to no good. None of them looked like they had worked in a while. All of them looked out of place in such a nice house.

Her surprise was wearing off, in time to note that a couple of the men had shown surprise, too, at her own appearance. It didn't take long to realize why, though, when they started talking around her, all at once, so it was a bit hard to keep up.

"It be another lady."

"Is, ain't it? You thinkin' wot I'm thinkin'?"

"We can send the other one to collect a ransom for this'n, I'm thinkin'."

"Was thinking the same thing."

"Glad we think alike." This was said with a chuckle. "This could turn into a mighty fine line o' work, it could."

"Not to mention, I'm in no hurry to give up that soft bed upstairs."

"You have the money, lady?"

It was the first remark directed at her. She was still grappling with the notion that they were thinking of keeping her there, if she had understood their meaning correctly. She hadn't figured out a way to reasonably dissuade them of that notion yet, so a bit of stalling was in order.

"Well, now, I'm not so sure I know what you're talking about," she replied, then tried a bluff. "And just what are you doing in my house?"

"Your house? The gent said it were his house."

"What gent?"

"The one we tossed in the cellar, which is where you'll be heading if you ain't got the money."

"Well, when you put it that way, I'm sure I can come up with some money," she told the last speaker. "How much did you require?"

"Is she fooling us? You didn't get a letter that brought you here?"

"A letter? Why, yes, but, well, I broke my glasses this week, and so I wasn't able to read it. Was it to let me know you apprehended someone breaking into my house? If so, you are to be commended, and indeed are in line for a reward. Is that the money you're talking about?"

They stared at each other, baffled for a moment, until one of them said, "Lady, just answer yes or no. Do you have forty pounds on you?"

That odd number made a bit of sense now, forty to be divided four ways, yet still a laughable amount. "Why, yes, as a matter of—"

"A simple yes or no!"

"She said yes," was pointed out.

A frustrated growl. "I heard her, but it weren't going to be simple."

"She's batty," was said behind her. "Don't even try to understand her."

"Just make sure she has the money."

Her reticule was grabbed from her hand. She objected to that, most indignantly. "Now, see here—"

"It's empty," was the next complaint from the grabber. "Now, why would she carry an empty bag?"

"Tol' you not to try to understand nabobs. They're all batty."

Another frustrated growl from her left side. "Where's the money, lady?"

"In my pocket, of course. Honestly, any simpleton would know not to carry money in her bag, when bags are a prime target of bag snatchers. You *just* snatched my bag, didn't you? I rest my case."

They again stared at each other, but in some serious annoyance this time. In fact, she wasn't all that surprised when her arm was grabbed in the next moment and she was marched directly upstairs.

She supposed she shouldn't have tried her silliness tactics on them. They weren't the least bit appreciative of it. But after hearing that they were thinking of keeping her there, she really did need a bit more time to examine all the ramifications of that. That she did at least in part, and didn't like her conclusions at all. So she now needed to figure out a way to not be kept.

That was paramount. After all, if she didn't come out of the house soon, her aunts would no doubt be coming in, and then they'd be kept, too. And if they were all three kept, who would there be to fetch a ransom from? Certainly not their distant relative who had gotten her great-grandfa-

ther's title and refused to even acknowledge them as relatives.

Being thrust into an upstairs bedroom
and having the door slammed behind her
gave her the bit of undistracted time to
think that she needed, or it would have—if
Mavis Newbolt weren't also there.

43

The room was dark. The only thing that told Sabrina she wasn't alone was the cranky voice that she recognized, coming from somewhere in the middle of the room, complaining, "What do you want now?"

"It's me—Sabrina," she said in the general direction of the voice. "Weren't you expecting me?"

"Oh! Yes! But what took you so long? I gave them the letter to mail days ago."

"I only just received it today."

"Bah, those idiots," Mavis said derisively. "I should have known they wouldn't know how to post a letter. Well, no matter, you're here finally. And I can't tell you how much I appreciate your coming."

"Don't mention it," Sabrina replied. "I'm

just surprised that you would contact me. I really thought the letter was a joke."

A sigh. "If only it was. But I'm sorry, Sabrina, truly, to have involved you in this. I simply couldn't think of anyone else to contact nearby. It would have taken so long to reach my parents, and besides, they think I'm still at Summers Glade and I didn't want them to think otherwise. They'd be quite upset with me to know I left there but didn't come straight home, and then that *this* happened."

Sabrina decided not to mention yet that they already knew their daughter wasn't where she was supposed to be. She wanted to assure herself that Mavis was all right first, and she had to see her to do that.

"Is there no lamp in here that can be lit? It seems rather odd, talking to you in the dark."

"There are several, yes, but I didn't think to be conservative. I've already used up the fuel in them, and they won't replace it—probably wouldn't bother to look for the store of it, the lazy sods," Mavis added bitterly.

A moment later, though, moonlight

streamed into the room as Mavis opened the curtains at both windows. Since Sabrina had been several minutes in the total dark, that little bit of moonlight was almost as bright as a flamed light.

"Better?" Mavis said, coming back to sit on the edge of the bed where she had been.

"Much," Sabrina replied, and moved to sit next to her for a closer examination.

Mavis looked fine, though, if quite rumpled. She was fully dressed, but in the same clothes she'd been wearing when she left Summers Glade, and it looked like she hadn't removed them once. She'd been sleeping in them, and just using the bed as more of a pallet, not turning down the covers, even though they would have given her some welcome warmth. The room wasn't too cold, though, which suggested the fireplace had been fueled earlier and had just burned down to nothing. That Mavis had her coat near to hand meant she was probably used to the cold intruding late in the night.

"Have they been feeding you?" Sabrina asked with concern. "Treating you well?"

"Yes, I've been fed, but mostly with

loaves of bread they steal, I don't doubt, since I can't imagine them baking them. The house wasn't well stocked with food, just a few stores, and they no doubt went through that very quickly. As for how I've been treated, well, I've been kept locked up here and left alone for the most part."

"What exactly happened here?" Sabrina asked next. "Is this your house?"

"No, it belongs to my cousin John. We arrived late at night, having come here directly from Summers Glade. The house was somewhat of a mess, which is why John suspected it had been broken into. We didn't expect to find the intruders still here, though, and sleeping upstairs. They were as surprised as we, actually. They'd apparently found the house empty and decided it would make a nice place to live for the winter, or until the owner showed up. Vagrants, the lot of them, or so I've gathered."

Sabrina had come to that conclusion as well. "I take it there was no time to summon the authorities?"

"There was no time to think of anything *logical,* if that's what you mean. That should have been our first recourse. I know it. You know it. But John was too furious to be thinking of doing things in the proper order, I suppose. Understandable, of course. They had broken into his house, were still here. He really was livid. But he really shouldn't have tried to physically evict all four of them himself."

"*All* four?"

"I know, even if he was a bloody Corinthian, which he's not, those odds are a bit much. And they were scrambling to escape, after all. So everything might have been fine if John hadn't chased after them in his rage. When he tried to trounce one of them, the other three came to their friend's rescue and John ended up being the one trounced."

"Was he hurt bad?"

"More his pride than anything else, I imagine. Their victory over him emboldened them, though. They tied him up and put him in the cellar, then locked me up here. It was another few hours before they came up with the ransom scheme and I was ordered to write that letter—for a mere forty pounds. Can you believe it?" she added with an indignant snort. "My parents are worth—"

"I know it's a silly amount," Sabrina cut in. "But probably not to them, and redundant. They have guns. Did they have them before?"

Mavis frowned, hearing that. "No, I saw no weapons before. My, my, they're really embracing the criminal path, aren't they? They must have acquired the guns since this started, probably stole them like they have the bread. That was really stupid of them. Someone might really get hurt now."

"As long as it isn't us."

"Oh, I wasn't worried about us. They're more likely to shoot each other. They *do* seem like complete incompetents. I doubt they've ever done anything like this before, so they don't really know what to do. I wouldn't even be surprised if this whole ransom thing was just a delay so they could stay here longer. They do seem to love it here, but then, of course, they would, if they'd been living in the streets."

"Gathered that myself. And they've already come up with another reason to let them stay longer. They plan to keep me now and send you for another ransom."

Mavis made a choking sound of frustration. "Absolutely not! I didn't ask you here to put you in the same deplorable situation as I. They are idiots. There is no other explanation. Well, we'll just have to inform them that this is *not* how this is done."

"That isn't all that needs explaining," Sabrina said, her worry sneaking into her tone. "I'll have to let them know that others will be arriving here if I don't leave soon. You've dealt with them for a few days. Will that work to get them to take their ransom and run?"

"Will someone be arriving?"

"Yes, my aunts will." Sabrina sighed. "They're waiting outside in our coach."

"Oh, dear," Mavis said, and then when they heard some door pounding coming from downstairs, "Oh, *dear.*"

44

It all happened too quickly, Raphael putting his shoulder to the door when it wasn't answered soon enough, breaking the lock on it—he had a strong shoulder—then muttering, "What the hell?" just before he slumped to the floor.

With the lantern they had set on the back porch, Duncan saw him falling, saw the weapon in the hand of the man who'd clubbed him over the head with it, and dove at the fellow. A shot was fired.

Shrieks of startlement were heard from in front of the house, from somewhere upstairs in the house, from the next block. The shot had echoed loudly through the quiet neighborhood at that hour of the night. The stench of gun smoke filled the air. The bullet had passed near Duncan's neck, and had been heard clearly, which was probably why he was angry enough to seriously bloody the man's face before he was done with him.

They should have approached this with more caution, rather than the impatience they were both feeling. But after two days of searching, having doors slammed in their faces, being chased by dogs, and finally being led to this place by an urchin through backyards and over fences, rather than down the front street, then finding that the house looked deserted . . . well, that hadn't inspired calm emotions.

He spared a moment to wonder who he had beat unconscious. He didn't think it was John Newbolt. One of his servants, perhaps, who had understandably come armed to investigate what most likely sounded like someone breaking into the house. Bedamned. They'd have some explaining to do now. The authorities would no doubt be arriving soon, after all those shrieks he'd heard.

He spared another moment to make sure Raphael wasn't dead. He wasn't, was even starting to groan a little. He went to fetch the lantern from the porch. The urchin had disappeared, not surprising.

Coming back into the kitchen where the two bodies were sprawled, Duncan had only enough time to set the lantern down on a table before two more men appeared in the open doorway that led farther into the house. One had a pistol trained on him. He hadn't thought to pick up the gun on the floor that had been used on Raphael's head.

"Wot the 'ell?"

"What happened here?"

"A wee misunderstanding, I'm thinking," Duncan explained. "I'm here tae see John Newbolt, or rather, his cousin. You work for him?"

An exchanged look between the two men, before one said, "Shore we do, but this ain't the hour to come visitin'. Come back in the morning, gent."

"I'll stay and see tae my business, if it's all the same tae you."

"You'll be leaving if you know wot's good for you," the one with the weapon said, and just in case Duncan hadn't noticed it, he waved it about in front of him now.

But the other intervened and said cordially, "That's fine, we'll take you to Mr. Newbolt. He'll likely be glad o' the company."

That it was said with somewhat of a snicker wasn't Duncan's first warning that something wasn't right here. It was that they would call Newbolt "Mister" when the man held a minor title, according to Rafe, title enough for his servants to refer to him as Lord Newbolt.

The lantern Duncan had brought into the kitchen illuminated the short hallway and into the larger entry hall, though by then the light was extremely dim and there was no other to be had. He should have brought it with him. One of the two men should have thought to do so as well. It seemed strange to have no light inside the house unless everyone in it had been asleep, and yet the men had all been fully dressed, so apparently hadn't come straight from their beds to investigate the noises at the back of the house.

Those noises, though, had obviously woken the whole house, including those upstairs. At least that was what he figured when from the corner of his eye he saw the ripple of a skirt at the top of the stairs. He started to turn that way but felt the pistol poke into his back, insisting he continue on where they were leading him.

That was pretty much the last bit of warning he needed that something was definitely not right here. He'd explain later if he was wrong, but right then he turned on the man behind him, knocked aside the arm with the gun, and slammed his fist against his nose. The fellow flew backward, toppled over a hall table, and didn't move any further.

The other man, who had been in the lead and was now behind him, growled and jumped on his back, wrapped his arms around Duncan's throat and tried to choke him. He wasn't succeeding, not even a little, though he probably thought he was, because he laughed triumphantly. Duncan, thoroughly annoyed by then, dragged the skinny little fellow around to the front of him, held him there as he drew his fist back, then watched him scream and faint before he could hit him. Disgusted, he let him drop to the floor.

And then he was incredulous to hear a voice he had no trouble recognizing, despite the anger in it. "How *could* you just ignore his weapon like that?"

He didn't answer that, demanded instead, "What the hell are *you* doing here?"

She didn't answer either, still intent on her original question. In a furious tone, she said, "You could have been killed just then!"

Duncan realized then what was the cause of her anger and tried to shrug it off. "When you've a bleak-looking future, lass, the threat o' danger just doesna hold the same meaning as it might when all is right wi' your life."

"Reckless, no matter how you put it," she pointed out stiffly.

He wasn't going to argue the point. "You'll be answering my question now."

"Yes, certainly—if you've taken care of all of them," she replied.

"All of who?"

"The poor wretches who broke in here and foolishly held Mavis and John captive all week. There were four of them in all."

"I've only encountered three—"

"Then we'll lock ourselves in up here until you're done. But do be careful. At least three of them had guns and—" She paused when a new pounding began, at the front door. "That will probably be Mickie, our coachman. Let him in. He'll help you look for the last fellow. And John's in the cellar. Please make sure he's all right."

He stood there for a moment after she disappeared back into the dark of the upper hall, still incredulous that she was there, even more incredulous at how bossy she'd just been. But then he smiled, remembering her angry upset over his wee brush with danger.

45

Upstairs, Sabrina returned to Mavis's room and, feeling around the doorknob for a latch, which was easy to find, locked them in. She was still amazed that the door hadn't been locked from without, as it had been when she'd been brought upstairs. She concluded that she'd annoyed those men so much with her chatter that they'd simply forgot to lock the door again after thrusting her into the room. If she'd known, she and Mavis could have vacated the house already and been away in the waiting coach out front. The authorities could have returned to release Mavis's cousin. Not that it mattered now.

"We've been rescued," she told Mavis. "Well, almost, or at least, in the process of being rescued, so we should stay here until all is secure."

"By whom?"

"Duncan MacTavish."

"But what's *he* doing here?" Mavis asked.

"Looking for you, I don't doubt. Actually, I believe Lord Neville has had people looking for you since you left Summers Glade, so your parents are aware that you're not where they thought you to be."

"Oh, bother, now I'm going to be in for it," Mavis groaned. "Whyever would Birmingdale be looking for me?—Unless, hmmm, never mind."

"It's all right," Sabrina told her, realizing the direction her thoughts had just gone. "I know all about what you witnessed at Summers Glade the night you left."

"You do?"

"Yes, Duncan told me."

"Well, I suppose that shouldn't surprise me. You did seem to be very good friends with him."

"Yes, friends," Sabrina said in a voice that was starting to turn maudlin. She gave herself a mental shake. She was not going to let that "just friends" destroy her composure at a time like this. "But why did you leave the party so suddenly that night?"

"Why did you?"

Sabrina blinked. "Excuse me?"

"I saw you run off earlier in the evening, saw Duncan leave to follow you. I was hoping, I really was, that something would come of that, that he'd be asking you to marry him." A sigh. "But I guess he just wanted to make sure you were all right, because not an hour later, there he was trysting with that witch, so they'd obviously made up. It was the last straw for me. Ophelia had won again. She gets anything and everything she wants."

"It does seem that way, doesn't it?" Sabrina agreed with a sigh of her own.

"The funny part was, I'd really thought the world was righting itself finally when Duncan broke that first engagement with her. She'd instigated it, but it really did backfire on her, *and* she realized too late that he was a prime catch after all. Then to find out that it was only temporary, that she was going to get him after all—it was too much for me. Women like Ophelia win no matter what they do wrong. It just isn't fair! And for her to win again, so soon after she tried to blacken my name and convince everyone that I'm a liar, which isn't the least bit true, but . . . it brought me to tears. I had to leave, and quickly, before I made a fool of myself."

Sabrina understood that well enough, when the exact same thing had happened to her. She'd had to leave for the same reason, before the tears she couldn't hold back embarrassed her royally.

"So you came directly here?"

"Yes. I needed a little seclusion to gain a proper perspective again so it wouldn't bother me anymore. I thought it would only take a day or two—but those fool vagrants changed those plans."

"In the case of time, yes, but did the seclusion do as you'd hoped it would?"

"Yes, actually. I've concluded that I'll always hate Ophelia. She's just done too much to ever be forgiven for, and not just to me. But I'm not going to let it bother me anymore. I'm simply going to stay far, far away from her from now on, and try to forget she even exists."

"If you've always hated her, why did you chum about with her?"

"Because I didn't always hate her. She and I were actually childhood friends, believe it or not. We were very close, close enough that I was often at her house and saw firsthand how her parents spoiled her. So I understood a little why she was the way she was, and tended to forgive her for it—until I met Alexander."

"Alexander?"

"The man I fell in love with. He was actually courting me as well. And he knew Ophelia, assured me he wasn't impressed with her beauty. She didn't like the way he was completely ignoring her, though, and she set about to change that. And the very day she started giving him some of her attention, he fell into the 'worship the goddess' crowd of fools. He stopped calling on me. He started calling on her. I was devastated. And the worst of it was, I knew Ophelia didn't want him for herself, she'd just been annoyed that he could ignore her. Just as soon as he started worshiping her, she dismissed him from her mind. Of course, it was too late for me. He tried to court me again, but I wouldn't have him. Ophelia's other friends might not mind taking her leftovers, but not I. I *should* have forgiven him. I knew what he felt for Ophelia wasn't real, was just the awe of her beauty. But I was too stubborn, and he ended up marrying someone else."

"I'm sorry."

"Don't be," Mavis replied. "Much of it was my own stubborn pride."

"But you were still friends with her after that, weren't you? Or did this only just happen?"

"Actually, I did end our friendship back then, but she came to me and begged me to forgive her, swore she didn't try to steal him from me, and if he could turn his affections so easily to someone else, then he wasn't worth having. Be that as it may, I let her talk me around because we *had* been such close friends. But it was never the same again between her and me, and slowly I just got more and more bitter, watching the way she manipulated people to always get her way, watching her spiteful little antics whenever she got jealous of someone. Even you were one of the victims of her jealousy."

"Me?" Sabrina almost laughed at the very notion of anyone being jealous of her, but Ophelia in particular.

"I'm not talking about normal jealousy," Mavis clarified. "She's never really been interested in any man in particular, to become jealous in the normal way. And I know you probably won't even believe this coming from me, after she publicly branded me a liar, but she's the one who started up that old family scandal of yours again. It wasn't just a slip of the tongue on her part either. She did it deliberately when she noticed the attention you were getting from a few of her regular admirers. That's what she was jealous of. She really can't stand it when she isn't the absolute center of attention. Just thought you ought to know, since you still seemed to be chummy with her yourself."

Sabrina was a bit incredulous. She didn't doubt what Mavis had just said. She just found it rather extreme, that Ophelia would do something like that for such a petty reason. It wasn't that she had been devastated that the old scandal had made the rounds again, nor that her chances for marriage had been ruined. But if it had been some other girl who took the matter more seriously, devastation could have been the result. Did Ophelia not *think* of the consequences of her actions? Did she just not care whom she hurt?

"I had already realized that Ophelia has never been a friend to me," Sabrina admitted.

"Good. At least you aren't being fooled anymore, like poor Edith and Jane are. For myself, I finally began to really despise her, and the only reason I continued to be in her crowd was I was waiting, hoping, that someone, anyone really, would finally put her in her place. I just wanted to be there to see it. Petty of me, I know. But she never has received her comeuppance and probably never will."

"Perhaps it will help you to know that Duncan doesn't really want to marry her."

"Then why were they having a lovers' tryst?"

"They weren't. What you walked in on wasn't what it seemed."

"Oh, come now, Sabrina, don't be naive," Mavis scoffed. "Ophelia was half clothed. They were obviously about to get into bed."

"In a room she shared with many others? When any one of those others could have arrived at any time?"

Mavis frowned. "I didn't consider that. Then what was he doing there?"

"Letting his temper get the better of him, or so he confessed to me. He was confronting her, had sought her out to demand answers, nothing more."

"Now, *that* doesn't surprise me. She is well known to drive people to rage, the result being they do things they wouldn't ordinarily do."

Sabrina blushed slightly, to have her own appalling reaction to Ophelia that night described so perfectly. "Yes, well, they are engaged again, but only because she convinced his family that you would spread the tale of it to ruin her. This is why Lord Neville has been looking for you. He doesn't want Duncan to marry her. Duncan doesn't want to marry her either. But he can't in good conscience not do so, when it was his own temper that caused him to be there and would result in her ruination if he doesn't marry her."

"Good Gawd, you mean she won him because of *me?* I've handed him to her on a silver platter, as it were? Oh, no, absolutely not. If that is the only reason he is marrying her, then he will have my assurance that what I saw will never be told to anyone. Her blasted reputation is quite safe in this instance, if it means she *won't* get what she wants—finally."

Sabrina smiled, relieved for Duncan's sake at least. "I rather thought you would feel that way."

46

Sabrina expected Duncan to be knocking on their door any time now. She didn't expect the door to open without her aid, but that it did, the reason being she'd forgotten there was a key to it.

The fourth ransom demander stood there just inside the doorway, key in hand. He was the one who was less unkempt than the others, the one without a weapon—at least, none that he'd revealed thus far. Which didn't mean that he didn't have one on his person somewhere, just that he seemed the less dangerous of the lot—so far.

His first words didn't give cause for alarm either. "Come along, ladies, I'm here to save you. There's a bloody big Scotsman on a rampage downstairs."

"That Scotsman happens to be a friend of ours," Sabrina pointed out.

"I was afraid of that," he said, chewing at his lower lip in a way that revealed just how worried he was now. "Well, one of you is coming along with me, to save me, then. And I'd rather it not be you, Miss Never-Shuts-Up."

Sabrina, a bit indignant over his description of her, replied stiffly, "You are *not* inconveniencing my friend here any further than you already have in detaining her here. If you mean to save yourself, I suggest you get to it. There's a window right there."

"We are *up*stairs," he complained, as if she had overlooked that fact.

"So? I would imagine any fall you might take on your way down will be less painful than if Duncan MacTavish gets his hands on you."

He turned more fully to face Sabrina to argue with her. "Now, look, lady, I'm the one in charge here, and I'm not about to give up using one of you as my ticket to escape this mess, especially when you didn't even give us the bloody forty pounds you owed us!"

"Well, if that's all you still require—"

Sabrina didn't need to finish. Mavis, quite familiar with the room in the dark, had managed to find something heavy to use as a weapon and took the opportunity of his turning his back to her to bash him over the head with it.

She then set the object down, dusted her hands briskly, and said to the unconscious fellow, "That was for feeding me only bread."

Sabrina started to grin, but the door opened again. It was Duncan this time, and after he stared a moment at the man on the floor, he glanced at her and said accusingly, "I thought you were going tae lock yourself in."

"Well, I did," she replied uncomfortably in her own defense. "I suppose I forgot that he had a key that might circumvent that."

"Did you now?" he said in a disgusted tone as he hefted the unconscious man over his shoulder. On the way out the door, he added, "You can come downstairs now. Newbolt has gone tae fetch someone tae collect these fellows."

"He was all right then?"

"Aye, he's fine, more embarrassed than anything else, that he let riffraff get the better o' him. Och, and a wee bit angry o'er it, I might add."

"Did you let my aunts know that you have everything under control?" she asked as she followed him downstairs.

"When I didna have this fellow yet, nor even know your aunts are here? Where are they?"

Sabrina blushed slightly, to have forgotten that she hadn't mentioned their presence yet. Adventure just wasn't her cup of tea, she supposed, when it caused her to make one blunder after another.

"They're outside in our coach. I'll be right back then," she said, and hurried out the front door before he noticed her embarrassment.

It took a bit longer than she imagined to reassure her aunts that no one was in any more danger. She'd been inside the house too long for them not to have gotten extremely upset. But as soon as they started to argue with each other over whether they should return home immediately or try to find an inn open at that hour, she knew they had calmed down enough for her to go back inside the house for a moment.

She still had to give Duncan the good

news, that Mavis wasn't going to tell anyone about what she'd seen that night at
Summers Glade, if Mavis hadn't told him
herself by now. Mavis had followed her
downstairs, so she might have assured
him already that he didn't have to marry
Ophelia.

She was surprised to find him alone by
the stairs, and not exactly looking like
someone who had just performed a very
nice and successful rescue, nor someone
who'd been saved from a marriage he
didn't want. He looked like he'd just lost
his best friend.

She was alarmed, demanded, "What
happened?"

He barely glanced at her in his dejection.
"She willna help me, lass. She flatly refused
tae keep silent if I dinna marry Ophelia."

Sabrina frowned. "Nonsense, she already assured me she would."

"Then she lied tae you. She's delighted
tae be able tae serve Ophelia her just deserts. Her words exactly. And she willna
discuss it further."

Sabrina sat down on the stairs, a bit
dazed in her confusion. "I don't understand.
She thought you were already engaged to

Ophelia again, that that's why you were with her that night. It made her miserable to think that Ophelia was again getting just what she wanted. That's why Mavis left. She was completely disheartened. But when I explained to her what had really happened, and that you were only marrying Ophelia to protect her reputation *because* of what Mavis saw, she swore she'd never tell. Why did she change her mind, Duncan? What did you tell her?"

"The truth."

"And I didn't?" she asked in a bewildered tone.

"Aye, you did," he assured her. "There was just a wee bit more that you didna know aboot, and I didna think tae keep from mentioning. I was forgetting how much the lass hates Ophelia. I was appealing tae her compassion only, but it apparently takes second place tae her desire tae have Ophelia no' get what she wants for once."

"What truth?"

"Ophelia doesna want tae marry me, any more'n I do her. After a talk she had wi' Neville, where he explained tae her the responsibilities she'd be facing as the next marquise, she's determined that being m'wife will be tae much a chore for her. Rafe was right, 'twas only the title she was interested in, no' me in particular, and now that the title entails more'n she was expecting, she wants oout o' the engagement again."

Sabrina didn't know whether to laugh or to cry. She was relieved, greatly, that Ophelia didn't want Duncan, that she'd never really wanted him, only what came with him. But she was going to get him anyway, because of the way she was, because she'd created such baleful feelings against her that her onetime best friend would rather get revenge on her than do what she knew to be the right thing.

"I'll talk to her again."

"You're welcome tae try, lass, but I saw it in her eyes, the triumph I just handed her, that she now has the means tae get e'en wi' her enemy. She'll no' be giving that up."

47

Duncan had been right. Mavis was unmovable in her decision to take her revenge and run with it. She was also angry with Sabrina, thinking she had deliberately kept the more important part of the situation from her, and wouldn't believe that she simply hadn't known about it. That didn't help at all to make Mavis see reason, quite possibly gave her an excuse to ignore anything Sabrina had to say.

She'd scoffed at the notion that Duncan was the innocent party in this and the one who would really be getting hurt by it. She'd pointed out that men didn't take marital commitments as seriously as women did, that many of them didn't even try to hide their infidelities anymore, and the gossip mills supported that contention.

"He'll have his mistresses to keep him happy and the most beautiful woman in all of England as his wife to be envied for," Mavis had told her. "So how could he not come out ahead in this? It's not as if he had someone else that he wanted to marry, or he would have done the asking and then none of this would have occurred."

That point had stabbed home directly, if unintentionally. It was yet another reminder of how unrealistic Sabrina's own hopes had been. But she had thrust it aside with her other dashed hopes.

However, having exhausted all the "decent thing to do" points, Sabrina was forced to resort to, "She's going to make his life hell. Would *you* want to spend the rest of your days with her?"

"I wouldn't. I'd lock her away and let her out only for holidays, and maybe not even then. I'd make *her* life hell, believe me, and do so without the least bit of guilt, knowing it's what she deserves. I hope, I really do, that Duncan MacTavish is smart enough to do just that. So go home, Sabrina. I appreciate that you came here to help, but you're wasting your time now."

It had been one of the hardest things

Sabrina had ever had to do, to come back downstairs and have to shake her head at Duncan. This had been his own last hope and now it was gone.

He had apparently expected no other outcome, however, because his expression didn't change, not that it could have gotten much more dejected at that point. He did gather her in his arms, though, to thank her for trying. And it was like heaven and hell for those few moments, savoring the feel of him, yet knowing it would probably be the last time she would ever be that close to him.

Duncan and Raphael rode along with their coach, escorting them back to Oxbow, which her aunts had decided would be the best course of action, despite the lateness of the hour. Sabrina hadn't even known that Raphael had been there with Duncan until she was already in the coach and they were on the way, and she could vaguely hear his voice outside complaining of a wicked headache.

The return trip seemed to go much quicker, and Sabrina was in bed before dawn after all, though it was close, less than an hour away. She had managed to keep from crying until then, but as soon as her head touched her pillow, all the emotions of the last week converged on her again—and the knowledge that Duncan would probably be married before she woke.

It wasn't any more painful to rise in the afternoon and know that Duncan's marriage had become a fact that morning. That surprised Sabrina. She had anticipated being devastated again. But after thinking about it, she realized there was no difference for her either way. Loving him, she hurt *for* him, but it wasn't as if she might have been able to have him for herself if there were no Ophelia.

Her own worse pain had occurred earlier in the week when his grandfather had warned her what Duncan's real feelings for her were. Until then, she had still harbored a small hope that if he didn't have to marry Ophelia, he might marry her instead. But it wouldn't have happened, at least not for the right reason, which Archibald had pointed out to her. She would never be more than a friend to him—but some friend she was, to have missed his wedding.

It annoyed her now, that she'd missed it. Archibald had told her that Duncan would be needing his friends today more than ever. And she couldn't help recalling how sad he'd looked last night, just before he hugged her.

She hoped her aunts had at least gone to the wedding. They'd all been invited. But considering the hour they'd gotten to bed, they'd probably overslept, too. It was too bad Duncan couldn't have done the same. She was sure he would have liked to. But no doubt someone had woken him. It was *his* wedding day, after all.

Coming downstairs a bit later, she found at least one of her aunts up and about, and on her way up to fetch her, or so Alice indicated when she said, "So you *are* up then? I wasn't sure."

"Yes, did you go to the wedding?"

"Good heavens, no, we needed *some* sleep. But I don't doubt we'll hear all about it for the next month or two. Right now you have a visitor in the parlor."

Sabrina wasn't sure why she guessed it was Ophelia, possibly because she had been her last visitor. On her wedding day, though? Yes, she would want to gloat—no, actually, she was forgetting what she had learned last night, that Ophelia had changed her mind about wanting to marry Duncan. She was still incredulous over that. How could any woman not want a man who possessed all the qualities one could possibly hope for in a husband? But Ophelia had her own personal set of priorities, and Duncan just didn't fit in to them.

She would be there to complain then and bemoan the fate she'd been dealt, a fate Sabrina would have given anything to have for herself. Sabrina wouldn't tolerate it, not this time. She wouldn't pretend a friendship anymore, either, that had never been there to begin with, especially when she knew now how Ophelia had lied to her, manipulated her, and even set about to deliberately ruin her. Actually, she decided she would simply show Ophelia to the door.

Determined to do just that, she was quite deflated to find Mavis waiting on her in the parlor instead. She even blushed slightly over the mean thoughts she'd just had about Ophelia. That Mavis was looking a little embarrassed as well gave her pause, though.

But it was easy enough to guess why the other girl would be uncomfortable. Mavis probably wanted to explain why she had refused to help Duncan, was probably suffering a guilty conscience for it now. She wasn't really a bad sort, after all, just unwilling to give up her one chance for revenge against someone she felt was so deserving of it and wouldn't get it any other way. Not that any of it mattered now, when it was too late.

"I came to apologize," Mavis began.

"There's no need."

"Yes, there is. I *knew* I wouldn't do as I said last night. I should have indicated as much to you, or at the very least offered you some doubt, so you wouldn't have left thinking the worst of me."

"What *are* you talking about?"

Mavis sighed. "I just wanted to savor, for a few hours at least, having the power to destroy Ophelia's happiness in my hands. And I just wanted her to know it, for a short time. She really does need to learn that the horrid things she does will come back to haunt her, and this was one instance to prove it to her."

"For a short time?"

"Yes, I intended to stop by Summers Glade today on the way back to London, to let Duncan know that he doesn't have to marry her, at least not to save her reputation on my account. For me to spread the tale of the compromising situation I came upon would make me no different from her. It's something she would do, hurting someone else just to get what she wants, and the day I start behaving like her is the day I hope someone locks me up and throws away the key."

Sabrina grinned. She would have laughed aloud in her relief, but managed to restrain that impulse. She didn't want Mavis to know just how happy she was for Duncan.

"Then you've already told Duncan?"

"Well, no," Mavis said. "I was hoping you would come with me. I rather suspect he will be annoyed with me for letting him think, even for another day, that he still had to marry that witch."

It was like having the ground open up and swallow her. Sabrina found the shock was just as bad, especially after her momentary relief.

"You didn't know the wedding had been scheduled for this morning, did you?" Sabrina asked in a dull, lifeless voice.

The immediate loss of color to Mavis's face was answer enough, but she said, "How could it be so soon? It takes three weeks just to post the banns!"

"Unless a special license is obtained, and Lord Neville apparently had one in hand long ago. Due to his advanced age, he didn't want any time wasted, once Duncan made his choice of bride. Understandable that he'd like to see a great-grandchild or two before he passes on. But in this case, the rush was to circumvent a scandal as well. After all, they didn't *know* that you wouldn't say anything about what you witnessed."

"Good God, if I'd known there was a time constraint . . . I confess I even considered keeping silent for at least a week, but felt that would be too long to let Duncan go on thinking he had to marry Ophelia. But I didn't think a few hours would matter overly much, when he would probably be sleeping through most of them. Oh, God, I'm never going to be able to forgive myself for this."

Ordinarily Sabrina would have tried to ease the other girl's misery, a natural impulse for her, but for once she couldn't manage to even try. It wasn't Ophelia's life that was ruined, whether she thought so or not, due to Mavis not fessing up to her intentions immediately, it was Duncan who would have to live with the results.

"Perhaps it isn't too late," Mavis added, grasping at straws.

"They are married. That's too late no matter how you look at it."

"Yes, but there is still another way to get out of a new marriage, well, as long as they haven't gone straightaway to bed to consummate it, and why would they when they don't even like each other? They could get an annulment, which is certainly more acceptable than a divorce."

Sabrina couldn't manage to see that as an option. "Based on what grounds?"

Mavis waved an impatient hand. "How should I know? But I'm sure *something* can be suggested. Perhaps her parents haven't let anyone know how they feel about the renewed engagement. If so, then they can claim they are against it and she married without their permission."

"When they were so set on the marriage themselves?" Sabrina reminded her.

"Sabrina, you aren't helping with this skepticism," Mavis complained. "We need to at least let them know this is an option, and *before* any consummating gets done that would remove it as an option."

We? Sabrina wondered how she had gotten volunteered to participate in this nonsense. Mavis was forgetting that Ophelia had let all and sundry know how much her parents were for the marriage, so much so that they refused to listen to her own heart. Nor did she want to be the one to have to tell Duncan that he was stuck with Ophelia now simply because neither of them had thought to tell Mavis when the wedding was to be, when they both *could* have mentioned it to her last night.

48

The wedding party was still going on, though some of the guests were already departing. This was why Sabrina and Mavis arrived unnoticed, entering Summers Glade just as a small group was leaving, and Mr. Jacobs busy elsewhere rather than attending the door.

They weren't completely unnoticed, though. Raphael Locke, looking very handsome today in his formal wedding attire, was leaning against the open doorway to the drawing room, where most of the remaining guests were gathered, and happened to be facing the hall, having just said good-bye to the departing guests. Drink in hand, eyes a bit red—whether from lack of sleep or one too many drinks was debatable—he probably wouldn't have been standing very steadily, which was why he was using the doorframe for some support.

"I know some women like to arrive late to an event, to make an appearance, as it were, but this is taking late arriving to extremes, ain't it?"

Raphael's remark, loud as it was so it would reach them across the hall, caused both women to blush. Neither Mavis in her traveling clothes, nor Sabrina in her simple day frock and walking coat, was dressed for a wedding, which was already causing some small embarrassment to them. They had opted for haste rather than dressing appropriately, and had come here straightaway after deciding they should, so drawing further attention to them was not what they were hoping for.

Sabrina briskly closed the space between her and the young duke-to-be so she wouldn't have to shout back at him. "If you don't mind, we are not here for the celebration, if it can be called that, but to try and offer a solution that might work to cancel the unwanted occurrence. I think it's a waste of time myself, but Mavis is desperate to make amends now, so here we are, and we do *not* need attention drawn our way, thank you very much."

She had whispered, but in a thoroughly scolding tone, which had him grinning at her and saying, "Oh, I just love riddles. How many guesses do I get in figuring out what you mean by that?"

Sabrina tsked at him, deciding he was indeed quite foxed. "They are still here, aren't they? They haven't gone off yet on a wedding trip?"

"If you mean the bride and groom, they are indeed still here, moping about. Ophelia was last known to be in her room pouting, and I believe Duncan has entrenched himself near to the brandy supply. If he gets married today, he's bound and determined not to remember it."

Sabrina was sure it was Raphael who wasn't going to remember today, and frowning at him, demanded, "What do you mean, *if* he gets married?"

"Why, that the wedding hasn't occurred yet, of course," he replied nonchalantly.

Sabrina felt her earlier rush of relief again soaring through her, but she curbed it this time. She wasn't going to leave herself open to the disappointment that was bound to follow if she was misunderstanding again what she was hearing.

"They really haven't married yet?"

He smiled at her. "No, they really haven't."

She smiled back at him, letting the relief flow unchecked now, and what a heady feeling it was. Yet it was the very last thing she expected to find here, and it didn't take long for her confusion to take over.

"Why not?" she asked him. "I thought they were all in agreement that any postponement would be detrimental to Ophelia's reputation."

"Assuredly it would be, under the circumstances, but this isn't a real postponement. From what I gather, and I wasn't there to witness it, mind you, but Duncan mentioned that Neville was quite annoyed when told this morning that Mavis wasn't going to cooperate in keeping things hush-hush. So it didn't surprise me, really, when he conveniently had a relapse just as the wedding ceremony was commencing this morning. Was rather well done, if I do say so myself. Had to be carried up to bed and the doctor fetched."

Sabrina frowned. "Convenient? Are you

quite sure he hasn't taken a turn for the worse?"

Raphael chuckled. "Well, considering that Duncan let it slip that his grandfathers had gotten into an argument about which one of them should have the honor of doing the collapsing, yes, I'm quite sure."

"Oh," Sabrina replied, finding it a bit hard to believe that the esteemed Lord Neville would even agree to such trickery, let alone perform it.

Seeing her doubting expression, Raphael added, "It's just a delaying tactic, and one that won't last very long. But apparently Neville seems to think that if he can talk to Mavis himself, he can make her see reason. And if not, then he plans to call in a few debts to use against her father to make *him* make her see reason. He immediately sent someone to Manchester to fetch her, now that her whereabouts were finally known. Good of you to bring her here yourself."

Fortunately, Mavis was still standing by the entrance and didn't hear any of that. "I didn't bring her, she pretty much dragged me here with her. She was devastated thinking she was too late to fix this mess, and was going to suggest an annulment might be arranged."

"Too late? I was under the distinct impression last night that she was determined to have her revenge against Ophelia. What changed her mind?"

"She was only determined that Ophelia should think so for a little longer."

"Not very kind of her, considering Duncan was getting slapped with that revenge as well."

"I agree, but I do understand, knowing a bit more now about why she despises Ophelia so much. And she did intend all along to come here today to make her assurances. But no one had bothered to tell her that the wedding was to take place this morning. She was basing her time schedule on the posting of the banns, so thought she had ample time to put a stop to the wedding."

Raphael shook his head in amazement. "My my, assumptions do have a way of kicking you in the ar—ah, teeth occasionally, don't they?"

Sabrina cleared her throat but still couldn't help grinning at him as she replied, "Indeed, I've been losing a few teeth myself lately."

That caused Raphael to burst out laughing. Unfortunately, the sound was highly inappropriate with the deathbed-vigil atmosphere that the house was currently in. After all, the guests were waiting to hear how serious Neville's collapse was, so laughter, under the circumstances, would indeed draw immediate attention.

Raphael, half foxed as he was, didn't notice, but Sabrina blushed to her roots when every eye in the drawing room fixed on her in stern disapproval. She quickly stepped to the side of the doorway, out of the path of those eyes.

She felt like kicking Raphael for making her forget herself like that, enough to answer him with her old habit of trying to get a laugh out of him. But then she started. It had been so long since she had felt like making anyone laugh. That the impulse had resurfaced was actually a relief. It indicated that the horrid misery she had been wallowing in really was on its way out the door finally . . .

49

The laughter in the hall drew Duncan with only a mild curiosity. Ordinarily he wouldn't have bothered finding out the cause of it, but he was hoping for a distraction, even a small one. Anything would be preferable at the moment than sitting around waiting for his wedding to begin, or at least pretending he was waiting, when he already knew it wasn't going to begin, at least not today.

Neville had no intention of "recovering" until he had his chance to talk to Mavis Newbolt himself. He had maintained from the beginning that that was all it would take, but if not, then he fully intended to coerce her father into using parental authority to assure her silence instead. But the girl had to be available for either course of action to work, which she hadn't been until now.

Duncan wasn't depending on either occurrence happening when, from all accounts, Mavis's father was reputed to be an uncooperative individual, and Mavis was adamant in her own stance. Neville was too dependent on the power of his position to work wonders.

Duncan was more realistic in knowing that Mavis only had to tell one person, just one, for a rumor to start. And she only had to claim she'd already done just that, whether she had or not, for Neville's plan to go by the wayside.

But any delay was welcome, even one caused by a pretense, which he hadn't exactly agreed to—not that he'd been asked his opinion in the matter. His grandfathers, once again, were making decisions for him. One of these days he was going to have to set aside his desire to not hurt Archie's feelings and tell him plainly to stop meddling in his life.

The trouble was, Archie still saw him as a lad, when he wasn't. And loving Archie as he did, his impulse was to protect his feelings, not hurt them. But he didn't have that impulse where Neville was concerned. And it made him distinctly uncomfortable every time Neville "helped" him, feeling the way he did about the old man. And this wasn't the first time that Neville had done something that caused Duncan to be grateful to him.

Neville hadn't argued even once when Duncan broke the first engagement, while Archie had done his share of complaining about that. And Neville had told Duncan quite frankly, after this current mess began, that if he chose to not marry Ophelia, he would support that decision and do his best to see the girl wasn't ruined because of it. That Neville couldn't guarantee she wouldn't be ruined was the only reason Duncan hadn't been able to accept that option, much as he would have liked to.

The gratitude that kept sneaking up on him didn't change Duncan's feelings about his English grandfather, however. That the old man was behaving like a real grandfather now didn't excuse his complete absence in the first twenty-one years of Duncan's life. He hadn't cared enough to make himself known to Duncan in all that time. Duncan wasn't going to care enough to open his heart to him now.

Duncan set his brandy aside now and sauntered out to the hall. He had wanted to drink himself into a stupor, but for some reason, the brandy wasn't affecting him at all today. Too many churning emotions, he supposed. But suddenly he was glad of that when he saw Sabrina standing there with Raphael.

Raphael's laughter was now quite understandable. Sabrina. Sabrina and her flair for easing a troubled heart. Duncan acknowledged a stab of jealousy, that Raphael had been the recipient of her charm just now rather than he, but he pushed that aside. He was too glad to see her to let trifling emotions interfere and ruin her efforts.

"I didna think you would come t'day," he said, drawing her eyes to him.

She gave him a brilliant smile, one filled with joy and laughter, the kind of smile he had come to enjoy seeing from her, but hadn't seen since his reengagement to Ophelia. Under the circumstances, it was quite jarring.

So was her quick rejoinder. "We're still friends, aren't we?"

"I was beginning tae wonder," he said carefully, trying to hide his confusion.

It didn't work, his frown quite obvious, but even that had her grinning at him to disconcert him further. Why *was* she so happy of a sudden? Just because she'd probably learned from Raphael just now that he wasn't married yet and why? Did she really think that Neville's ploy was going to be the end of it, after she had herself tried to change Mavis's mind last night to no avail?

That Raphael was grinning widely at him, too, was the last straw, causing him to demand, "Oout wi' it. What's got you tae acting like giggling cherubs?"

"Here now, I object to that description, indeed—" Raphael began indignantly, but Sabrina interrupted him with what did indeed sound like a giggle.

"I rather like the cherub part myself," she said in a confiding tone. "I can just see myself with wings, fluttering here and there and shooting arrows of merriment at everyone in passing."

Raphael rolled his eyes. Duncan glowered. Sabrina really did giggle at that point.

But then she took pity on Duncan and

explained, "I have good news, excellent news—actually, it's the most wonderful news." But before she said what it was, she chewed at her lower lip and confessed, "Come to think of it, though, it could be seen as bad news as well."

"Bad?"

"Well, that you'll have to start looking for a bride again could be seen as bad news, considering you weren't having much fun doing it before."

He sighed at that point, finally figuring out what she was talking about. "Lass, what Neville is trying is no' a guarantee o' anything."

"No, no, that isn't my news, that's your news. *My* news is that Mavis misled us last night. She did it intentionally, though she now grievously regrets doing so. But the truth is, she had no intention of letting you be forced to marry Ophelia on her account."

It didn't quite set in yet, that he was free of Ophelia. He did notice Mavis by the front door, though, wringing her hands and looking like she was about to be marched off to a firing squad.

"Go easy on her," Sabrina whispered,

following his gaze. "She thinks you're already married and is castigating herself over her tardiness. She had thought that Ophelia, in marrying you, was getting what she wanted, that she'd won yet again. But when you told her that Ophelia was against the marriage now, well, she just wanted her to suffer a bit more, to think that there would be no escaping it."

"And me."

"No, not you. She didn't think it would hurt you too much, since she did plan to save you before you actually did marry. She just didn't know the wedding was to happen this soon. She thought she had plenty of time to come to the rescue, as it were, that today would have been soon enough to tell you, on her way back to London."

"Then why is she here now, if she thinks the wedding took place?"

"To try and make amends by suggesting an annulment. I didn't think it would do any good myself, and it might not have. Ophelia's parents were too pleased to have you for a son-in-law, after all. Not that it matters now, thanks to Neville's tactic. It's over, Duncan."

It took hearing her say that for it to really sink in. Duncan's first impulse was to grab her and hug her, and he did just that. That she laughed and hugged him back was almost more of a relief than his not having to marry Ophelia now, when Sabrina's recent reticence toward him had been greatly contributing to his misery.

But he wasn't able to savor his relief, nor the exquisite joy in being able to hold Sabrina close for a few precious moments. Ophelia's voice, coming from the stairs behind them, was like a splash of icy water designed to separate them, and it did.

"You could at least make a pretense of being a gentleman and wait until this farce of an engagement is officially severed before you show where your true affections lie," was said with dripping scorn. "Of course, common courtesy can't be expected of someone only newly come to civilization."

50

Duncan turned slowly to face Ophelia, who had stopped halfway down the stairs. His anger was most definitely pricked over her remark, but it was tempered with the fact that, thankfully, he was never going to have to deal with her again after today.

So his tone was only mildly revealing of his dislike when he told her plainly, "Lass, if I was the barbarian you keep alluding tae, we wouldna have been engaged again, even if this whole bluidy gathering had witnessed me in your bedroom that night. I wouldna have given a single thought tae yer reputation, you ken?"

"But you were responsible!" she reminded him, even as her cheeks pinkened over his frankness.

"And your point being? Or do barbarians suddenly have a care for responsibility?"

"Oh, very well, so you *aren't* a barbarian," she replied testily.

"Amazing day, I think I'm actually going to faint," Raphael interjected with a snide chuckle. "The ice queen has made a retraction."

Ophelia turned to give him a withering look, but noticed Mavis instead. Her gasp was audible. And she completely forgot about the threesome at the bottom of the stairs as she hurried down the last few steps and across the hall to her old friend's side.

"Mavis, I *knew* you would come before it's too late. I knew you couldn't overlook our years of friendship. You *have* to forgive me. You can't let me suffer for the rest of my life over a few paltry words that you *know* I didn't mean."

Duncan rolled his eyes over her description of what it would be like to be married to him. They had followed Ophelia to Mavis's side, in time to hear her beseeching speech. He might have remarked on that "suffer" part, if Mavis weren't looking quite confused now.

Her confusion was understandable, though, when she asked, *"Before* it's too late?"

She was looking at Sabrina for confirmation. Sabrina smiled at her and nodded. You could almost see the weight leave the girl's shoulders and then the very second that Mavis realized that she held the winning hand again, and that her nemesis was there for her to play it on.

Ophelia didn't miss the implications in that question either. "You thought we were already married? So you came here to gloat instead?"

"Is my name Ophelia?" Mavis shot back. "Gloating is what you do so well, my dear, not I."

Ophelia stiffened. It was obvious that she would have returned the insult in kind, but she didn't dare to do so. It took her a moment, though, to gain enough control to keep her spiteful tongue leashed for once. She was still under the assumption, after all, that she needed Mavis's cooperation, and she wouldn't get it if she lambasted the girl in her typical fashion.

"Then what are you doing here?"

"As you've surmised, I thought that the

wedding had already taken place. It's logical then, that I might come by to wish the
happy couple well, isn't it?"

Ophelia all but snorted. "Happy? When
we despise each other?"

Mavis pretended incredulity. "You mean
there's actually a man alive who hasn't
dropped at your feet in adulation? I'm
shocked, indeed I am."

Ophelia's lips tightened and her voice
lowered to a confiding whisper that she
thought would reach only Mavis. "He's not
English," she said, as if that were the only
possible explanation there could be.

"Lucky him, if that's what it takes to not
be blinded by you."

"Takes much less than that," Raphael interjected with a grin.

Ophelia, reminded that she wasn't alone,
turned a glare on him and said, "Do you
mind? I'm having a private conversation
here."

"Don't mind a'tall, dear girl," Raphael rejoined. "But that don't mean I'm leaving.
No, no, wouldn't miss this for the world, I
do assure you."

"Miss what?" Ophelia snapped at him.

"Seeing me grovel? Do you all detest me that much?"

Not one reply was forthcoming to deny it, which was probably why Ophelia's cheeks blossomed just then with bright color. She would have left them there then. It was apparent that she wanted to run. But she couldn't leave Mavis yet if there was the slightest chance that she could turn the girl back to her favor.

To that end, she tried to ignore the three interlopers, as she saw them, and faced Mavis again. But Mavis was giving her a curious look now, and she wasn't long in revealing the reason for it.

"Two men, Ophelia?" she said, feigning incredulity. "And neither of them smitten by your glorious self? Does that not give you a clue?"

"What *are* you talking about now?" Ophelia demanded impatiently.

"That maybe it's not them? That maybe it's you? You've been slipping up, Pheli," Mavis said, using the childhood name that Ophelia had long ago forbidden her friends to use anymore. "You've been revealing your real self much sooner these days, be-fore you have a chance to fool anyone new you meet with your pretenses. People sim- ply aren't as blind as you think they are. Some are even seeing quite clearly that there's nothing but blackened, bone-chill- ing ice beneath the pretty surface you pre- sent to the world."

That last disparaging remark actually provoked a gasp out of Ophelia. She still couldn't leave, though, much as she might want to.

Duncan was beginning to feel a bit un- easy himself. From what he was hearing, he would have to surmise that Mavis would never help. Ophelia must be coming to that conclusion herself. If he didn't have Sabrina's assurance of why Mavis was there, this conversation between the two lasses would be the last nail for him . . .

"Are you done insulting me?" Ophelia said in a tight voice that cracked for the briefest moment, just enough for anyone paying attention to hear the hurt inside.

Mavis didn't catch it herself, though even if she had, she might not have ended her diatribe just yet. This was her moment of revenge, after all, and Duncan was wise enough to stay out of it, even if he was starting to feel a bit sorry for the blond beauty.

"Since when is the truth an insult?" Mavis countered.

"Very well, so I am the most despicable person imaginable. My fiancé has assured me of that. Sabrina has assured me of that. Even Locke there has assured me of it. With so much evidence against me, it must be so."

She was definitely revealing the hurt now, but Mavis was unmoved by it. "Oh, *please,*" Mavis said derisively. "Don't think you can use those tactics on me, Pheli. You forget, I *know* you. I know how you'll use every trick in the book to get what you want."

"I know you as well, and we both know you'll end up regretting what's been said here. You simply don't have it in you to be this vindictive, Mavis. You know you would rather forgive me. We've known each other too long—"

"I recall forgiving you once before," Mavis cut in tersely, some of her inner anger showing now. "But what good did that do? Did it change your ways? Did it stop you from ruining other people's lives like you did mine?"

"Honestly, Mavis, I thought we agreed you were better off without Alexander."

"You tried to offer that as a consolation, but it didn't work. My heart still wouldn't reconcile to my loss. Instead of getting over it, I grew so bitter that I barely recognized myself anymore. And the *only* reason I continued to abide your presence is I have been waiting all this time to witness your downfall."

Ophelia was apparently surprised over this last revelation, enough to protest with feeling, "Mavis, you can't hate me this much!"

"Can't I? Have you yet to realize, Pheli, that no one likes you? You don't have a single real friend, because you end up using them all, and contrary to what you might think, we're not all so stupid to not realize it."

"That's not true," Ophelia said in a small voice. "Jane and Edith are still my friends."

"Are they?" Mavis rejoined, stabbing her point home. "Are they here for your wedding then? The wedding of their 'best' friend?"

Ophelia's silence was telling. And if that weren't answer enough, the abject expression she momentarily revealed was. Mavis's smile, which could only barely be called one, still revealed her triumph over it.

"As I thought," Mavis continued. "Even Jane and Edith have finally seen the truth, haven't they? But then how could they overlook it any longer when you turned on me right in front of them? They know now that you can't be trusted. Of course, they've always known that really, when they spend most of their time with you trying to soothe your ruffled feathers, because they *know* you'd turn your spite on them just as easily as anyone else."

"I wouldn't."

"Good God, Ophelia, lie to others all you want, but don't stand there and lie to me! I was *there* when you burned them in the past, when you turned your vicious tongue on them more than once. And for what? For some minor trifle not worth mentioning that you just happen to take offense at. But then you take everything as a personal affront, because everything must revolve around *you.*"

"I can't help my temper."

Mavis shook her head. "You can. You just never try. You'd rather make excuses, even to yourself, to explain your nasty retaliations. What does that say for you, Pheli? That you still behave like a child? That you never grew up? Isn't it about time that you did?"

"Enough. You've made your point."

"Have I? But has it opened your eyes? I doubt it. You'll make your excuses, call me a fool and a liar, and go about your blithe way, ignoring anyone's opinion but your own just as you always do."

"I can't very well go about any blithe way when I'm stuck here . . . Mavis, I'm begging you—there, I've said it. Is that what you came here for? To hear me beg? Are you happy now? *Please* don't make me have to marry a man who despises me."

Mavis shook her head again, this time in amazement. "You see how self-centered you are, Pheli? It never even occurred to you that I might have come here for Lord Duncan's sake, did it? As it happens, that's exactly why I'm here, to end a tragedy, because that's what any marriage to you would be. My silence is assured on all accounts, but *not* for your sake. You I wouldn't help if you were drowning. It's for Duncan, because no man deserves to be stuck with you for a wife."

That was Mavis's last word on the subject; in fact, she stepped around Ophelia, giving her her back, dismissing her ex-friend from her mind completely to address Duncan now. "Lord Duncan, I'm sorry, truly sorry, I didn't make my assurances to you last night. I've let my association with Ophelia nearly destroy my own integrity, though that is no excuse and I know it."

"Nae, lass, dinna trouble yourself o'er it," he replied, giving her a smile. "My relief is tae great tae do aught but thank you for it."

She nodded curtly, still embarrassed that she had let him suffer in doubt even one extra day. She then turned to Sabrina and took her hand to squeeze it.

"Thank you for reminding me how heartwarming and selfless real friendship is, Sabrina. I'll be proud to call you a friend henceforth, if you'll allow me?"

"Certainly," Sabrina replied. "But you sound like you're leaving."

"I am. I can't delay getting home any longer. I imagine my father has a long list of punishments awaiting me, and I'll deserve every one of them."

Ophelia slipped away from them unnoticed. She knew they wouldn't care. She also knew she could contain her emotions no longer and sought a private place to release them. She ran back upstairs, but rounding the corner of the hallway at the top, she collided with Raphael Locke.

He had slipped away unnoticed as well, just before she did, and with the express purpose of catching her alone, having guessed which direction she would take. He'd listened to most of Mavis Newbolt's allegations, things he'd been unaware of, and he didn't feel that Ophelia was quite contrite enough for all the trouble she had caused.

He had meant to have a few disparaging words with her himself. He hadn't expected to find tears running down her pretty face, however.

"By God, they're real, aren't they?" he said, setting her back from him to touch a finger to her wet cheek. "And you thought to not share them with anyone? I'm impressed."

"Leave . . . me be," she choked out.

He didn't. Awkwardly, and utterly amazed that he had the impulse, he drew her back to him and let her make use of his shoulder. Appalling shortcoming of his, to be a sucker for tears, real ones, that is, but there it was, and he was bloody well likely to regret it in this instance.

He sighed inwardly, but there was no help for it. Ophelia's narrow body was trembling with emotion, and it was incredible just how much emotion was pouring out on his shoulder. Not that he thought the ice inside her was melting. No indeed. Never would he think that. The Lockes did not raise fools.

51

Amazing how quickly Neville "recovered" from his collapse after being informed of Mavis Newbolt's brief visit. He even came downstairs himself to make the announcement official, that the two young people had decided not to marry after all, and had severed their engagement amicably this time, it being a mutual decision.

Of course, following that announcement, he pretty much booted those remaining guests out of his house. He did so diplomatically, but did so nonetheless and with concealed relish. By that evening, Summers Glade was actually empty again as it should be, well, except for one unwelcome guest he still couldn't get rid of yet and wouldn't, until Duncan found himself a real bride.

That guest sat across from Neville that evening in the formal dining room. They were sharing an aperitif while waiting for Duncan to join them for dinner. With the dilemma of the Reid marriage out of the way, the somewhat temporary truce they had been under in their mutual opposition to it was pretty much at an end.

Congratulations over with and thanks given that Mavis Newbolt turned out to be a decent lass after all, Neville and Archibald were back where they had started, in disagreement over how to get Duncan married.

"He'll have to go to London," Neville said, seeing no other solution himself.

Archie groaned. "Gawd, I've heard the devil hisself lives in yer London."

"What utter tripe. Our London is no different than your Edinburgh, I'm sure."

Archie snorted. "Ye ain't sure, since ye've ne'er been there."

"And you've been to London?" Neville countered. "When was that?"

Archie bristled, being put on the spot like that, and maintained, "That's neither here nor there. A big city, nae matter the country 'tis in, isna the answer. What's wrong wi' anither gathering here, eh?"

"This house will *not* undergo another invasion," Neville replied adamantly, which was the same as saying that he simply wouldn't tolerate another mass of strangers peeking into his every nook and cranny. "The social Season is still in full swing in London. Invitations can be easily obtained to all of the upcoming affairs of note, and more will pour in once Duncan makes an appearance there."

"There'll be far tae many lassies in a city that big," Archibald pointed out. "How will the lad e'er be able tae make a choice—"

"Archibald, haven't we been over this ground once before? As it happens, and it can't be disputed, London *is* the place that all the marriageable young women flock to each Season. It's a well-known marriage mart. If Englishmen have managed just fine finding their wives there for years, myself included, why then wouldn't Duncan be able to? And no one said you have to accompany him."

"Then ye mean tae?"

Neville shuddered at the very thought.

"No, actually, I was thinking of asking young Locke, who seems to have become quite chummy with Duncan, to take him around and introduce him to all the right people."

Hearing the end of that as he entered the room, Duncan said, "If there's any asking tae be doing o' friends o' mine, I'll be doing it. The both o' you are really going tae have tae stop treating me like a bairn in swaddling that canna do a bluidy thing for himself. And no' that I'm conceding one hundred percent that Rafe is a friend, but what is it I'm tae ask him tae do for me?"

"Get you immersed in the London Season."

Duncan, about to take the chair between the two old men, paused with an appalled look. "Whatever would I want tae do that for? Archie, you told me yourself that place is a hellhole nae sane man would want tae visit."

Archie coughed uncomfortably. "Well, whether it is or no', Neville is sure that's the place tae be finding yer wife now. And I'll hae tae agree wi' him," Archie said, gaining a raised brow from Neville since he had just got done disagreeing with him, which he ignored for the moment. "We've had an unpleasant detour, but 'tis time tae be getting back tae the matter at hand, which is finding ye a wife."

"Then rest easy," Duncan replied. "I've already made my choice if she'll have me."

"Who?" Archie asked in surprise.

Neville, figuring out the "who" part and not all that surprised, but not all that pleased either, dropped a hand over his eyes and mumbled the least of his objections. "She's not titled. You can do better."

"Who?" Archie repeated, glaring at Neville now since he seemed to know but hadn't warned him.

Neville didn't notice the hot look, with his hand still covering his eyes. But Duncan answered for him. "Sabrina Lambert, o' course."

Archie did some brow raising now at his grandson, both of his bushy arches shooting straight up in surprise. "There's nae o' course aboot it, lad," Archie admonished. "She's a friend. Ye dinna marry yer friends, and ye dinna hae tae marry this one tae keep her friendship."

"Much as I'd like to see you married soon," Neville said, adding his own misgivings. "I don't want you marrying for the wrong reasons either."

Duncan didn't take offense, he even smiled as he replied, "Either o' you consider I might have more feelings for her than friendship?"

"Nonsense," Archie abruptly snorted. "Ye assured us otherwise, if ye'll recall. And she's no' e'en pretty. There is nothing wrong wi' valuing a friend, but ye dinna need tae take it tae extremes."

"Archie, she has more beauty within than anyone I've ever met. Besides, you've been blinded by Ophelia, and now find every other female lacking in comparison. I wasna impressed wi' Ophelia, so I find Sabrina more than lovely. I find her perfect, actually."

"She does have her good qualities," Neville put in. "But she also has a scandal on her back that she will never be rid of."

"A silly scandal that's bluidy well groundless," Duncan pointed out, and then challenged, "You're afraid o' a wee scandal, Neville?"

"Not at all. I even happen to agree it's silly. It's still not something we want in the family if it can be avoided. But if you tell me you're in love with the chit, then by all means, marry her."

"Bedamned, Neville," Archie blustered at that. "Can ye no' see the lad is deluding hisself? Dinna be encouraging this nonsense."

Duncan was amazed, once again, that Neville was taking his side, albeit with protest, but his support was nonetheless there. Archie, on the other hand, didn't surprise him at all in the stand he was taking.

"Archie, let me worry aboot m'feelings," Duncan said as he stood back up. "You trusted me tae run your many businesses. Trust me tae know what I want and why I want it. And I think I'll be paying the lass a visit right now."

Archibald dropped his head on the table the moment Duncan left the room, even banged it a few times in his frustration. Neville, unimpressed with the theatrics, waved away the servants who chose that inopportune moment to come in with their dinner. Drink was more in order at the moment, at least for his Highland guest.

"You're taking this too hard," Neville suggested as soon as they were alone again.

Archie looked up to scowl at him. "Am I? Can ye nae see what a mistake this is?"

"Not if he loves the girl."

"Bah, that's the bluidy trouble. He does love her. I dinna doubt that one bit. But it's nae the love a man gives tae a wife, ye ken?"

"Love is love—" Neville began.

"Nae, there's many a difference," Archie interrupted, stressing, "She's a dear friend o' his, and that's what he loves her as. But because this friend happens tae be a lass, he's got it mixed up in his mind that what he feels for her is the same as the mating kind o' love, when it isna. Och, ye see what happens when men make friends o' lasses?"

"And what if you're wrong?"

"I'm nae wrong. I know the lad. He's been lacking really close friends in his life, and now he's found one, he's loath tae risk losing her. He's thinking marriage will keep her always by his side, and sae it will, but he'll nae be happy wi' it in the end. And he'll be finding that oout as soon as he tries tae bed her, and finds he'd rather be playing a bluidy game o' whist wi' her instead."

Neville couldn't help it, he burst out laughing. "I swear, Archibald, the way you think sometimes boggles the mind. Hasn't it occurred to you yet that what might have begun as friendship could have progressed to something much deeper? Not all love occurs immediately, you know. Occasionally it simply grows on you."

Archie snorted. "Love, aye, but lust is either there or it isna, and he doesna lust after this lass. Now, what hope is there for a marriage that doesna start wi' good, healthy lust, eh? E'en the kind o' love that grows on ye at least begins wi' lust. Wi'oout it, there's nothing tae work wi', nothing tae get any feelings at all started, you ken?"

Neville rolled his eyes. "I think when Ophelia Reid branded Duncan a barbarian, she would have been right on the mark if she'd named you instead. Feelings can *change,* Archibald. Friends can become lovers. Enemies can become friends and vice versa. If everything was writ in black and white as you seem to see it, this would be a very dull world indeed."

52

He might not have been allowed to see her. Duncan realized that after he arrived at Cottage by the Bow and Sabrina's aunt Alice, who let him in, gave him a disapproving look because of the late hour. But tsking and mumbling that he wasn't to stay long and *should* have come in the morning, she still took him through the dining room to a pair of French doors that led to a small garden and pointed him in that direction.

He found Sabrina there, bundled in her winter coat, sitting on a stone bench in a pool of moonlight. That was the only light available, since that side of the house was dark, but it was ample once his eyes adjusted to it. The garden was nearly barren of greenery at that time of year, but was probably quite pretty in summer.

He didn't wonder why she chose to sit there in the midst of winter. He knew by now that she simply preferred to be outdoors, no matter the time of year, and apparently no matter the time of day.

"Are you no' cold, lass?" he asked as soon as he reached her.

She had glanced his way when he stepped outside, watched him as he walked toward her, all without a change in her expression. No curiosity about why he was there, no surprise, almost as if she'd been expecting him, despite the lateness of the hour.

"No, not a'tall," she said simply.

"I'm thinking you'll like the Highlands," he remarked nonchalantly.

"Why do you think so?"

"Because most visitors, e'en Scots Lowlanders, dinna take the time tae really look at what's around them in the high country, but you, you wouldna be rushing tae get back indoors where 'tis warm, now would you?"

She smiled. "Probably not, but that can be said of many people and in most any place, even here. Look," she added, pointing up. "A winter moon is a thing of beauty, no matter what country it appears in, but rarely does anyone stop to marvel at it."

He chuckled. "Point taken, but I marvel that it ever appears in your cloudy English skies."

"Do you still hate it here?"

"Nae," he assured her. "There are some things English I've come tae love."

Sabrina smiled to herself, but then she didn't read any hidden meaning in that statement, was just glad that he was no longer so averse to his new home. She had left Summers Glade today with a lightened heart. It had nothing to do with herself, had everything to do with him. She was simply happy for him, that he had escaped a marriage he would have hated.

She didn't move over when he sat down too close to her on the bench. She was comfortable with him because of their friendship. It was only when she began thinking of him as other than a friend that she got disturbed by his closeness. But those kinds of thoughts had been put to rest after her talk with Archibald, and for her own peace of mind, were going to stay buried.

He still had to get married. He would

probably be going to London now to accomplish that. She rather thought that was why he was here, to tell her he would be leaving for a time. She was going to miss him, terribly, but she had to get used to seeing him only infrequently now. When he came back, he'd have a new wife . . .

"Are your aunts watching us from one of the windows?" he asked her suddenly.

"Quite possibly."

"I dinna care, I'm still going tae kiss you."

It was too unexpected. And so swiftly was she gathered in his embrace and his lips were covering hers that there was no time for a single thought before it was happening. He *was* kissing her, thoroughly, deeply. And the second the surprise left her, she realized she didn't want to think, or analyze, or do anything other than revel in the joy of being in his arms once again.

It was so selfish of her. It was giving him the wrong impression. But she just couldn't help herself. It was going to be the very last time she could touch him, taste him, dream for a few moments that he could be hers. She was going to have to insist that it never happen again. She'd stay friends with him, but not if he kept thrusting temptation at her. And he probably didn't even mean to. This was probably just his way of sharing his relief with her, but—good God, did Highlanders really kiss their friends this way?

She had her answer in the next moment when he leaned back to gaze into her eyes and said simply, "Brina, lass, will you marry me?"

For the longest while she just stared at him, every one of her fanciful hopes realized in those few words of his. She had to savor the joy for a few moments more, to hold back reality and the pain, the pain that was going to rip her to shreds as soon as she answered him. But since she knew what her answer would be, what it had to be, the joy didn't last long for her. She tried to retain it, but her emotions just wouldn't cooperate, and if she didn't get it over with quickly, she was going to start crying all over him.

She ought to explain, but in the end all she could get out was, "No."

He wasn't expecting that answer. His expression said as much, the surprise, the hurt he quickly masked, the stiffness that came next. But he wouldn't leave it at that, either. He asked her, "Why not?"

It was incredible, how many difficult things she'd had to do where this man was concerned, and this was probably the worst, to try and hold back her own anguish long enough to make him understand. "You're my friend, Duncan, the closest I've ever had, actually, and I have a great care for you as my friend. But to try and make more of what we feel than that would be a mistake."

She should have said more, she really should have, but the words were starting to choke her. She stood up, turned her back toward him, before he sensed what she was really feeling. The moon helped, going away, leaving the garden in dark shadows. If he could see her face just then, he would know that she hadn't meant a word of that. The tears, pouring down her cheeks now, unable to wait any longer, would tell him plain enough.

And with the pain was a rage, too, toward his grandfather. She hated Archibald just then, for warning her, for preparing her for this. Why couldn't he have left her ignorant? Would it really have been so bad for her to marry Duncan? She would have loved him enough for the both of them. She could have made him a good wife.

But she was deceiving herself. Marriage needed more than just one side of it doing all the loving. They would have just lived together, as friends. That wasn't a marriage. And eventually she would have come to resent it, too, that he didn't really love her as she wanted to be loved.

She tried to dry her eyes before she faced him again, without him noticing that was what she was doing. She thought she succeeded. It didn't matter. He'd silently gone.

53

Duncan didn't head straight home, when he knew his grandfathers would both pounce on him to hear if he was engaged again or not. He had no desire to discuss it. He went to the inn in Oxbow instead, or more exactly, to the tavern side of it, and bribing the innkeeper to stay open when the man tried to send him home, got quite thoroughly soused.

He did manage to find his way home eventually, though he fell off his horse twice, at least he was pretty sure it was twice, and might have stayed put on the cold ground if the animal didn't repeatedly blow some very fetid hot air in his face. He suspected it might have been his own breath coming back at him, but that was neither here nor there, when he wasn't in good enough condition to tell the difference.

Nor had he managed to avoid his grand-fathers. They both still pounced on him the moment he stumbled through the front door. Mr. Jacobs had had sense enough to go to bed, but Neville and Archie, despite it being the middle of the night now, had both waited up for him.

Not together, though. Archie came out of the drawing room to help Duncan off the floor, where he managed somehow to land again. Neville was at the top of the stairs asking if he should fetch a footman to carry Duncan to bed.

"I can bluidy well heft the lad m'self," Archie blustered indignantly.

"Then do it," Neville called down.

Duncan, who would have much preferred to just sleep there on the floor in the hall, had a vague suspicion that Archie really was going to try to carry him up the stairs, stubborn Scot that he was, and no doubt break his back doing so. Which was why he drew on the last bit of steam in him and got up those stairs himself, pausing only long enough to raise a lopsided eyebrow at Neville, who was standing there in his bed robe holding a lamp aloft.

For the lifted eyebrow, he got back a very English sounding snort, which started him laughing. He hadn't known that snorts could be differentiated by language, and found the knowledge quite amusing.

"Now tell me," Neville was heard behind him as he careened down the upper hall in what he hoped was the direction of his bedroom. "Since you know him so well, is he foxed this time from celebrating or drowning his sorrows?"

"Shhh," Archie hissed back. "Dinna be reminding him o' what he's tried tae forget in drink."

"Not celebrating then." Neville sighed.

Duncan, wondering why they thought drink had any effect at all upon hearing, propped himself up against the nearest wall and said, "She wouldna have me, flatly refused tae marry me. Yet she returns my kisses as if she'd drag me tae her bed if she could. I dinna understand, Archie," he complained, but then he glanced accusingly at Neville, asking him, "Is that some English peculiarity in your lasses here?"

"That they might want to drag you off to bed? Or that they still won't marry you after they get you there?"

"Aye, that."

Duncan suspected the old man wanted to laugh, but he managed to keep a straight face when he replied, "I wouldn't know. Honestly haven't had that many women who want to drag me off to their bed."

Archie was less restrained, he did laugh—at Neville. "Now, why am I no' surprised?"

Which got Archie a glare, another snort, and nearly lost them the lamp, since Neville marched off with it. But he did come back with it after a moment, set it on the nearest hall table, and stiffly said, "For the lad, so he doesn't break his neck. And we'll discuss in the morning what sounds like a misunderstanding."

The last was said with yet another glare in Archie's direction, which instead of further amusing the old Scot, caused him to wince this time. Duncan didn't notice, demanded, "What misunderstanding?"

"The one you just complained about not understanding," Neville replied.

That, of course, was much too cryptic for Duncan's whisky-soaked brain to try to grasp, so he didn't try. Instead he stumbled the last few feet to what looked like his bedroom, and pushing his way in, managed to do his falling this time on a soft bed. He'd worry tomorrow about whether it was his room. As long as no one was shouting at him to get out, his mind took the opportunity to stop functioning.

Waking the next afternoon—he managed to sleep that long—Duncan was treated to the reminiscent scene of finding someone sitting beside his bed again, waiting for him to awake. It was Archie this time, and although he was pretending to be asleep as well, Duncan knew better. The irony wasn't lost on him, despite the wicked hammers pounding on his head. Both times had been after he'd drowned himself in drink.

Archie, cracking one eye at him, said pretty much the same thought. "Ye sloshed yerself when ye got engaged but didna want tae, now ye've done it again when ye did want tae, but couldna. Is the after pain worth it, lad, when the forgetting is only temporary?"

"Nae, no' worth it at all. And you'll be regretting sitting there all night just tae ask me that, when your auld bones creak now for a week."

"Let me worry aboot m'auld bones," Archie replied as he sat up and stretched. That they both heard a few creaks as he did so caused him to softly chuckle.

Duncan rolled to a sitting position on the side of the bed himself. He did so carefully, but it still didn't help. Obviously he hadn't slept quite long enough to get all the liquor out of his system yet. Next time he thought that drink would be the answer to his problems, he decided he'd just ask someone to shoot him instead.

Archie, watching him, said uncomfortably, "This should probably wait until yer feeling better, but m'conscience says otherwise."

"If you mun scream at me, do it in a whisper," Duncan replied.

Archie winced. "Any screaming gets done will probably be coming from ye."

That got Duncan's undivided attention. "Conscience, eh? Verra well, what's bothering you?"

"That yer taking the lass's rejection sae hard."

Duncan raised a brow, but that hurt. He tried a scowl instead, but that hurt, too. He finally just put his head back in his hands and mumbled, "Was I tae rejoice that she doesna love me in the way I love her?"

"Yer sure then, that ye love her that way?"

"Would I have asked her tae wed me if I still saw her just as a friend?"

"Aye, I was afraid ye'd do just that, just tae get the marrying o'er wi'." Archie sighed. "But then the last word I had from ye on the matter was yer assurance that she was only a friend tae ye."

"And so she was—then. The irony is, 'twas your own insistence that men and women canna be true friends that started me looking at her differently. And I found I liked what I saw, verra much so. In fact, I had the devil's own time, after that, keeping m'hands off o' her."

Archie closed his eyes with another sigh. "Then I hae some apologizing tae do. I'm afraid I may hae influenced her rejection o' ye."

"Dinna be absurd," Duncan scoffed. "You canna change how she feels."

"Nae, but from the talk I had wi' her, I may hae convinced her tae no' admit how she really feels."

Duncan went very still as he stared at his grandfather. "What talk?"

"I thought I was doing the right thing—"

"*What* talk?"

"Last week, when I saw her in Oxbow. I warned her that ye might be coming tae her for marriage, if ye could get oout o' marrying the Reid lass, but that it'd be for the wrong reasons if ye did."

"Bedamned, you told her I felt nothing more'n friendship for her?"

Archie cringed, though Duncan's tone wasn't as harsh as it sounded. "Aye, but then I was sure that is all it was, when ye had assured me o' just that, and I didna want tae see the tae o' ye making a serious mistake in thinking ye could base a marriage on it."

Duncan's scowl suddenly turned into a grin when he realized, "Do you ken this means she really loves me?"

"Aye, that is a possibility."

"More'n that. I'm realizing what a fool I

was no' tae listen tae my heart, when I know she has more'n a tepid care for me. I let a few words o' denial destroy my common sense last night."

"I'll talk tae her, lad," Archie said gruffly. "And tell her my mistake."

"Nae." Duncan shook his head with a smile. "She needs convincing that I really love her, and if I canna do that m'self, then I dinna deserve her."

"Ye can forgive me then, for interfering?"

"Dinna fash yourself, Archie, I know you meant well. But for this devil damned headaching that's going tae keep me from going tae her right this minute, aye, you can wallow in guilt a bit longer for your part in that."

Archibald snorted and headed for the door. "If I'm going tae do any undignified wallowing, then ye might as well suffer the full brunt o' yer *own* foolishness," he said, and slammed the door shut soundly, knowing full well he'd be leaving some serious groaning behind him, which he did.

54

She couldn't get to sleep, of course. Sabrina hadn't thought she would, any more than she'd been able to last night. It was odd how a broken heart did that to you, made sure you fretted and analyzed and went through every imaginable "what if," and in the end, still stayed broken, when if the heart would just have a bit of pity, the pain could be ignored for a brief time in sleep.

She tried reading this time, though, and had brought to bed a book that had put her to sleep numerous times before. It didn't work. Had she really thought it would? When deep down she knew that she was probably going to lose even her friendship with Duncan now? How could what they had shared ever be the same, after all, when he had foolishly tried to make more of it, without having the real feelings that were necessary to make more of it?

He was deceiving himself, and in the process, had nearly deceived her as well, but only because she *wanted* to believe that he could love her. She did know better, and somehow had lost sight of the simple facts, that she wasn't a great catch, wasn't the type of woman who could turn men's heads, didn't possess the kind of beauty that could attract someone as handsome as Duncan was. She had tossed aside her common sense because of a few kisses and . . .

Well, they really hadn't been friendly kisses. But then making love to her hadn't been a friendly type of thing to do either. *But*—and this was what she had overlooked—that was in her opinion, a woman's opinion. Men must obviously view it quite differently.

She was doing it again, analyzing, dissecting, driving herself deeper and deeper into moroseness, when the facts simply weren't going to change. She left her bed. She paced some. She stopped by the window, opened the drapery, but the moon was hiding, giving her nothing much to look at outside. Perhaps a long walk—no, then she'd have to dress again, leave her aunts a note . . .

She moved to the fireplace, which was keeping the room pleasantly warm. She should put it out, turn off the lamps, too. Of course, a completely dark room hadn't helped last night. A warm glass of milk then. At this point she'd try anything to get some sleep so she could stop thinking.

She fetched her robe and went down to the kitchen, but shortly thereafter she was dragging her feet as she returned to her room. The milk hadn't made her drowsy. She was still wide-awake, and even more so when she opened her door and found Duncan sitting on her bed.

She doubted her sight, of course. Her imagination had brought him there, had even removed his coat for him, because she knew how indoor heat tended to bother him rather quickly. Just wishfulness. He wasn't real.

"Since it was already late t'day afore I felt fit enough tae come," Duncan told her, "I decided tae make sure it was late enough that there'd be nae aunts peeking through windows this time. O' course, I hadna quite figured oout how tae get tae you wi'oout waking the whole house, until you appeared at the window."

It was the brogue, which she knew she couldn't duplicate with any degree of accuracy, that convinced her he wasn't just a trick of her mind, that he was really there. "You came through the window?"

"Aye, and had a devil's time reaching it. That tree oout there didna want tae cooperate. I think I broke a few o' its limbs."

He looked contrite. She was still too amazed at his presence to think straight.

"But—why?"

He left the bed, approached her, closed the door behind her that she'd been too startled to realize she was still holding open. She moved away from him, over to the fire, starting to feel . . . agitated. That didn't deter him; he followed again, took her hand so she wouldn't move off a second time.

"I've come here willing tae make a fool o' m'self if I'm wrong, but I have tae be telling you, Brina, that what I feel for you is nae longer just friendship."

She groaned inwardly, knowing full well she wasn't going to be able to survive with any degree of composure if he was going to try to convince her that he loved her, when she knew he was just deceiving himself. Archibald's warning hadn't just been heard and filed away for vague reference, it had repeated itself in her mind countless times, had been drilled home into her heart.

He wants ye near tae hand is all. He showed how far he's willing tae go tae hae ye near, by bringing ye tae the gathering, e'en though it brought Ophelia as well. He'd move ye intae Summers Glade if it werena inappropriate. I'm thinking he'd marry ye just tae get ye there permanently. He values yer friendship that much. But it is only that. Dinna let him fool ye intae thinking there's more tae his feelings. Ye'd both sorely regret it if ye do.

She tried to hold those words up as a shield now when Duncan continued, "Archie admitted tae me what he told you, but he was wrong—"

"No," she interrupted. "I've hated him for telling me, but he was right, we—"

"Be quiet and let me finish," he admonished gently. "I dinna mean his intentions. Those were fine and noble. I mean he was wrong in what he thought. I did indeed tell him a while back that we were only friends, and it was the truth at the time. I felt a closeness tae you that I've ne'er experienced afore wi' any other, and truthfully, lass, I didna think o' you any other way until Archie tried tae convince me that men and women canna be friends, that sex will get in the way o' it. Dinna be blushing now. There's nae polite way tae explain this. It was after he had that talk wi' me that I started seeing you as more'n just a friend, as the bonny lass you are. You can blame Archie if you like, but I'm no' blaming anyone for what I feel for you now. It's no' what it was, lass."

This was more painful than she could possibly have imagined it would be, because she wanted to believe him so much—but couldn't. Archie had been right, Duncan just wanted her near to hand, and this was the only way he thought he could accomplish it. And he'd just said it himself, that he'd felt a closeness to her that he'd never experienced before. She was his best friend, but because she was a woman, he was trying to call it something else.

She turned away from him to face the fire. "It is what it was," she said sadly. "You've just come to realize that I'm not as accessible as you'd like, that you can't visit me anytime you want, that you can't wake me in the middle of the night to share your thoughts, that you—"

His chuckle cut off her words, and her gasp as well, as he wrapped his arms around her from behind. "And what is this, if no' the middle o' the night?"

"You know what I meant. You can't be climbing trees every night. And you'd have the neighbors gossiping about us if you tried to see me as often as you want. But then you know that, which is why—"

His arms squeezed her to silence this time. "You're a stubborn lass, so I'm going tae speak plainly. Every time I see you now, I want tae drag you into my arms and make love tae you. D'you really think that that has anything tae do wi' friendship? I'm fighting wi' m'self right now no' tae kiss you. Brina, I love the fact that we were friends first, and I love thinking that we always will be, but I have tae be more'n that tae you now. I want tae be your lover, your protector, your provider, *and* your friend, but I canna be all o' that unless you'll marry me."

"You're killing me," she choked out.

He swung her around. "Look at me! Do I look like a man who doesna know his own mind? And if you tell me nae, I swear I'll cart you off tae the Highlands and live wi' you in sin. After nine or ten bairns, *then* you can tell me I dinna love you like I know I do."

"I meant I couldn't breathe."

"Oh," he said, but he caught the twinkle in her lavender eyes and laughed as he drew her back into his arms. "You believe me now."

He wasn't asking, nor did she need to confirm it, though she did say, "Any man who would want that many babies from me must love me."

"It hurts how much, lass."

She cupped his face in her hands, leaned up to kiss him softly. "No, it only hurts when you can't share it. We're going to share it now, Duncan."

"Then I hope you'll be understanding that I canna fight this any longer."

"This" was kissing her, and no soft pecks for him. His mouth took hers voraciously, the culmination of untold frustrations, the release of the hopelessness they'd both experienced too much of. Passion exploded between them instantly, but it was mixed with so much joy and relief, it was more a unique emotion, theirs alone, theirs to share.

Sabrina wanted to laugh in her happiness, but didn't want to stop kissing him long enough to do so. He must have felt the same, for his lips formed an uncontainable smile even as they seared hers.

They dropped to their knees together on the rug before the fire, still kissing, hands still grasping. The bed, only steps away, was too far for the kind of urgency upon them. Undressing, even, wouldn't part their lips. Not surprisingly, a few buttons went flying along with their clothes, into different parts of the room.

The heat from the fireplace, the heat from their bare skin, the soft fur on the rug in sensual contrast, all were conducive to quick repletion, yet Duncan still delayed. The first time they had made love had been in utter darkness. There was ample light now, and he wouldn't have been normal if he didn't want to feast with his eyes, as well as his hands and mouth, on the woman he loved.

"I'm glad this beauty has been so well hidden, lass. Had other men possibly guessed, they would've been lining up wi' proposals."

She blushed, yet it was a most pleasant embarrassment. She had always thought herself a bit too plump, even if in the right places, but his eyes told her he found her luscious curves rather perfect. His hands did as well, kneading, caressing, gripping when the passion flared to near unbearable heights, soothing as he tried to prolong the exquisite moment. All the while his mouth ravished, sucking at her breasts, her lips, her neck, her earlobes.

They were both still on their knees, so it was a surprise when her own left the floor as he grasped her hips and dragged her up against his hardness, a surprise and sensual delight. But that wasn't his only intent, she found, as one at a time he wrapped her legs around his hips, and she realized in amazement that he was going to make love to her like that as he slowly entered her.

She held on to him tightly with her arms and legs, though it wasn't necessary, he had complete control of her weight, holding her to him, his hands gripping her cheeks and directing her own movements. He controlled the pace as well, and the depth, slow, hard, yet not deep enough, teasing. Not until he knew she was about to climax did he impale her fully, so deeply it wrenched a scream of pleasure from her that thankfully was muffled by his mouth.

She was smiling, afterward, when he finally lay down on the rug and gathered her close. "I didn't exactly mean that kind of sharing, you know."

He chuckled. "I know."

His hands were still caressing her softly, possessively. She still wasn't the least bit tired, but was now glad of that. She would be most happy, in fact, to snuggle there with him all night.

After a moment more, though, she sniffed the air and said, "You might want to remove your shoes from the fireplace, especially if you're still wearing them."

His first reaction was to burst out laughing, and he did. Her remark, out of the blue and so casually spoken, was just too bizarre. But then he also smelled what she did, leather burning, and sat up immediately.

"I'm no' wearing them, but I suppose I will need them tae get home." He made a sour face as he rescued the smoldering shoe that had managed to fall too close to the fire. "We'll be married t'morrow, so I can be removing m'shoes properly for bed. Neville has a special license for it, so there's nae reason tae delay."

"No," she said.

"No?" he roared, and pounced on her, pinning her flat on the rug, thinking he had more convincing to do.

"No," she repeated, smiling up at him. "We're going to let my aunts arrange this wedding. They've planned it for years and years. I'm not going to deny them their day, and lording it over their friends, what a fine catch I made."

"Oh," he replied, contrite, but then, "How long will this arranging take?"

"Two or three weeks at the very least."

He groaned. "Could we no' sneak off tae

Gretna Green for a quick wedding, then come back and have another?"

"No, that wouldn't be the same, but I'll arrange for some roof work to be done on the house."

"Och, I'm afraid tae question that, but what the devil do roofs have tae do wi' weddings?"

"Not much, but it will leave a ladder handy outside my window until we actually do get married."

He gave her a very beautiful smile. "You'll be protecting m'shoes then?"

"Oh, absolutely. I might even keep my room quite chilly, just for you."

He chuckled. "You're joking, but you'll ne'er need a fire when I'm around, lass, I promise you."

"I wasn't joking," she corrected him. "I was counting on you keeping me warm."

55

The next weeks dragged by slowly for Duncan, though they weren't unpleasant since he spent many of the days with Sabrina. It was simply his impatience to have her for his wife before something went wrong again to prevent it. Not an unreasonable worry, and nothing at all to do with his lady.

She had assured him that she loved him, even that she had realized it much sooner than he did, and he had no doubts there, just his own amazement that he'd been blind not to see it sooner. They had just had so many obstacles thrown in their path that he wouldn't be able to relax fully until the wedding was an accomplished fact.

It was amusing, though, sitting back and watching the bickering that went on between her aunts and his grandfathers, who each had his or her own ideas on how this grand wedding was to proceed. And it was particularly amusing that the aunts won out in the end on every single disagreement— accept those the two ladies had with each other.

The wedding ceremony was going to take place in Summers Glade, because it really was the only place in the area big enough to accommodate the guest list, which included the entire village of Oxbow. Neville nearly collapsed, for real this time, when he heard that every one of the neighbors he'd managed quite nicely to ignore all these years was going to be invading his house.

He had protested long and loud, but with Archie feeling "the more the merrier" and so not supporting him in this, Neville was quite outnumbered. He might have turned his house over for the ceremony, but that was about the extent of his say-so in anything else having to do with the wedding.

He *had* continued to grumble about it, until Sabrina told him, "Look at it this way. They might have excluded you from the guest list, considering you haven't been on the best of terms with them for a good many years."

"From my own house?" he'd said incredulously.

"Certainly. You don't think a minor detail like that would stop my aunts, do you?"

Amazingly, he'd burst out laughing and replied, "I'm almost sorry I missed the fight."

Sabrina had blinked at him and then laughed as well. And to Duncan's chagrin, they had been quite chummy ever since.

Archie, still feeling bad about his interference which had been such a blunder, had been profuse in his apologies to Sabrina, but in her typical way, she had put him completely at ease with just a few words, and now they were quite chummy as well. In fact, if Duncan didn't manage to actually drag her away for a little time to themselves, both his grandfathers were pretty much monopolizing her when she came to visit Summers Glade with her aunts.

But Duncan's wedding day did finally arrive, and unlike the last one, which he had dreaded to his depths, this one he couldn't have been more eager for. Raphael returned for it and in his annoying fashion did his fair share of teasing and insisting that he'd known all along which leg shackles Duncan would prefer.

Duncan took it all in good spirits. He didn't think anything could possibly annoy him today, he was so happy. And then something did . . .

He was in his room dressing for the wedding, or to be more precise, allowing his valet to dress him this once, to the little man's delight. Archie was there as well to keep him company, or as he'd put it, to distract him from getting the usual wedding-day jitters. Not that Duncan was the least bit nervous, and he assured Archie of that.

Impatience was all he was still feeling, and it had increased abundantly because he hadn't climbed the ladder to Sabrina's room these last four nights. Not that he hadn't wanted to, but she had stayed up late each of those nights with her aunts, going over all the last-minute details of the wedding, and he hadn't wanted to exhaust her by keeping her up even later. But it hadn't been easy, staying away, and now he sincerely hoped he could be patient enough not to drag her off to his room immediately following the ceremony.

And then Neville arrived.

The old man's attitude had been much changed since Duncan had announced he was marrying Sabrina. Aside from a few grumbles that he'd have to be putting up with Alice and Hilary Lambert now on a regular basis, he seemed genuinely happy for Duncan. And Duncan's attitude toward him had also undergone a change—at least on the surface.

He wasn't as stiffly formal or cold when in Neville's presence now, though that was entirely Sabrina's doing. Duncan simply had no room for anger in his heart anymore, when she filled his heart with such joy. It didn't mean that he had forgiven Neville for ignoring him for most of his life, just that he wasn't going to let his bitterness over it interfere with his present happiness.

Neville didn't stay long, had merely come by to warn that the hour was approaching, as if Duncan hadn't been watching the clock diligently, and to offer a few words of wisdom. Now, whether he was joking or not was undetermined, since he said it with a straight face.

"My advice to you is what my own father told me when I married your grandmother. Love your wife, but don't let her lead you around by her little finger. But if she does anyway, make sure you enjoy it."

Archie laughed. Duncan grinned despite himself. But after Neville left, his expression must have reflected a bit of what he still felt toward that particular grandfather, at least enough for Archie to notice and remark on.

"I've come tae like that auld bastard, now I've seen for m'self that he means tae do right by ye. Dinna be telling him that, ye ken?" Archie said. "But I'm thinking 'tis time I told ye a thing or tae that yer no' aware o'."

Which was where Duncan got annoyed. "Now o' all days is no' the time tae be talking aboot Neville."

"Nae, I'm thinking there's nae better time, lad, or am I wrong that ye've no' accepted him yet as close kin? And he is that, as close tae ye as I am."

"Aye, but wi' a huge difference, Archie. You were there for me my whole life, there tae advise, tae cuff me when I needed it, tae teach, tae—"

He couldn't finish. He was getting choked with emotion again, and appalled at himself for letting it still bother him so deeply, that Neville hadn't cared enough about him to contact him, let alone meet him, before he was ready to collect his promised heir.

"Och, laddie," Archie said as he came forward to put an arm around Duncan's shoulder. "I didna ken that was the source o' yer anger. I thought 'twas only that ye had tae come tae live here."

"Had I no' come here, Archie, I'd ne'er have met Sabrina, so I canna object tae that anymore. I'm e'en looking forward tae taking o'er my duties here. Idleness doesna suit me well at all, as you know."

Archie nodded, but still added, "It wasna that Neville didna want ye here much sooner than now. He did. 'Twas yer muther's decision, that ye should hae the stability o' knowing only one home whilst growing up. Neville would've *preferred* that one home be here in England, but yer father ne'er would've agreed tae that, and rightly so. Neville conceded, because it was in yer best interests."

"We're no' talking aboot tae homes so far apart the distance would make visiting impossible, Archie. You made the trip here, e'en at your age, and Neville wasna older than you when I was born. Yet he ne'er once came tae meet me, did he now? I didna exist tae him until 'twas time tae fetch me, just like one o' the bluidy art pieces he collects."

The bitterness was spilling out now in Duncan's tone and expression, impossible to mistake. Archie had known it was there, buried deep, had even been somewhat pleased that it was, not wanting to share the lad's affections. But he had come to see how selfish that was of him.

Archie said simply, "He came, lad, more'n once."

Duncan went very still. "When? When I was tae young tae remember?"

"Nae, he ne'er actually reached the Highlands. The first tae times he tried, the weather turned him back. The third time, the weather did him in. He got sae sick he nearly died. He's no' been able tae get anywhere near cold weather again, no' e'en the paltry cold they hae here. Ye dinna think he likes these hot rooms he mun suffer, do ye? Nae, he finds them as uncomfortable as we do, but his doctors hae given him nae choice in the matter. And all because he wanted tae visit and get tae know his only grandson."

"Bedamned, why did he ne'er say so!" Duncan's emotion exploded.

"Possibly because he didna ken that that's what was bothering ye, and I didna help matters by telling him 'twas coming here that had ye in such a lather. But he's always had ye uppermost in his mind, lad. Yer muther diligently kept him apprised o' all aspects o' yer growing up, and if I didna do the same in the later years, he hounded me aboot it."

"I'll be back," Duncan managed to get out through the knot that had grown extremely large in his throat as he headed for the door.

"I've a wide shoulder—" Archie started to offer, but was cut off.

"Faugh."

Archie chuckled, pleased with himself for getting that misunderstanding cleared up, and thinking the lad just needed a few moments alone to get his emotions back in hand. But Duncan needed more than that.

He found Neville just leaving his sitting room to go downstairs for the ceremony. The old man started to say something, but Duncan didn't give him a chance. He gathered that frail body in his arms as he would a child and hugged him carefully, if fiercely, all of his pain and anger and bitterness washing away in that simple contact.

Neville was surprised, so much so that he didn't know what to do with his own arms at first, and then he did, so overcome with emotion that moisture gathered in his eyes. He wasn't a demonstrative man, but that hug meant more to him than he could possibly say.

They were neither of them embarrassed when they separated; they were in fact both grinning. It was simply such a relief to own up to the simple fact that they cared about each other. No words were necessary at that point to say it any plainer.

But Duncan did say, "I wish I had known you sooner. I'm going tae feel cheated when you're gone."

Neville smiled. "Then let me borrow one

of Archibald's more colorful phrases and tell you not to fash yourself over it. I've decided to live for a few more years."

Duncan chuckled at him. "That was your decision to make, was it?"

"Well, actually," Neville admitted, "for a very long time now I've had no *reason* to cling to life. I'm beginning to think that that's been part of my decline, and why my health continued to deteriorate to the point that I wasn't expected to live out the year."

"I take it you're feeling better?"

Neville winked at him. "Don't tell Archie this, but I'm quite determined to outlive him now."

They both laughed.

56

They were married amidst family and friends, and quite a few sentimental tears were shed that day. Quite a bit of laughter, too. It was a joyous occasion for all concerned, and Sabrina's aunts even managed not to bicker—too much.

Hilary was heard to tell Neville after her second glass of champagne, "Well, if *you* hadn't refused to let her see us after the scandal broke, it might not have had such an impact."

"My daughter was sick that summer, you twit. She wasn't seeing anyone but her doctor."

"We couldn't have been told that? Instead of having the door slammed in our faces?"

"Bloody hell, you women exaggerate to

extremes. No doors were slammed on you, though I swear, I'm going to make sure Mr. Jacobs learns how to do just that."

Hilary huffed off, but Sabrina caught her smirk as she did. So did Alice, who remarked next to her, "She's going to delight in tweaking his goatee on a regular basis now. Be good for the old coot, to get some spice added to his life."

Sabrina grinned. "Speaking of spice, I noticed Archie had you blushing quite a bit earlier. I think he likes you, Aunt Alice."

"Humph, that man would flirt with anything wearing a skirt, I'm sure," Alice replied, though there was a sparkle in her eyes as she said it.

"I'm not so sure about that," Sabrina continued to tease her. "In fact, I wouldn't be surprised if Aunt Hilary finds herself living quite alone soon, poor dear."

"Now, don't you worry about my sister. She made the decision years ago that she'd live life to the fullest, which included experiencing more of it than an old maid would."

"You don't mean—?" Sabrina couldn't quite manage to say it.

Alice nodded. "She's been seeing that

nice widower Sir Norton Aimsley from over Manchester way for years. In fact, I don't doubt that they were quite put out when you moved that ladder to your side of the house recently."

Sabrina blushed, and not just over imagining her aunt Hilary having trysts with lovers. Alice's remark meant that her aunts hadn't been fooled in the least about the roof needing repairs.

"Why don't they get married?"

"Because she won't leave me, and I refuse to live with her *and* her husband. But I expect that we'll be rearranging our priorities now that we've seen you so nicely settled."

This was said with a grin, and Sabrina didn't doubt that Alice was thinking about Archibald MacTavish again. She was thinking herself that if those two did happen to get married, Alice would see to it that Archie came often to England to visit, and she knew Duncan would like that.

But before she could tease her aunt about that, her husband came by to claim her attention—goodness, how nice it was to think of him as her husband now—and drag her out of the ballroom where the ceremony had taken place and refreshments were now being served.

She got the distinct impression that he was actually going to leave the celebration with her, to sneak off as it were, so they wouldn't have to go through yet another round of congratulations. But it was still the middle of the day! They were expected to remain in attendance for at least a few more hours.

But he was indeed heading straight for the stairs. So he was quite chagrined to find both his grandfathers sitting there on the bottom steps—she was amazed herself that they would sit there of all places. They were having a friendly, or not so friendly—it was hard to tell—disagreement over something.

That something was easy enough to figure out when Archie, noticing Duncan with Sabrina's hand in his, said to his grandson, "Tell him. Ye'll hae the first bairn afore the end o' the year."

"Sooner than that if you'll be getting oout o' m'way," Duncan replied.

Archie chuckled and stood up. Sabrina blushed profusely. Neville rolled his eyes toward the ceiling.

But that wasn't all Duncan had to say on the subject. To his grandfathers' surprise, at least to Archie's, he added, "No' that it will matter all that much when the first bairn comes along. 'Tis time you both know that I'll no' be dividing my family as you were planning for me tae do. You both have created these empires, and you currently have one heir quite capable o' seeing tae it all. When one o' *my* heirs is ready tae share some o' the responsibilities will be soon enough for him tae do so. So stop your worrying aboot it, and let me do the worrying from now on."

He didn't give them a chance to argue with him about it. With Sabrina's hand still in his, he passed between them and marched up the stairs with her.

But behind them, they could hear Archie say, "I told ye he was quite capable o' being our only heir."

"You said no such thing, but as I recall, I did," Neville replied smugly.

"Well, I thought it," Archie protested.

At the top of the stairs, Sabrina whispered to Duncan, "That was nicely done."

Duncan paused long enough to kiss her, a possessive kiss, a teasing kiss, a kiss that was very—arousing. "D'you think so?" And then quite huskily, "Then I wonder what you'll have tae say aboot the rest o' what I'm meaning tae do just now, because, lass, I have missed you."

"But you've seen me everyday," she pointed out, quite misunderstanding.

"Nae, I've seen you, but I havena seen you."

The "rest" wasn't just more kissing. No, the "rest" began when he tossed her over his shoulder before he continued on the way to his room.

Sabrina wasn't going to say it aloud, but that had been rather barbaric of him. Then she chuckled to herself. It was going to be interesting, having a Highlander for a husband, interesting and so very wonderful. And the only wondering that she actually did, was if she would ever get over the amazement that her dreams really had come true.